MIXED IN

CATHERINE HAUSTEIN

Cheers!
Cathy Haustein

CITY OWL
PRESS

MIXED IN
Unstable States, Book One

CITY OWL PRESS
www.cityowlpress.com

Cover Design by MiblArt. All stock photos licensed appropriately.

Edited by Amanda Roberts

For information on subsidiary rights, please contact the publisher at info@cityowlpress.com.

Print Edition ISBN: 978-1-944728-12-0

Digital Edition ISBN: 978-1-386-64903-8

Printed in the United States of America

To Kathi

PRAISE FOR CATHERINE HAUSTEIN

"Haustein creates her world with subtlety and intelligence which captures the imagination. Wonderfully entertaining, Mixed In delivers a powerful message with an admirable and honest grace. The reader can look forward to more tales from this author with anticipation. Well done!"
- *InD'tale*

"The author introduces an entertaining cast of characters, while warning us of what could be."
- *Author Lee Joanne Collins*

"Catrina bucks the typical trend you see of female scientists in pop culture. While she's a dedicated scientist, she refuses to let people see her as a one-dimensional nerd girl -- she also has aspirations for sex, romance, and having a family. This was a fantastic, sexy read, and the main character's struggles are very relatable for all women. Would definitely recommend!"
- *Book Reviewer*

"Hilarious, life-affirming, politically provocative . . . I loved seeing the world from the viewpoint of a chemist! A page-turner plot and clever writing."
- *Cynthia Mahmood, Book Reviewer*

"From romance to mystery to intrigue, Mixed In offers the reader a little bit of everything. Catrina and Ulysses's unlikely union sets the stage for all sorts of situations that occur throughout the book, keeping the reader interested from start to finish. Love how the author inserts tidbits of knowledge at the beginning of each chapter! Love the dialogue throughout the book that builds the characters. Loved the book!"

- Ann V., Book Reviewer

"A unique love story that will suck you in, take you on a wild ride, and spit you back out on the other side with a smile."

- Karin A Van Wyk, Book Reviewer

CHAPTER ONE

Creating a beer is much like breeding a dog. Dogs have that one tricky gene, number fifteen, that can cause height variation between five inches and seven feet, more than any other land vertebrate. (Imagine humans ranging from two to over thirty feet tall.) Hops are complicated, having intricate aromas, regional differences, and changing chemistry upon brewing.

Sipping the dark and sylvan house ale, I studied the wavy-haired bartender. A pretty man with smooth skin, a dark mustache, and little sideburns, he resembled Nikola Tesla, who despite his love for frequency and vibrations, was said to have died a virgin.

I'd taken refuge in Union Station bar after the bus blew a tire on a pothole as I rode home from work. I hadn't been in this neighborhood before, although it was only a few streets and a couple of turns away from Cochton Enterprises where I worked. I'd looked at it through closed bus windows, pretending that I wasn't gawking at the residents loitering on cracked sidewalks in front of a bar, an abandoned grocery store, and a laundromat with a window boarded with plywood. I'd never planned to set foot here. Other passengers had stood beside the bus on the fragmented sidewalk and called for rides. I'd foolishly bolted into the first place I'd seen, seeking shelter from the cold drizzle and urban neglect. Officials in black bomber jackets and belts covered with devices that hung like pinecones walked past the window. Those belts loaded with technology confirmed my suspicions. I was in a bad neighborhood.

I wasn't a citizen of this city-state, carved out of Iowa, with a name pronounced "Cock-Ton" like an enormous penis. I was a chemist from Michigan on a work visa and didn't worry about the officers. I had a permit to be here and, unlike most of the population, to have seeds. This was my first month in the country, and I was struggling to understand my new home and connect with the people here.

I looked up numbers for a cab. Tiffany lampshades diffracted light above the bar. A hundred years had flown by without touching this spot. There was even a huge painting of President Ulysses S. Grant behind the bar above the mirrors. Despite the sidewalk cracks and the officials stepping over them outside the window, Union Station was clean.

"Want another?" asked the bartender, coming over to my booth. He was dressed in black wool pants and a black T-shirt with "Union Station" stamped in gold block letters on the pocket. He wasn't wearing a wedding ring. Of course, that meant nothing.

"It's good. What do you call it again?" I wanted to be friendly. I'd met few citizens and made fewer friends in my time here.

"Rainy Day Dark Ale. Perfect for today. I brew a small batch when I can. Most people who come in just want CochLite. You have good taste."

"This is your brew? I love the aroma. I'll take one more," I said.

The bartender brought me an amber glass and read my company nametag pinned to my jacket.

"Dr. Catrina Pandora Van Dingle."

I snatched off the tag and put it in my pocket. My name had always been embarrassing for me and what kind of person sits in a bar wearing a name tag? I might as well have worn a "Rob me" sign.

"It's a Dutch name," I said quickly. "What's yours?"

"Ulysses." Now this bar was making sense. Union Station. U.S. Grant. He had to be the owner. Ice balls ticked the street-facing window as the temperature dropped below the freezing point.

"You work for The Company, I see." His deep voice poured from his chest as easily as beer from a pitcher.

"I do. I study chemicals in plants. I'm analyzing beans grown from seeds found in an old pair of pants." Too much information. I should have stopped at do. The man leaned towards me so I went on talking.

"The original beans were found in antique corduroy trousers purchased at an estate sale by Bert Cochton." Bert was a history buff who specialized in buying up old Civil and Revolutionary War clothes abandoned in attics. Part owner of Cochton Enterprises, he had a dream about these beans the moment he got his hands on them—that they would lead to something great. When a Cochton has a dream, no one in Cochtonville stands in his way.

Ulysses said, "I see. Well, better call somebody for a ride if you're waiting for the bus. Things here don't get fixed quickly, as you know."

"I *don't* know. I've only been in Cochtonville for a month."

"Oh. Welcome to the city." I'd saturated him with information. He went back to the bar as I dialed for a ride. Fifteen minutes passed. No luck getting a cab.

The lights of the Pavilion of Agriculture snapped on and most of the bar's patrons drifted out the door—a three-inch-thick Prohibition-style affair with a rectangular peephole—leaving me alone with the bartender, a couple kissing on the couch in the corner, and a man and woman playing pool. The man wore a newsboy cap and thick plastic glasses. The woman, hair shimmery with henna (2-hydroxy-1,4-naphthoquinone) was in a tight red dress with a little bow under the left breast. In contrast, I wore a cropped jacket over a green polo, with the gold C for "Cochton," purchased at the company store. Cochton Enterprises liked us to wear insignia clothes. It made us appear professional. I unclipped my hair and let it fall like a sandy flag.

The woman from the pool table glided over to the blue-backlit bar, graceful in her heels. She had twenty-pound breasts and a ten-pound ass, and I was insecure in her presence. She shook her hair at the bartender and let it drape over one eye. "Hey, Ulysses, get me a drink of water."

Surprisingly, she came to the booth and sat across from me.

"He's being friendly to you 'cuz he's in the doghouse," the woman said. Here was the first person in Cochtonville who'd approached me when it had nothing to do with work or commerce. "Hey, Ulysses, how about some snacks?" she called.

"He's being friendly?" I said, confused.

"He usually don't talk to Company people much. I got no prejudices. Nothing much to hide. I'm Maven, by the way."

"I'm Catrina."

The weather report was on the television. An "arctic invasion," the forecaster was saying.

The bartender put a basket of pretzels in front of me and handed Maven her water.

Maven chomped a pretzel. "I'd hate to be on the road with this ice. Lucky all I have to do is walk the streets. Ulysses, give me some of what's behind the counter."

"That, my dear, will cost. Cash money this time," the bartender said, reaching into his pocket and tucking something in her palm.

She snapped her fingers shut to hide it. "Put it on my tab."

He put a hand on his hip. "Maven, let me know if you're going to die soon."

She opened her leather purse and blinked. "What you mean by that?"

"I've carried you this long. I might as well be a pallbearer and finish the job."

She slipped the small item into her purse. It dropped in silently. The bartender went back to the bar and stood behind it. The man in the cap joined Maven and me in the booth.

"Ulysses talks tough, but he'd be nowhere if it weren't for Bernadette. She's the real manager of this place," he said. "They're both the proprietors, but she's the one with the business sense."

"He's the creative one," Maven said. "They're having another tiresome fight. That's why she's not here."

"They'll get over it," the man said, bug-eyed behind his glasses. "They've got to."

He went to the pool table and put a cue between his legs.

"Hey, baby, you can lead a horse to water. Who'll play break the law with me?" He wiggled it at me.

"Go home, Ernie Ray," Ulysses said from behind the bar. "You'll get me arrested. This nice woman here probably agrees that all deviants need locking up."

Ernie Ray put his pool cue on the table. "Hey, man, is this some kind of acid test? I'm not going anywhere." He sat next to me again. I inched away. I wasn't quite used to so many locals in one spot displaying their strange attitudes and archaic speech patterns, as if they'd been dropped into a time hole by their separation from the rest of the United States.

"Welcome to the joint." Ernie Ray huffed his stale popcorn breath in my face, as if all he ate was free bar food and he was eager to share the experience. "You're cute. Single?" He had a prominent brow and hairy eyebrows. He'd hit on a sore topic. I was single but didn't want to be single forever. My parents had expressed worry that this place was known to be prudish and I'd never find a man. My granny was concerned I *would* find a man— an oppressive one. I wasn't sure I had room in my life for a man at all, and yet, I wanted more than just a life in the lab. I wanted kids, a family, everything good that a person could experience.

"Aren't you getting a little too personal?" I asked, crossing my arms over my chest. He was the desperate type. He made me uncomfortable. I was sure I'd caught a glimpse of him slumped against the door the last time the bus had zoomed past.

Ulysses came over and leaned on the booth. "Ernie Ray, find

that guy who pays you ten to go down on him. I'm trying to keep a decent place here."

"I wouldn't be caught dead doing that for only a ten," Ernie Ray said in all seriousness.

"Walls talk, Ernie." Ulysses pulled him from the booth. "And accidents will happen, pal."

"Wait, wait. One poem for her. It's called 'Toast to a New Girl.'"

"Poem?" I asked. The media here was twenty-four-hour news. It surprised me that people even knew what a poem was.

"Make it fast," Ulysses said. "Watch the words."

Ernie Ray shrugged off Ulysses's grasp and steadied himself. He recited with a deep croak.

"Let's drink to getting hard
To holding the line
To cornering the market
To hiding all women in the suburbs
Only wearing Floyd."

He bowed. I wasn't sure if I should clap or not. This whole thing had me uncomfortable.

"Did you like it?" he asked eagerly.

"What did it mean? I can't say I understand poetry. Is it all about emotion? Sincerity?" I couldn't classify this guy. Maybe he was one of those who came with special-handling instructions.

"Exactly," he said.

The door opened and a man in a tan uniform came in with a keg on a cart. "Delivery," he said brightly, shaking precipitation from his short hair.

"In this weather? You're a juggernaut," Ulysses said, following him as he wheeled the beer to the cooler behind the counter.

Ulysses unlocked a drawer. He counted out bills and gave them to the man and asked, "Need a tip?"

"Sure do," the guy replied. "Brings a man out on a night not fit for sewer rats."

Ulysses reached under the cash tray, palmed something, and shook the man's hand, giving him what he'd taken out.

"Be gentle," Ulysses said. "And be careful on that ice."

"Will do," said the man, a common-looking, middle-aged fellow. I couldn't imagine what he might be getting for a tip. He slipped out with a rattle like a specter of smoke or a final breath.

"Me too," Ernie Ray said. "I need a tip."

"When you deliver something useful," Ulysses said.

"I delivered a poem to the new girl," he said hopefully.

"More like a nightmare." Ulysses took Ernie Ray by the arm and walked him to the door.

"It will be when Bernadette finds out. I won't tell if you tip me. This girl isn't even your style. Hardly worth the risk."

"All right, I've had enough. Get out." Ulysses tossed him into the icy night.

"Chickens will come home to roost," Ernie Ray yelled as Ulysses shut the door.

"That wasn't called for. You know he's not playing with a full deck," Maven said.

"You too," Ulysses said, opening the door. "Time to go to work."

"You're kicking me out?"

"I am. I'm closing early." He called to the kissing couple, "You two, the couch is finished for the night."

Maven tossed her hair. "No need to bite my head off. You're all sizzle and no steak. Do you think I'm playing gooseberry?" She put her purse under her arm, strutted to the exit, and slammed the door as she left. A few seconds later, she opened it. "Ernie's making a fountain on your wall." After the couple slunk past her, she slammed the door again.

I took a deep breath while Ulysses leaned over me and closed wooden blinds with a clatter. It had been a while since I'd smelled a man's t-shirt. If not for the beer, his molecules invading my nose would have made me nervous.

"Dr. Van Dingle, were you planning on meeting someone here or getting a ride?"

"I'm calling a cab, but I'm not getting through. Do you have a phone that works?" I asked in frustration. This place was playing catch-up on everything except growing food.

Maven poked her head in the door. "Ulysses is a one-off! He always runs back to Bernadette." Ulysses went and leaned on the door, forcing her back out.

"She's right," he said as he snapped the lock on the door.

"Are you going to keep that door locked?"

"Just for the next five minutes. Another beer? On me." He pulled out a phone. "I'll see if I can get through."

"I'm near my capacity. This stuff is good. Dreamy. I mean creamy."

"Glad you like it. Made from rainwater and the best of secret ingredients." He put down his phone. "No answer and no use leaving a message."

"I could figure out your secret. I'm a chemist after all."

He sat down across from me. "You'll never get a secret from me." Did he have dimples?

I eased myself into the coziness of the place. "Are you going to join me, or must I drink alone?"

"I don't drink on the job. It could lead to bad habits." Ulysses had baby blue eyes and thick lashes, I noted, in case I had to give a Patrol report.

"You're closed. You even pulled the shades."

Five hours of lost signals, a discussion on importation and chemistry of hops, one locked door, a microwaved pizza, and two beers beyond my limit later, Ulysses turned off the light over the bar. I wasn't sure what my options were. There had to be a hotel within walking distance. The weather was too bad for scary weirdos like Ernie Ray to be slinking around. Only the officers would be on the sidewalk.

Ulysses stood with his arms folded across his chest. "I live above the bar. I'll bring down a blanket and you can sleep here." I watched him open a door next to the beer cooler and climb a narrow set of stairs. He had a nice butt and a steady walk with an easy gait. For a second, I was embarrassed by my staring at the butt of a man instead of considering his mind. Was it so wrong? I was a professional woman with a promising career. I could objectify a man I'd never see again, couldn't I? The only dangerous objectification was internal objectification that limits a person's scope of experiences and leads to shame and depression. Did I learn that in college or was I drunk?

My equilibrium off kilter, I sat listening to the city, waiting for Ulysses to return with a blanket. It was dead still except for the tapping of ice on the window. It gave me the creeps. The floor of the bar was all footprints and popcorn. The booths were about four uncomfortable feet long. This dreamy bartender had me lusting to whiff his t-shirt. Grant's portrait was looking sexy. I'd slip out and find my way home before I grew more ridiculous. I went to the door, stood on tip toes, unbolted it, and poked my head out. A sheet of ice twinkled over the gnarled sidewalk. The bus was still there, frozen in place, listing a little or maybe it was *me* being unsteady. *Not a sole around.* Ice pellets pinged on the streetlights. Down the block, one flickered and went out. A siren's scream exploded across the city. I leapt back, my heart pounding in my throat. A robotic voice, loud enough to blast paint from a building, bounced through the city. "Alert. A security violation has been reported. Citizens, remain inside." I slammed the door and covered my ears, refusing to panic.

Ulysses came down the stairs. He had no blanket. "Don't worry. We get warnings all the time."

"What's it mean?"

"If you go out, the Vice Patrol will use you for target practice."

"What about Maven?"

"Every person for herself at times like this."

His gender-inclusive language warmed my flustered heart—he was a magic number, an island of stability. I liked him. I trusted him. Autonomous pheromones and perspiration sprouting under his arms, he reached over and locked the door. "You'd better come upstairs and sleep on the futon. I got a roommate, a woman, so you won't be in danger except maybe from her. I'm on her bad side tonight. All my fault, I'm afraid. Stay quiet and away from windows."

"I can take on any woman." The beer had me cocky.

"No, honey, believe me. Not Bernadette. She never loses.

CHAPTER TWO

Yeast is a round, single-celled organism that changes sugar into alcohol (ethanol) and carbon dioxide—waste products produced when oxygen isn't present. This process powers the yeast. Yeast metabolism causes bread to rise and gives booze its buzz; Brewer's yeast is a strain of Saccharomyces cerevisiae.

I trembled as I followed him up the narrow staircase. The apartment was wood paneled and dark, and the futon was covered with some sort of chenille that might have held a large quantity of dust. Ulysses took a blanket from the back of the futon and spread it out. I sat down carefully as the apartment spun. The alcohol had changed the density of my blood. How could I have let this happen? He went into the kitchen and came back with a glass of orange juice.

"Drink this. It'll help you keep ahead of that hangover." He was right. I had to get more water into my blood.

I tossed down the juice and regretted it. My stomach was a vat of acid.

"Sorry to have served you so much. It's against my principles, really. You've got an honest smile. Can I get you anything else?"

"The bathroom," I said, my mouth dry.

"This way." I followed him down a hall. He turned on the light to the bathroom.

"You gonna be okay?" he asked kindly.

"Of course. I'm a scientist. See you later. I can handle this," I said with false confidence, pulling the door closed.

The bathroom was a spiraling cenote blue with a shiny, brown tile floor and neatly hung white towels. He hadn't lied about the woman. A used tampon was in the toilet, and the bowl was filled with diluted blood. After taking more than the average mammal urination time of twenty seconds, I stood up stupidly looking at the bowl, paralyzed by such a simple decision. She hadn't flushed. Should I? Did she know I was here, or was it a secret that would be revealed with a flush? My stomach made the call for me. I vomited, hitting the bowl neatly. All my laboratory experience with volumetric pipets made me an expert at delivering fluids from one place to another. I wiped my mouth with toilet paper before flushing the evidence and slinking like a stray cat back to the lumpy futon in the living room.

Snuggling dizzily under the covers, I thought I wouldn't sleep. But I must have because I woke as my hair was being yanked. Bernadette had a tungsten grip, enormous boobs, bobbed brown hair, and Hello Kitty pajamas.

"How cute. Cock-a-doodle-do. It's morning. Now get the fuck out of here." She tossed me onto the floor. She could pull off being beautiful while throwing more shade than Mt. Hood. Apparently, she thought that since she was gorgeous, she could push me around. I was barely awake and did a stupid thing. I wobbled to my feet and slapped her. The crisp crack of my fingers smacking right below her cheekbone was no louder than fingers snapping. I hadn't used all my force. I only meant to shock her enough to defend myself.

She stepped back in surprise. "Bitch, you'll pay for that *and* the free drinks you got! Ulysses! Get this *thing* out of here."

Wearing only sweatpants, Ulysses bolted from the bedroom. "No trouble, no trouble," he said. "Trouble brings trouble."

Bernadette grabbed for my purse, and I tucked it under my arm like a running back with a completed pass.

"I'll pay," I said, angrily thrusting out my arm to keep her away as she rushed forward.

"No! On me!" Ulysses said. He hurried me down the stairs into the bar. I could smell his yeasty morning breath. He was shirtless and I could see a tattoo of Ulysses S. Grant on his deltoid.

"So sorry, Dr. Van Dingle," Ulysses said as he scooted me out of the door. The ice had melted.

After I made my way to the bus stop, I fished through my purse for gum and a hairbrush. Ulysses ran out of Union Station with a cup of coffee and a bag of corn nuts. "Here. You're gonna need this," he said, putting the mug in my hand and the snack in my purse. The bus pulled up. Ulysses and I shivered together on the curb as the bus doors swung open. He was shaking in the wind. A car honked. We touched hands. He was gone and I was on the bus bouncing over potholes.

In the lobby of Cochton Enterprises, a company specializing in agricultural products with their tentacles in diverse ventures, the three cast-metal statues of the Cochton heirs with their thin noses and squinty eyes glared at me accusingly. The gum-chewing security guard stood beside them.

This company was the heart of Cochtonville. Cochtonville might be a called a company town, except that it was completely divorced from and antagonistic toward the United States, especially Illinois, an agricultural rival. I flashed my ID to the guard. I was disheveled and smelly. I was lonely here. I had to admit it to myself. Being in the bar shined a spotlight on it. I came here to do science. I *had* to do science. It was a part of me. But it was only one component of my whole self. It was the part I understood, the concrete side of me. My other ingredient was missing in the tangle of life's madness. The situation reminded me of what I'd learned about chemistry back in the 1800s when chemists didn't grasp that air was a mixture of gases. They didn't understand why sometimes air burned and other times it suffocated. Then they figured out that oxygen was combustible gas and nitrogen was a noncombustible gas and that they mixed together to make air. There was more to air than a simple vapor. There was more to me too, but I didn't know what it was. Or maybe I was still a little drunk.

My boss, Dr. Mike Watson, stood in the doorway of his office and frowned as I passed him. He followed me to my lab. His white hair sprung from his head like a flame, and he sported a gray flannel suit with a yellow tie patterned with hexagons. The shelves in my lab were built for someone six feet tall, and I reached on tiptoe for my volumetric flasks. I wanted to get right to work, be a go-getter. My spine felt hot with the intensity of his eyes on my khakis. Wearing the light-colored material while being a light-colored person gave me the uncomfortable sensation of not wearing pants at all. I was being too sensitive. This wasn't a sensitive place, and I'd best get used to it. At the same time, I kind of *wanted* a man to look at my ass, as long as it wasn't Mike Watson.

"Dingle," he said as I opened my lab notebook and recorded the parameters. Today I'd be getting my first large sample of *Muscuna cochtonus*, the beans found in an old pair of pants. It was a bad day to have a hangover.

"Coming on time is important." He stroked my arm, the one I wrote with, so that my entry for the "run conditions" smudged. I tried not to lose my temper as he bungled my last name yet again *and* was touching me. I had to keep my annoyance to myself. It wouldn't be professional to go off on him and I'd already slapped the wrong person once today.

"Please, Dr. Watson, this is a new method. I need good notes." I was too fatigued for all of this.

"Good notes? Would you be a good *girl?* You make it hard when you don't follow the rules and then...." He paused. I wasn't sure if he was being intentionally sexual or just being a chemist. I wanted to slap him, but not as much as I wanted to study the new beans Cochton Enterprises had procured.

"Then what?" I whispered.

"I explode," he said, as if he was unstable.

"Dr. Van Dingle? I've got new beans for analysis." Dr. Natharie Nair, a botanist about five years older than I was, stood in the doorway with a packet of red mottled with white *Muscuna cochtonus.*

I dashed over to Natharie. "So good to see you, Dr. Nair." My head was bursting with ideas of what these beans could be used for —biofuels from the oils, food additives from the alkaloids, phenols, proteins....

"Get to work," said Mike, pushing past us. "You smell like a bar."

Natharie had grown the vines that had for so many years been lost to history. She had a huge specimen in the company greenhouse, her first attempt at growing this rediscovered species. It was a fifteen-foot-long vine crawling over the greenhouse glass and bursting with jasmine-scented blossoms that were a fluorescent indigo. She'd named it Mother. The whole company knew about Mother. Now the botanist had a two-pound bag of Mother's offspring, a nutritious feed crop that didn't need fertilizer, beans being legumes and fixing their own nitrogen. My job was to complete an analysis of their content and identify a unique molecule that could be used to sell the beans as having a secret ingredient. It was a marketing ploy, but the truth was all plants house unique chemicals. Finding one would be fun.

Inside me burned the spirit of adventure that every scientist has. Some travel the globe. Some work with dangerous substances, walk to the edge of volcanoes, or cohabit with gorillas in the wild. For me, it was living in Cochtonville. I was unattached and had nothing to lose. But we always have something to lose, don't we? I just didn't yet know what it was.

My lab was meticulously kept and filled with chemical instruments that made precise measurements. There were a dozen jars of leaves and seeds on the bench top. Volumetric flasks lined the shelves above the pH meter and analytical balance. Sunlight streamed through the windows. Below, the Cedar River with no cedar trees in sight rushed between dirty buildings and past the processing plants of Cochton Enterprises. Somewhere out there was my boarding house, the Brownstone Inn. I was happy to have found it. Not only was it cozy, I'd been told by HR that it was "against morality" for a woman to live alone in Cochtonville and a boarding house was considered respectable. City buses, slow even from this perspective, chugged through the streets. I was soaring above Cochtonville, formed fifteen years ago, 325 square miles in size—between that of Hong Kong and Singapore.

"Dr. Van Dingle?"

"The beans!" I said to Dr. Nair. "I can't wait to get started. I have the method all ready."

Natharie gave me the sample of beans. "Were you having a spot of trouble with Dr. Watson?"

"Yes." I felt the seat of my khakis as if I was the one who'd done something shady. "Are my pants too tight?"

She took in my rumpled clothes and probably my pallor. "He's a lecher, as are most bosses here. The only thing he respects is another man. Looks like you've maybe got one."

"Not exactly." My face grew hot at this suggestion. "I got stranded in the ice storm. There *was* a handsome man, but he wasn't single."

She held up her left hand to show a sparkling engagement ring. "I bought it myself. Worth every penny. There aren't any harassment laws here. No way to protect yourself."

Genius, although I didn't want a big ring. It could get caught on the lab equipment.

"What if I say I have a man back home?"

"Good idea. Especially if he's burly or has a black belt," she said. "Be sure to mention your hometown boyfriend to Rhonda, the office manager."

Less than an hour later, a man about my age came into my lab. He had a shy smile and hair the shade of pimento with an amateurish close cut, the kind a child might get at the hands of his mother. He and I both looked geeky in our attire purchased from our employer: insignia polos, tan pants, flat shoes—you get the picture.

"Dr. Jester Rana, synthetics," he said, shaking my hand. "My lab's down the hall."

"Dr. Catrina Van Dingle, analytical chemist. Do you have something for me? Do you need anything?" I asked, glancing at his hand. No ring. Of course, that didn't mean a thing.

He held a screw-top vial the size of a tall shot glass. "I do. Can you tell me how many components are in this mixture?"

"I can."

"I can't disclose what it is. It's got something to do with the containment of hogs."

"Doesn't most everything around here?"

"They're smart, you know. They have the intelligence of a three-year-old human." He gave me the vial.

"I thought I'd be seeing more of them. They're in shelters as I understand it. That was in the news back home."

"Yes, eight thousand or more in each confinement building. You can't take photos or write about it. Interferes with commerce. You'd be brought before the mayor and the city manager." He had a wholesome look—like Archie from the comics.

"You can smell them, though, can't you, when the wind is right?"

"The stink is much worse than the individual chemicals. We consider the vapors harmless."

I took a strip of label tape and put it on the vial. "At Purdue, scientists found that pigs can sniff the difference between spearmint and peppermint. That's my area. You know, plants and the chemicals in them. What's your lab number again?"

"Four twenty-seven. You know, like seven times sixty-one. Dr. Van Dingle, I like your...." He stared at my polo and swallowed. "Your lab." This guy was nice. "You're new here. Are you single?"

I wrote *427.1* on the vial. He was as bold as that bar poet, but certainly seemed safer.

I smiled. "Yes."

He leaned on the lab bench. "I want to get married. Have some little ankle biters. I'll be a good dad. Not like my old man."

I took his bait. "Sometimes I get the idea that since I'm a female scientist, I'm expected to not want to get married or have kids. I'm not some kind of paradox. A male scientist can want that without anybody thinking twice about it. Mendeleev didn't just father the periodic table. He had six kids and two wives."

Jester moved away from me. "If you're thinking of bigamy, it sounds like something they might execute you for here. You're new. I gotta tell you, we don't have set punishments. They fit the person, not the crime. It prevents deviants from doing a cost-benefit analysis."

We were looking at each other intently now. He was strong and secure. He could be a rock of a partner, a guide to this crazy city-state, and despite not needing a man, I wanted one. I was determined to have everything any other woman could have. I would do it all.

He leaned forward. I tilted my head up. Even though his breath smelled like hotdog, I was eager to kiss him, to experience a local guy up close, make some memories on this blank slate of a place. You can learn so much from a kiss. If I liked him, I'd surely like it here. Everything bad from the rest of the world would be left behind in the rush of the take-off. My future was riding on this kiss.

He leaned toward me and said, "You're amazing. I love your science. But I'll clue you in."

I said, "Yes."

He said, "I need to marry a virgin."

My hand flew from my lap and I slapped him.

CHAPTER THREE

Malt is made from germinated barley or wheat that has been heat-dried. Malt adds enzymes that convert starch to sugars during the brewing process. Light beers have malt that has been dried at low temperatures and contains more enzymes. Dark beer contains fewer enzymes but more dark, heavy, flavor-rich melanoidins. Malt contains lipids (fatty components), and these will form foul, cardboard-tasting substances if oxygen is present during the brewing process. Malt provides proteins that fortify the structure of the foam on a head of beer.

Saturday night, lonely, bored, and disgusted with myself for slapping two people in one day, I roamed the neighborhood near the inn and window-shopped at nearby stores. The antique store, Odd and Ends, had a window packed with cast-iron toys, ceramic crocks, and advertising signs. I went in, looking for an old book or watercolor—a relic of Cochtonville's past as a normal place. Even in here, the only things in frames were yellowing certificates, photographs of street scenes, and reproductions of portraits of famous white men. There wasn't anything beautiful. I found a black-and-white photo of Ulysses S. Grant from 1843, heavy-browed and serious with greatness behind those eyes like my Ulysses and his tattoo. It was the size of a postcard in a thin, gold frame. To cover up my motivation, I snatched a photo of Louis

Pasteur, his famous quote penned on the back: *Science knows no country, because knowledge belongs to humanity, and is a torch which illuminates the world*. I paid for them and left quickly, embarrassed for my strange attraction to all things Ulysses.

At No More Lonely Nights, a lingerie store, I bought a pair of silky pajamas. I wore them that night on my trips from my room upstairs to the parlor to get the cookies put out by Jan and Hans, the owners of the Brownstone Inn Boarding House. I wore them to breakfast too, as Jan, in a blue fleece bathrobe, poured coffee and brought out plates piled high with fruit and muffins.

"New clothes and new habits. You've met somebody." Jan studied me while maintaining the tact and reserve of the matron he was pretending to be. He dressed as a frumpy woman by day to appease the sensibility of Cochtonville, which didn't approve of two men sharing a bedroom even in their own inn.

"Not really met. Just ran across someone interesting."

"Did you? How interesting did it get?"

"Not very. He's with someone."

"The spark's been lit none the less," said Jan, putting a pastry on the white china plate in front of me. "Have a blueberry tart."

Valentine came to the table. Valentine was a doctor at the prison, one of the main employers in Cochtonville besides Cochton Enterprises. She was near my age and similar in height. If we both hadn't been so busy, we would've been best friends.

"Catrina's lovesick," said Jan, dishing out scrambled eggs.

"I never said that!"

"You don't have to say it. I see it in your eyes. And in your pajamas. And that night you didn't come home."

Valentine sipped her orange juice. "A man from work?"

"No. Not him."

"He's taken," Jan added, pouring orange juice for Wilma as she sat. Wilma was about sixty years old with long hair that fell to one side in a white braid.

"Taken. Story of my life," I said.

Valentine swallowed a forkful of eggs. "How did you meet this guy?"

I fumbled with my napkin. "I ran into him one rainy day."

"Sounds kind of dangerous," Wilma said. "Some chance guy. That's a good way to end up chained to a basement wall."

"Oh, Wilma, you watch too much television. Not every man is a sexual predator," said Jan.

"In any case, be careful," said Valentine.

"No worries. I won't be seeing him again. Or any man from the looks of it."

Wilma waved her hand. "Who needs a man? You can do everything you need all by yourself."

"Safely in private," said Valentine matter-of factly.

"Ladies, I disagree," said Jan. "There's something about a man that can't be replicated. Wilma, I applaud you for trying."

"It's time for that party we talked about the night the tornado passed over," Wilma said.

Shortly after I'd arrived, the tornado sirens had gone off around midnight. Jan and Hans had lead us through the kitchen to the shelter beneath the house, a cellar filled with canned goods, flashlights, and magazines. Without a wig and close shave, Jan looked remarkably like a man. Finally, shivering with fear at the sound of the wind rushing above us, I blurted out, "Are you male?"

"Of course," he'd said. "Do I really look like a frumpy woman?"

Jan explained that he and Hans shared a room, and since it was against the law for two men to do so in Cochtonville ever since it became a city-state, he pretended to be a woman during the day when people might see him.

"People vote for this kind of oppression?" I asked.

Hans explained, "We don't have elections here. People got sick of the ads, and the Cochtons got sick of paying for them."

"Never fear, we have our own ways of lifting the skirt of the law, so to speak," added Jan.

Wilma huffed. "Some of us pull down its pants and whack it on the butt. Are you with us, new girl?"

"If we live through this," I said, hugging my knees as I sat on the cement floor of the cellar.

"We'll have a party," Wilma said. "The kind you mustn't tell anyone about. Can you keep a secret?"

While we waited for the storm to blow itself out, Wilma compared tornados, engorged parts of clouds that cause damage, to men she had known. Wilma was divorced, which made her a second-class citizen here—unable to get a steady job and without a retirement account. Valentine and her husband, Trent, an engineer who traveled out of the state frequently, confessed they used birth control. When they had enough money saved and paid off her loans, they would move to a place where it was legal. I told them about Devil's Bargain, a drug I'd made from plants and sold to football players in high school so they could get high. It had happened long ago but was enough of a confession to win me a shred of trust.

That's how I found myself on Sunday afternoon in the living room of the Brownstone Inn in front of a popping fire, behind closed blinds and a locked door, looking at plastic wands spread out on the oriental rug. We weren't talking magic wands.

Wilma, a salesperson for Just Be You Sex Toys, said, "Women of all ages and morphologies, it's best to take things in your own hand. I'm here to confirm that relationships can be difficult. Men can be scarce."

"Or dangerous," said Jan. He was at home with himself, wearing a tailored shirt, his black hair cut close.

"Might travel for business like Trent does," said Valentine.

"Or be liars," I added.

Wilma said, "They might not always be able to get hard thanks to diabetes, smoking, or alcohol."

"Or high blood pressure medication," added Valentine.

"Too old," Wilma said. "Once women get beyond menopause, they get more sexual while the men their age get less sexual. Many women find it necessary to take things into their own hands."

"And everyone should," said Valentine.

"They're undependable," Wilma said. "One minute on, the next minute off. That's why over half of women and forty percent of men use a vibrator for masturbation or partnered sex. Thirty percent of women use a vibrator as a sleep aid. Use is associated with a positive sexual self-image."

"They are normal and healthy," affirmed Valentine.

"So of course they're banned in Cochtonville," said Jan.

"Over half?" I said, surprised I'd somehow missed out on something so normal.

"Yes," said Jan. "Not common among the devout but for everybody else."

"This product will help you keep your sanity." Wilma pointed to the sample merchandise. "Let me introduce you to the Randi line for women, Candi for men, Rod and Dodd for two women, Glen and Gwen for a hetero couple, Dolly and Molly for two men. These are our introductory units. They come in pink, granite, or automaton-silver, small, medium, large, and canyon. For those who want a quieter ride, we have our upgraded Whisper line."

"This looks like it will give you some quality pleasure." She handed me something the size of a flashlight and shaped like a cross between a penis and a tulip. "This is our Lepus Maximus," she said proudly, as if she'd hand crafted the thing.

"It looks awfully big," I said, turning it over in my hand. "And plasticky. Are there side effects?"

"Rarely," Wilma said confidently. "Occasionally numbness following rough use is reported."

"Can you become addicted?"

"We recommend a break on occasion if you find yourself needing top speed at all times."

She picked up an even larger wand that had prongs on the side. It was gray-green with flecks of white and gold peppered across the head. "We call this one the Klondike," she explained. She handed it to Valentine. "Don't go for the zone right away; massage all parts of your body."

Valentine ran the wand up and down her thighs.

Wilma eyed Jan.

"The Jack for you, maybe." She handed him something smooth and black, much like a jackhammer with ridges.

"Turn them on now," Wilma said. My wand made a hum and sprang to vibrating life with such force that I nearly dropped it.

"You might need rotation. Push the second button. Or the third button for rotation and vibration."

"No," I said. "Not that!" I threw it on the rug. It kept going. Already it didn't need me. Everyone gawked at me. "My ex studied those movements in molecules," I said shyly.

Wilma picked up a smaller, pointed device half the size of a banana. "How about this one? Deep pulse."

"That sounds interesting," I said. The smaller one looked easier to hide, although I wasn't sure from whom.

"Are these illegal?" I asked.

"Only if you admit what they're for," Wilma said.

I took it from Wilma and held the little pink thing it in my palm, happier with the girl talk than with the promise of sexual pleasure. I hadn't experienced much of that yet and compared to the others, this looked innocuous.

"That's perfect for you," said Jan. "I like the way it looks in your hand."

Valentine was pushing buttons on the Klondike.

"What do you think?" asked Wilma.

"I'm liking it," said Valentine. "Reminds me of Trent."

I felt pressured to buy something. I was curious and hopeful that this was an antidote for wanting a man who was all wrong for me.

"This size suits me," I said. "A simple starter model."

"It will keep you out of trouble," Wilma assured me. "Next decision: battery or charge?"

"Curing lovesickness takes a lot of time," said Jan.

"You'd be changing a lot of batteries," said Valentine.

"Charge. I hate changing batteries."

"Solar, conventional, or both?"

So many choices. This sex toy business was a mature industry. I was becoming overwhelmed.

"Both," I blurted.

"Noise level?"

"Are we talking me or the vibrator?" I asked. "Hey, am I the only first-timer?"

"We all have them," said Valentine.

"Even I do," said Jan. "And a penis ring. I'm jealous of you gals. A man comes with his penis and surrounding areas. A woman puts her whole self into it, with no rest in between if she wants. Or so Wilma's told me."

"It's why you should be careful who you love," Wilma said. "Life is too short to waste with the wrong man."

"You don't want a creep," said Jan.

"Test-drive first. You don't want anyone bad at it," said Valentine. "Life's too short not to have satisfaction."

"That's the whole truth," I said, not knowing exactly what I was talking about. My sexual experiences had been amateurish and I had low expectations for men.

"Don't rush into anything," said Valentine. "When you're new to a place, you're vulnerable."

"I haven't studied behavior," I said. "I only study plants. Even they have sex."

In the end, I put my hard money toward a silver Whisper Whizard shaped like a heart—chargeable both ways and silent—to be delivered the next evening.

At first, Whisper Whizard reminded me of sex with Rex in high school, and with Tudor in graduate school. I wasn't exactly lighting myself on fire with him. It was about as exciting as Kegel exercises, and after a while, I gave up. I wasn't sure what to say to Wilma at breakfast the next day. She believed in her products and their benefits enough to risk all for them. Maybe I was frigid even with myself. I was forever alone, I despaired, with holidays coming up and not even enough time off to go home. Luckily, she didn't ask how things were going.

At work I had lunch with Jester in the company cafeteria, a cavern filled with chrome and teak and carpeted in green with yellow squiggles, the word *Cochton* in cursive.

"How was your weekend?" he asked. He looked happy and sun-kissed

"Womanly," I said. "And yours?"

He didn't even ask me what I'd meant, which was good because I couldn't tell him. "Mine was cool. Super cool. I met someone." He took a bite of his burrito. Salsa ran onto his shirt.

"That's disgusting," I said.

"No. I went for a malt alone, and there she was. My shirt attracted her." He puffed out his chest and I read *Big minds for big yields—Bert Cochton*. "She asked all about my work and said it sounded fascinating. We went for two long walks."

"What does she do?"

"She's a hairdresser. Can't you tell?" He fluffed up his red locks. They looked silky, or was I being influenced by Whisper Whizard? "She's young. Younger than you, I'll bet. Smells like a woman. Maybe a little like acetone too. She hooked me up with some products. And I'll clue you in—her name is Jane!" He smiled into space until I wiped his mouth with my napkin.

"Isn't that sweet? I'll clue *you* in. It's not your shirt she likes. She's a gold digger!"

He took another bite of the burrito and it squirted all over my Cochton sweater.

I leaped up and blotted myself with a napkin. "Who takes casualties when they eat?" I dumped my meal into the trash and went to my lab, the only place in the building where I felt sane.

That night I took out Whisper Whizard. It looked so robotic and I felt so frustrated that I almost threw it across the room. I shoved it into the nightstand. As I did so, I saw the photo reproduction of Ulysses S. Grant in the gold frame. I propped him up on the mug from Union Station on the nightstand, took out Whizard, and switched it to medium speed. *It's on to Vicksburg. Full speed ahead, coming up from the South.* It wasn't like the other times. I was playing with myself, walking to the edge of something, moving ahead without worrying about my supply chain, with no fears, unconditionally marching. I was tickled, I was alert, I was beating with two hearts, quietly moaning, thrashing. A tingling went through me, then a shock wave, followed by an aftershock. I was victorious. I was so alive. Then came peace. I fell asleep blissfully, waking at midnight with Whisper Whizard in my palm. He was still buzzing as if nothing had happened between us. How realistic. It mattered so much less now that I had a "partner" who didn't care. I'd defined myself and my own parameters. I was experienced and I was truly flying solo.

CHAPTER FOUR

A thixotropic liquid will decrease viscosity and flow when pressed, like a drop of melted chocolate. These substances are called non-Newtonian fluids because their properties depend not only on temperature and pressure, but also on force. Melted chocolate, margarine, and catsup are thixotropic liquids.

The day before Christmas, Cochton Enterprises closed at noon. I was coming from the department store on that afternoon, walking in the wet fog that was trying to turn to snow. I'd purchased little gifts for those at the inn as I attempted to cheer myself up while facing my first holiday alone. Someone came up behind me and brushed past my left shoulder.

"Hey," I said as a man wearing a light parka, the hood pulled up against the dampness, passed me. I shook when he turned around to apologize. It was Ulysses.

"Catrina! Dr. Van Dingle. Remember me?"

He was windblown and wild-looking. I was so shocked to see him again, I could barely speak. "Ulysses. From Union Station."

"Good memory."

How could I forget? I'd slapped his girlfriend.

"Hey, I'm so sorry about that trouble," I said.

"I'm sure Bernadette started it. She's mean. What's in your

bag?" he asked casually. Shoppers zipped past us. Everyone else was in a hurry, and there we stood in front of the movie theater.

"Six pairs of slippers, three for men, three for women. Why?"

"They won't melt. I got some business with this theater. It shouldn't take more than thirty seconds. Are you busy? Want to come in with me and see this picture?"

"As in now? Today? With you?" I stupidly stammered.

He put an arm around me. "As in 'let's not miss the boat.'"

He exchanged a package the size of a cell phone for money and a pair of tickets. We sat in the back of the theater, nearly the only patrons. The plea to turn off phones was followed by a preview for *Flesh My Soul*, an obviously X-rated move. The picture began. The marquee had said *Disney Holiday*. The movie that came on was *Knights and the Prize*. It was a low-budget film, but I was determined to enjoy it due to the company.

Knights riding rhinos battled a dragon and cut off its head. Green blood squirted everywhere. When the victors returned to the castle, they could have sex with any one woman they desired as a reward. One chose a virgin; one chose a wild fortune-teller. We sat together not saying anything, his arm around my shoulder. He drummed his fingers on my collarbone during the sex scenes until I reached up and put my hand over his.

The third knight chose a married woman, the beautiful wife of a poor merchant. As their naked bodies rose and fell together, Ulysses whispered to me, "You deserve a better show. Let's go somewhere safe." His breath and the mention of safety sent shivers down my chest and up my spine. He flicked my earlobe with his wet tongue. A flood ran through me.

I didn't want him to see me as just a smart girl. I wanted to be the fortune-teller, wild-haired and experienced in such a way that no man could shame me or leave me. I put my hand on the firm bulge that had been in his pants throughout the picture, and I gave it a soft squeeze. "How about a fortune? You have a hard time ahead."

He cupped my chin, turned my face to his, and put his lips to mine. He was as hot as July and his tongue resolute. Melted chocolate holds its shape until pressed, and I puddled like melted chocolate. There was no doubt about the chemical delights and dangers of this moment. Oxytocin flooded through me, plying me, wearing away my resolve, and the testosterone from his lips made me want him more. His hand was under my sweater now, and mine was on his groin. Except for his erection and whatever was in his pockets, his whole body was thawing.

"I can hold your whole tit in my hand," he whispered. "It's efficient."

The only other two people in the theater were all over each other, the woman astride the man. She was wearing a dress under which anything could have been happening. Suddenly the screen went dark, and within a second the image of Bob Cratchit appeared. Ulysses pulled away. "Watch the movie. Vice Patrol. Oh shit."

"What's that?" I was shot through with vigilance and, although I tried to ignore it, fear.

Two men in unzipped black bomber jackets walked through the back curtain and into the theater. They held automatic weapons, and one man shot at the screen. Instinctively, I fell to the floor. It was sticky with what I hoped was soda. Ulysses bent down and whispered to me. "Sit up or these Washers'll think you're blowing me." He helped me back into my seat. I thought I might faint.

"What were you doing down there?" asked the big man.

"I lost a contact," I said, grasping at straws.

"It's a goner," he said, pointing the weapon precisely at the hair whorl on the crown of Ulysses's head.

"I guess so," I said, trying not to sound afraid. "Brother, let's go. I can't see a thing."

The shorter man with a nice body said, "Hold on. Hold on. We're looking for sexual predators. Have you seen any?"

"What do they look like?" I asked. As a chemist I knew that if handled properly, dangerous things could be safe. I summoned my steely nature.

"They're male of course," the big one said.

"I've seen men if that's what you mean. They're everywhere."

"Exactly right. No one is safe."

I grabbed Ulysses by his strong biceps. "I am. I have my older brother here to protect me. Alas, we must be going. I can't see a thing. Is that Goofy or Donald Duck? Would that be all right—if we left?"

The man with the hot body said, "Not so fast. Isn't this picture a little juvenile for you? Why're ya here?"

"Oh, we do it every year. A family tradition. I'm afraid I've ruined it."

He shined a flashlight in Ulysses's face. "You look familiar. You got ID?"

"Smells like hanky-panky in here," the big man said. The couple was headed for the door.

"I wouldn't know the smell," I said. I realized I'd been stupid. If he asked for an ID, I would be revealed to be a foreigner, not a sister. I burst into anxious tears.

"You're scaring her!" Ulysses said. "What crumbs."

"We keep the community safe. Are you safe?" asked the buff man.

"Only if you show us to the door, Officer," I said.

"'Officer'?" he laughed. "I'll let you go with a warning, miss." He handed me a plastic card. "Keep this with you at all times. Read it often." He shined his flashlight on it.

Warning signs of a sexual predator:
Unmarried man over the age of 25
Not stably employed
Finds relief in masturbation
Associates with foreigners
Promotes unrhymed poetry and disorganized music
Save your innocence. Report at once!
This message brought to you by Frani Foil, City Manager

"I see it's clear there are men to fear," I said.

"You get it. That's the ticket! There are those who are wicked," he replied, giving me a fist bump. "Now go home and be with family."

Once out on the sidewalk, Ulysses wiped his forehead and I laughed with relief.

"'Crumbs'?" I giggled. "What kind of word is that?"

"Gotta speak their language," he said. "Catrina Van Dingle, you've got me weak in the knees. When I thought I was going to lose it, you came up with that contact lens story. It wasn't true, was it?"

"Not at all. Popped out in a moment of panic. Do they swing those guns around for show or do they actually shoot people?"

"Of course they shoot people. They're not officers. We call them Washers."

"Washers? As in a spacer for a bolt? What do they do?"

He smiled. "As in they keep us from dirty laundry. Wash the windows of society. The filth. You know, unmarried people and other independent types. Catrina, forgive me. I don't know what I was thinking asking you to that movie except that I wanted to be alone with you in the dark."

The chemicals released from our kiss and my anxiety about the Vice Patrol had my head spinning. I took his arm. We walked together on the cracked sidewalks of downtown Cochtonville. The crowd had thinned since nearly everyone else had rushed home to loved ones. The department store hadn't yet closed. A lime-green, sleeveless dress with a 1950s-style flared skirt was in the window. I focused on it. In the twirl of my head and frosty breath, the dress was as a clear symbol. It represented the lost side of my life, the part that was spontaneous, like a candle burning. It was calling me.

"Hold on. I'm going in there and getting that," I said.

"You'll be damn cold."

"No, I won't."

"I still need something for my mama. Mind if I come along? I could use some female advice."

"Sure. What's she like?" I wanted to know something personal about him.

"Thirty-three years teaching at the public school. Romantic as all get-out."

A dirty movie and now a gift for his mother. Was this guy hustling me?

The department store in its final pre-Christmas frenzy was a sparkling tableau of kinetic energy. Moving mannequins in Victorian garb waved packages, drank from steins, and ate turkey legs. Women at the cosmetics counter accosted me with samples of perfume and eye shadow. To them, I was a blank slate needing to be adorned, and the man at my side, despite my lack of product, was an affront to their business model. Heeding my advice, Ulysses bought his mother a moon-phases bracelet with a little ruby at the half moon, the phase the moon would have been the night he was born, and a garnet and a crescent moon for this brother. I tried on the dress while Ulysses stood in the jewelry department and waited for the bracelet to be assembled.

I scowled in the mirror in the dressing room as the fluorescent lights flickered anemically. I needed to do something with my hair to make this work. I'd sent the clerk to get some matching shoes and stockings. Footfalls marked her return, or so I thought. When the curtain was thrown open, I screamed at the sight of a bug-eyed, bearded Santa Claus with thick glasses and a protruding brow.

"How about a sugarplum?" he said. "Half a loaf is better than no bread at all." He laughed. "I seen you coming in with Ulysses. April Fools!"

I surprised myself by being more angry than afraid. I lunged at him and pummeled his chest.

"Stop, stop, it's Ernie Ray. I'm no monster. I get ten bucks a day to dress up in this fat suit and listen to the greedy kids. Have some compassion for the working man. I was spoofing."

"Get the hell out of here, or I'll scream until you don't get paid."

Ernie Ray backed away.

The salesclerk came in. "How is that working for you?"

"The dress is lovely. Trouble is, I'm getting an unwanted visit from Santa Claus."

Ernie Ray said, "I thought it was the men's room. Don't it look like the men's room?"

"A smidge," the clerk said ignoring Santa.

I folded my hands across my chest. "Get this Peeping Tom out of here. He's a health hazard."

"That style becomes you. I brought you some Betty Grable pin-up pumps and nylons to go with it. We're closing in a few minutes. Will you be making a purchase?"

"Get this man out of here! Can't you see that he's unstable?"

"That bodice is low and you smell sultry. Perhaps you're tempting poor Santa. It's to be expected," the clerk said. "Did you touch her?" she asked Ernie Ray.

"Of course not," he said. "I've done nothing wrong. She's my buddy's rumpy-pumpy. I'm no gooseberry."

"Ulysses and her? I don't buy it," she said. "That dress is perfect for you. Shall I ring it up?"

I wanted the dress. I bought it. By the time Ulysses came to find me, Ernie Ray was gone, and I began to wonder if I'd imagined the whole incident.

We came out of the store to find buses stopped and restaurants closed. We set out for the Brownstone Inn together. We walked with optimism and oxytocin, already feeling like we'd known each other forever. Sunset fell early, and I suggested calling a cab as the snow dropped around us and wetted our packages.

Ulysses stood by the curb, stuck out his thumb, and a car pulled up. A white-haired woman leaned out the passenger-side window.

"You kids need a ride? Blizzard's on the way, they say."

Ulysses climbed in eagerly, and I followed. We cuddled in the backseat.

"Where you lovebirds going?" asked the elderly man in the driver's seat. I gave the Brownstone's address.

The woman said, "That's sweet. Wilma's place? You know her?

So do we." She smelled musky, like ambergris from whale intestines caused by irritation from a squid beak. The stuff was considered an aphrodisiac by some.

"I have slippers for her right here. Do you think she'll like satin?"

"If it feels good, she will," the woman said. "We all love Wilma and her parties. What would we do without her?"

I watched the windshield wipers clear away the snow as the musk from the perfume, the scrape with the Washers, and the closeness of Ulysses had me walking the edge of a dream.

"Who's Wilma?" Ulysses stood on the porch with me. Our arms were bursting with our purchases.

"She lives here. She's an entrepreneur, you might say." I unlocked the door, and he put the packages on the floor in the foyer. A twelve-armed chandelier twinkled overhead.

"Thank you," I said. He helped me take my coat off. Being near him in the old inn with its crackling fire had me cozy.

"Are you seeing your mom tonight?"

"Tomorrow. Alone tonight." He handed me my coat. I could tell he wasn't in a hurry to go.

"I have wrapping paper if you need some. Come on in. Wait here in the parlor."

When I came down, he'd taken his parka off and was sitting by the fire on the couch. His cardigan was open and the thin, black Union Station T-shirt under it pulled tight across his pecs. Snow was melting on his loafers.

I sat next to him and put my hands on his chest.

"It's not T-shirt weather," I said.

He jumped. "Yow. Your hands are cold. I was just planning to run out and take care of some quick business and then get back to the bar."

"It's become a long day," I said.

"It could get longer, and much warmer," he said, his eyes finding mine. He drew me to him, and our kiss had me again melting like chocolate into his soft lips. The smell of meat and spices and the sound of feet on the stairs parted us.

"Stay awhile. I can have a guest for supper. Put your shoes by the fire and let them dry."

"I'd love to. Were you planning to wear that dress?"

I hadn't yet decided where I would wear it. The company was having a party. I wasn't sure if I'd go without a date but knew I wanted that dress, even if Whisper Whizard was the only one who saw me in it.

"Should I?" I said.

"It's an occasion tonight. Or could be."

I ran up to change. I tossed my ugly Cochton clothes into the hamper with my moist, pink panties. I put on the sheer and lacy pair I'd only worn once when I was a bridesmaid in my cousin's wedding. I didn't like non-matching lingerie, so I threw my bra in the hamper too. I didn't know if I would invite Ulysses up. He always went back to Bernadette; he freely admitted it. I needed to guard my heart even though I didn't want to be alone in the windswept snow of Cochtonville tonight. Just in case, I put Whisper Whizard in the bottom of my underwear drawer alongside U.S. Grant. I slipped into the new dress and ran down the stairs, wondering if this wrapping might lead to some unwrapping.

"I need some help with the zipper," I told him.

The brief touch of his fingers on my shoulder gave me shivers.

He said, "You've got no shoes or stockings. Your toes will get cold."

"No," I said, "they won't."

His hands were shaking, and his nervousness drew me in. I wanted to be wanted, and this man seemed simple and willing, maybe easier to understand than others. If things didn't work out, the repercussions would be minimal since we hadn't a lab in common. I wouldn't have to see him again. I was giddy with the freedom.

He swallowed. "You have panties on?"

I spun around and looked him in the eye. "What kind of man asks that question?" I tried to sound coy. I wasn't usually flirtatious, but I wanted to be.

His winter-pale skin pinked. "You're snowing me, that's all."

I'll be bedding you if things go right.

"I'll let it go this time," I said.

We put the gifts under the fragrant tree, went to the dining room and took our places at the table with Valentine, Trent, and Wilma. Wilma regarded Ulysses suspiciously as he mentioned the couple who'd given us a lift. The oak table was covered with a festive, red table runner. Having had a humanities course titled Empire and Oppression in college, I was acutely knowledgeable of my own subjugation that could come with the intimacy I desired. We put our napkins on our laps. Hans poured red wine for each of us.

"Nice dress, nice man," said Jan, dressed in a poinsettia Christmas sweater. He served me a slice of thickly cut ham. My stomach dropped. I didn't want to eat a pig. I still remembered the smell of the hog confinement areas that had smacked my nose as I first drove into Cochtonville.

I reached for the fruit salad Ulysses handed me as headlights flickered past the window.

Wilma squinted at Ulysses as Hans lit red-candy-cane-striped candles on the table.

"Have we met before?" she asked.

Ulysses studied his plate. "It's possible. I have a business."

"I have a business too," Wilma said.

"In that case, we might know each other," Ulysses said.

"I've outgrown men," Wilma said.

"Our loss," Ulysses said, handing her a basket of cloverleaf rolls.

There came another headlight and the sound of car doors

slamming. Everyone exchanged uneasy glances. My stomach was already in knots at having this man I desired at the table, and each door slam sent my skin prickling at the memory of the Vice Patrol. Perhaps they'd followed us here.

Trent asked Ulysses, "What brings you here, anyway?" Headlights flickered outside.

Ulysses passed him the green bean casserole topped with french-fried onions.

"I'm beginning to wonder that myself," Ulysses said. He dropped a hand beneath the table and squeezed my bare thigh. "You're an engineer?"

"Yes, in robotics" said Trent. "I can travel between countries with a science pass. Valentine can't cross the border, Cochton's Edge, until her student loans are paid. Makes for lonely nights."

"I'm on my last year," she said.

I took a bite of the fruit salad—it contained gelatin and pretzels—while trying to decide what to do about the ham.

Jan and Hans sat at the table, and Jan raised a glass. "Holiday cheer!" We all lifted our glasses together.

After the toast, Hans took a bite of ham. He screwed up his face in disgust. "This is awful. Where did you get it?"

Jan drew himself up, offended. "It's a Cochton ham." He took a bite. "Oh, Lord. it's like eating a sweaty armpit."

"Like taking a drink from a urinal," Wilma said. "Not that I have."

"Essence of shit," said Hans.

Jan tossed down his fork. "That's it. I'm planting a victory garden in the spring."

Wilma spit a mouthful of ham into her napkin.

"Victory over what?" I asked.

"Over the hegemony of Cochton Enterprises. They control what we eat, what we drink, all means of production. I'm producing something they don't control." He gave me a full-frontal stare. "I'm sorry, Catrina. They're evil."

"Where will you get the seeds?" asked Wilma.

"They can be had," Ulysses said. "If you know where to look."

"We'll not be risking the safety of our guests by planting a garden." Hans stood up. "A little mustard and horseradish and this ham will be delicious."

Wilma turned as white as her hair as more lights illuminated the windows, then dimmed.

"Excuse me," she said, pushing away from the table and heading for the stairs to her room.

"I imagine you don't have loans," Valentine said to me as she tried to bring the conversation back to a respectable realm.

"No. It's partly why I went into chemistry. There are plenty of teaching assistantships and I had Cochton Enterprises sponsor my education. They're interested in plants, which was my research area."

"You're obligated," said Jan, as if I'd done something horrible.

"I studied plants because I was curious about nature's molecules and I didn't want to hurt animals."

The doorbell played cathedral chimes. Jan adjusted his wig. We sat without talking. Ulysses buttoned his sweater. The doorbell rang again. Hans plopped some condiments on the table, wiped his face on his apron, pushed in his chair, and walked through the dining room, past the living room with the oriental rugs and cozy fire, to the foyer with the chandelier. He cracked open the door.

"Is Catrina available?"

It was Jester. I recognized his slightly nasal voice.

I got up and went to speak with him. I passed Hans in the hall.

"It's for you," he said, his face stony.

Jester was on the porch with his entire extended family—an assortment of wives, children, and parents, the mother quite plump.

"Jester," I squeaked. "What a surprise!"

"You said you'd be alone tonight. We came to bring some cheer. These are my parents, Jack and Jill, my brothers Jordon, Jafar, Java, Jigger, and Juan and their families." The clan burst into "O Holy Night" that segued into "It Came upon a Midnight Clear" and topped it off with "Silent Night." They were surprisingly good and sweet-looking in their wool coats and knit hats with tassels. Some hats bore the name of the high school sports team, the Plough Boys. The snow was picking up. The night was crisp. Jill's face was shining in her conviction that no matter how much of her autonomy she'd lost, it was the right thing to do. I could see why Jester clung to his simple beliefs about love and family. For a man like him, this life offered little risk. Two children tussled and fell off the porch as the rest sang on. When they finished singing, I clapped.

"Merry Christmas, Catrina," Jester said. Even Jill, lowly, and yet, seemingly esteemed, beamed at me. "You sure look nice," he said.

"Thank you, I'd invite you in, but...."

Jester peeked in. Only Valentine was at the table. Everyone else was either under it or hiding in the kitchen.

"No sweat. I get it. Wood floors and wet boots don't mix."

I threw my arms around him and gave him a peck on the cheek.

CHAPTER FIVE

All elements larger than hydrogen and helium are made in stars. Comets mix solar dust through the solar system. The same minerals in a comet's tail can be found on the beaches of Hawaii. Being icy, comets carry water. Amino acids have been found on comets, and simulated comet crash conditions have caused amino acids to bond together, beginning the chain of life.

We lay together on top of my white comforter. My dress was bunched around my waist. Ulysses's hand was in my panties. I shuddered to climax beneath his skillful fingers as, still fully dressed, we kissed, with me not sure if he was Judas or the Frog Prince but charging ahead nonetheless.

"You're a sensitive woman," he said, giving me time to catch my breath.

"I-I'm self-taught as of late."

"Self-taught? I admire an independent woman. You were told to keep the supplies hidden, I hope."

This seemed too dangerous of a question even as we moved toward further intimacy. He could be an underground Vice Patrol for all I knew, or even a spy from my employer. Now that I thought about it, he could be anything.

"I'll never tell what I was told or not told. I need to keep some secrets from you. I can't let you unlock everything all in one night." I nibbled his earlobe and rubbed my cheek on his sideburn.

He licked my ear. "My guess is that you're not one to mess around. You get straight to the point. So a Whizard maybe. Automaton to avoid making a statement about race. I'd size you as a small." I tried not to reveal my shock at his accuracy.

"And you? Certainly you had a skilled professor in your past." He was the right combination of gentle and confident. My most previous lover, Tudor, had given me the impression of getting my oil changed, and Rex was nervously quick.

"Bernie and I were together for a long time. She's not one to hide her feelings or her wishes. We're still business partners. She's ambitious and an ambitious woman doesn't need a man. She wants me out."

"I don't want you out."

I took off his sweater and enjoyed the giddy feeling of having a man craving me, eating out of my hand.

He leaned over me, running his hands along my thighs. "I'd love to be in. How far do you want to go tonight?"

"Far enough keep you coming back."

"You want that?"

"I want a relationship. I want to come home from work and have sex. I love science, but I'm not monogamous with it. I'm just as normal as everybody else." If this was going to put him off, now was the time to find out.

He kissed my neck. "Oh-ho. I'll be back."

We were panting, each kiss chemically bonding us further, boosting our immune systems, washing us with well-being, shooting us with dopamine, making us foolish and reckless.

"You said you didn't want a one-off," he whispered, his body grinding against mine.

"I don't. Tell me now you'll see me again."

"I will."

"Make another date with me now."

Sweat poured off him. "Anything you want. Name the day. Tomorrow. The day after. I'm all yours."

I was breathless. "New Year's Eve. Be my escort to the company party."

He tensed and pulled away. My heart dropped. Of course he had a date. It was just a week away.

"A date to a *Cochton* party? New Year's? That's a big night at the bar."

I didn't say anything. I felt stupid. I didn't know what I wanted now, yet his honesty lured me in.

"I don't need to mess around with a taken man."

"It's not that. I'm not taken. You are. Taken by the Cochtons."

This had to be the worst excuse for a rejection I'd ever heard. *I don't like your employer.* How feeble. I shoved him off me. It wasn't difficult. He was halfway off already. I sat up and smoothed my dress. "It's not like I'm making bombs for them. There's a couch downstairs you can sleep on. Thanks for the nice time."

"I'm sorry. They make me nervous."

"Like being taken to a movie where men with guns show up and point them at you?" I twirled my hair into a knot.

"You're right. I'm sorry. I saw you again and did a crazy thing. I didn't expect the Washers to show up on Christmas Eve."

I was so mixed up. Why couldn't I attract a normal guy? I knew the answer before I even asked. It was because of that missing component. I wasn't whole. Neither was he. His fragile heart was squeezed into a million bloody tear-shaped drops. If we went any further, we'd be dangerous for each other. I looked at the floor. Our shoes were touching. They'd already made the decision.

"I can join you until nine. Come with me to Union Station after that. We're having entertainment." He resumed kissing my chest over my dress. "I'll want everyone to meet my girlfriend."

"Girlfriend?" Not only was it a childish word, a moment ago he'd been reluctant about me because of my employer. Now we were in a relationship. It was confusing. Then again, look how long he'd been with Bernadette. Clearly, he easily generated attachment molecules, attachment neuropeptides.

"Partner," he said, "if I may use that word. You don't want a one-off. What are you going to be after this? A two-off? You want something long-term. I do too. I do. I swear it." His hand was on my zipper.

I didn't believe in creationism for this very reason. Mother Nature was a capricious bitch. You wanted the very person you didn't know. The lust stage was brimming with risk, perhaps preparing a woman for childbirth. We'd have to use birth control. I wasn't taking a chance with this guy.

We were making our own Yule fire, and the spot where the blinds hadn't closed all the way was fogged over like a car after prom. He unzipped my dress and pushed it to the floor. He pulled his T-shirt over his head. The sight of Grant triggered a rush of lust. I undid the buttons on his pants and drew out his penis. He wasn't circumcised. I heard a crinkling. I reached into his pocket and pulled out a condom in a candy-cane wrapper. His pants were stuffed with them.

"You gotta know, honey, I sell condoms. It's the business I had at the theater."

My voice was shaky. "Lucky for us."

"It's illegal. It's Cochtonville's form of Prohibition. I'm a condom bootlegger. Bernadette is my partner in crime. That's why I almost shit my pants at the theater."

He was giving me reason to hesitate. This was the second time in my life I had given my heart to a man only to learn of a perilous secret he kept. No matter how innocuous I found condom selling, tangles with Washers and his ex were not going to further my career. My female predicament was clear. I could bed a criminal who used condoms, a good boy who did not, be wedded to Whizard, or give up passion entirely.

"How illegal are these condoms?"

He licked his lips. "We don't have to go all the way. We can take it slow or I can leave."

"Really illegal, in other words." What a fool I was to have this man here. He'd pulled me into a dangerous movie theater, yet I was getting ready to sleep with him and use an illegal condom.

"There's lots that's banned here. Ever notice that there aren't bookstores? No art on the walls that doesn't connect with agriculture? Those things are illegal too."

His eyes were smoldering. I tried not to let the ache in my genitals or the loneliness in my heart or the rush of adrenaline from the gun-toting Washers speak for me. How could one side of me be so rational and another side of me do stuff like this?

"Why do you sell them if it's banned?"

"They weren't always illegal. Everything here fell apart slowly. First, a governor was elected who was in the pocket of the Cochtons. They had the money to make him look like a saint. Before long all we had for an economic base was agriculture. It's not as if agriculture is bad. People need to eat."

"Yes. Those beans I'm studying grow on marginal land." How dumb of me to bring up work at this moment.

"See. The basic premise is good enough. It's been taken too far. Monoculture of thought."

"Like expecting a science girl to stick to the lab and not want kids or a family. You know, having a family and caring about someone other than yourself can bring inspiration. Pasteur lost three children to typhus. It inspired him to study infectious disease." I'd done it now. I'd used typhus as foreplay. Talk about a mood killer.

"Love and inspiration. You're right. I want kids and a family too, but I don't have the stability and never will."

But I do. It's what he wants from me. Whatever could I gain from him besides another orgasm?

He went on, the mood between us dying with each sentence. "I imagined a better life for myself. Cochtonville's shifting the sand beneath my feet. It became a city-state. Those with mobility moved away. This place needs people, so birth control was banned. I didn't want to go along with it, and neither did Bernadette. People should have kids because they *want* them. Just about everybody here is passively resisting. This is my resistance. Every now and then, somebody gets arrested and the rest of us go on. Shit. What am I doing here?"

He sat up and fumbled for the light on the nightstand. "I've said too much already. You're cute. I love smart women. I want a relationship. But you're with Cochton Enterprises. It won't work. This is stupid. I gotta go."

The company is what gives me stability, but I want this guy. I need a job, but I want kids. If I'm going to have kids, I need to start soon. No stable pattern, no map was revealing itself. I made a decision. I wouldn't let him go easily.

I fell into his lap as he sat on my bed. "I'm not from here. I don't know the Cochtons. Why should you be scared of me? What you're doing is noble. I admire it." I kissed his cheeks, his neck. He was a love hero. Even if he left me, I'd have no regrets.

Full of lust and relief, he kissed my breasts. It was dopamine surging, bonding us.

"I want to spread happiness," he said, pulling me onto the bed. "The missionary is the most intimate. Shall we start with that?"

I'd been starving for human touch. We were beating with four hearts. For a moment, I touched the divine. There was this man in my arms. No longer a stranger.

I was hard to impress with gifts. Rex hadn't even tried. He broke up with me before every Christmas and Valentine's Day, then begged for forgiveness to get me back. Tudor turned out to be married—the first perilous secret I'd learned about a man—and only bought what could have been explained as though he was buying it for himself, so a Merck Index and some AXE body spray were his unforgettable gifts. Ulysses didn't know me well enough to be worried as he handed me a little box the next morning. Inside was a necklace, a silver comet with diamond chips. I didn't know what to say. How had he known I was intrigued with comets and comet sampling and analysis?

"Stardust," he said.

Overwhelmed by the last twenty-four hours, the first time I'd spent a whole night in bed with a lover who satisfied me, and the streak of diamonds, almost in the shape of a sperm...I burst into tears.

"Oh no, not a crier," he said, sweeping me into his arms.

"Amino acids. The blocks of life. Comets carry them," I sobbed, trying to regain equilibrium. I wasn't one to appreciate emotions, especially my own, but the string of orgasms had released enough endorphins and other feel-good chemicals to give me the equivalent of a runner's high.

"Here's to life," he said, clasping it around my neck.

The phone rang. It was my parents.

"Happy Holidays, sweetie," said Mom as her face flickered on the screen. The image froze.

"Hi, Mom. It's a bad connection. This place is backward. Let's text."

Dad ducked his head into the picture as it kicked back to real time "We're sorry you're alone." Ulysses was under the covers licking my thigh.

"Ha-ha, no worries. Actually, ha, I'm not that lonely. I've met a guy."

"A scientist from work?" Mom asked.

"Oh no. Are you still there?" I replied.

It sounded like my mom was saying, "You're not getting any younger." Nothing like stating the obvious.

"I am today. Like a kid in a candy-cane store."

"Give me his name and I'll creep his profile," said Mom.

"Social media is kind of backward here, Mom, so don't bother."

"Pretty necklace. Is it from him?"

I touched my throat. "It is."

"Don't sacrifice your career," said Dad, who'd quit college to marry Mom and provide for me.

"Try not to scare him off this time," said Mom. "Be mysterious. Make him want you."

My brother Kevin's face popped in. "Could be your last chance."

"Be friendly," said Dad. "Just don't go too fast."

"Or too slow," Mom said. "And don't seem too smart."

"Or too stupid."

"Ahh, yes. Just right," I said, trying not to burst into ecstasy in front of my parents. Mom handed the phone to my granny.

"A man?" she said. "Be careful. You don't know that place. Have you read any good books lately?"

"There are no books here, Granny."

"Is it safe? I read that a reporter there was tossed in jail for using the term *manure spill*."

Mom snatched the phone away from her. "Did you get the gift we mailed? We thought it would keep you warm."

"Ahh, yes, yes, I did." My skin was flushing hot from what was going on under the blankets. "Flying pigs bathrobe. Not that I've seen a pig. I can smell them sometimes."

Even this talk wasn't bringing me down.

"We're proud of you for having such a good job and working so hard," Mom said.

Dad came into view. "Keep it up. Rome wasn't built in a day."

"I'd better go. Bad connection. I love you. I love you all."

I hung up and Ulysses popped his head up from the covers.

"You could have introduced me." He laughed.

"These are my parents. I want them to think I'm a good girl. You look like a horny rotter right now. Not a man to bring home to Mom and Dad."

He said, "You *are* a good girl."

"Good at it, maybe."

"Exactly. I'm going to release a special condom in your honor—a beanstalk. Meanwhile, are you ready for another candy cane?"

Luxurious winter darkness and the laughter downstairs covered the sounds of our morning lovemaking. By the time he left to see his mother, I'd memorized his body and loved every molecule of him.

CHAPTER SIX

Fermentation is a process in which yeast and sugar produce alcohol in an oxygen-free environment. Fermenting yeast is temperature-sensitive. Ale yeast favors 10–25°C, which produces fruity byproducts known as esters. Lagers are brewed at cooler temperatures and have fewer flavor components.

Most employees had the week between Christmas and New Year's off but, being new, without any vacation days, Jester and I were among those stuck at work. It was okay this way. Without interruptions from Mike, I'd gathered from a preliminary analysis that the beans were rich in oil and held potentially psychoactive compounds. I'd finished the analysis for Jester too—the one he brought me when first we met, the compound that had something to do with hogs. I was only supposed to confirm the chemical structure, but this gave me a clue as to what it did. It was an antiandrogen, working to lower testosterone, the male hormone. Either the pigs had acne or it was some sort of birth control. It didn't make a lot of sense. He'd mentioned that the male hogs were castrated and the females artificially inseminated until they became sausage.

I walked to lab 427 at the other end of the hall. Jester's lab didn't have the view mine did. It looked out over the manufacturing plants—their sprawling cement buildings spouting steam and, in the case of the ethanol plant, emitting a stale beer smell. The latter made me anxious. It reminded me of Union Station. Ulysses had barely texted me since our encounter. I tried not to let my heart sink to the pit of my stomach as I walked past the inane lettering lining the hall. *Success is in your hands and in your head—Aiyn Cochton.* She'd never been jilted, obviously.

There Jester was, in his goggles, gloves, and white coat, his head in a fume hood meant to suck away noxious chemicals. Despite the rattling hood fans, the lab still smelled like ethyl acetate, the non-acetone nail polish remover. We were both working alone in a lab, a violation of safe laboratory protocols worldwide, except here at Cochton Enterprises.

He closed the fume hood, which had been sucking in air like a vacuum cleaner. The room quieted. He took off his gloves and put them on the lab bench.

"Hi, Catrina." He checked his phone.

I held out my stack of papers. "I have your structural conformation. It's related to a natural product."

He didn't look up. "That's great. Can you text it to me?"

"It's right here in the report. "

"I don't think the phones are working right. I want to confirm my hypothesis by not getting your text. I can just feel my cortisol rising and my serotonin dropping with each second this phone doesn't ping."

"I know what you mean," I said. "It hurts so bad." I took my phone from my lab coat pocket and sent him a message: *Sophora root an Asian shrub.*

We stared at his phone. Nothing happened.

"Jiminy Christmas, what a relief," he said. "I haven't heard from Jane since Christmas Eve. I didn't know if she was mad at me. When we went to her house to carol, my mom asked her if she could cook a roast and invited herself in to inspect the housekeeping while Dad mentioned grandchildren."

"Ouch. What kind of a Christmas present did you get her?"

"A blender. A nice one."

"That's bland. Do you not have sisters to help you?"

"No, I don't. I have eleven brothers. Get with it, giving jewelry means you've made out. I could get fired if I look like a masher. We've got a morality clause in our contracts, you know."

I knew about the morality clause. It hadn't been important to me when I'd signed on at Cochton Enterprises. Not only would I keep away from married men, I was resigned to being a sexless smart girl when I'd agreed to it. Now I'd gone over the line—sex and an intimate gift from a petty criminal. I hardly knew what to wish for from my silent phone. I tugged the collar of my lab coat over the comet necklace.

Jester peeked at his phone.

"Sometimes they do this as a test. To make sure we can survive without communications."

"You mean people we've dated do this?"

"No. The establishment here. In case Cochtonville gets attacked, we need survival skills. It keeps us on our toes," he said. "Speaking of toes, do you have a date for the big shindig on New Year's Eve? We're all supposed to show up, date or not."

I put my phone in my lab pocket. "I don't know." *I don't know what I want right now.* It had all seemed so simple when I was with Ulysses. I hadn't been worrying about morality clauses or losing my job. If he forgot about the party, it might be easier.

Sirens cut the morning air. Not a blasting tornado warning siren, but a series of deep beeps, like Morse code.

Jester picked up his phone. "There it is."

"What now?" I said.

"Air raid," Jester said. "Probably a drill. I sure hope so."

We went to the door and flipped through the emergency booklet posted next to the jamb.

Tornado? No. Terrorists? Flood? No. Ebola? Alien Invasion? No. No. Air Raid! I read the instructions.

A three-minute pulsed tone will signal an air raid.

Secure labs. Extinguish flames. Lock solvent cabinet.

Move to lower level.
Duck and cover! (Place hands over head.)
A two-minute wail signifies all clear.
Someone had scrawled below, *Kiss your ass goodbye.*

"What's it mean?" I asked Jester. I had to admit, it had me sweating.

"Atomic bomb," he said.

"From where?" I asked.

"Illinois. The first bomb was developed there, you know. Right in Chicago, land of thugs."

"What type of atomic?"

"The worst, I imagine."

"An H bomb?"

"I really don't know. We've got to be ready, that's all. With our new products and small population, we're vulnerable to takeover. Let's make for the basement."

We headed for the stairs.

"Living here's suddenly got me on edge."

"Now you're getting it, kiddo. You're a fast learner. The good news is, we should be getting better phone service by the end of the day. Or we'll be annihilated. Either way, we solve the date quandary."

CHAPTER SEVEN

Ethanol is produced as a byproduct of yeast fermentation. It's toxic to blood and liver cells, harms the nervous system, and causes birth defects in mammals. It is highly flammable. Vapors may travel and ignite, creating a nearly invisible flame. It's also psychoactive.

I sighed with stupid relief when I received his text. *All clear. Pick you up at six NYE*

The party was held in the Pavilion of Agriculture that looked something like the Corn Palace in South Dakota but with its own parking ramp. A security guard was stationed at the entrance, and Ulysses had to sign his name beside mine on a form on a clipboard. We were together on paper—for better or worse.

The banquet hall was decorated with green-and-yellow LED strings and Mylar balloons shaped like ears of corn with smiles and pink pigs with floppy ears and lopsided grins. The atmosphere was innocent and childish, as if we could remain adolescents forever.

Ulysses was dashing in a white dinner jacket and bow tie even as he wrung his hands under the table. We sat with Jester and Jane, she with a beehive hairstyle and a tight, pink wiggle dress. All the other women wore gold or green dresses, some tight, some fluffy, as if Jane had missed a memo to wear the company colors. Unfazed, she talked nonstop, giving a running commentary about what each person was wearing. She declared my green dress enchanting yet daring and Ule, as she called Ulysses, an "it boy." She was copious in praise.

"Get some pointers from Ule," she told Jester, straightening the collar of his tweed sport coat.

As dinner was served, we were led in the "Cochton Enterprises Song of Strength," something I hadn't thought of since I'd sung its three flat notes at my half-hour orientation for work. I was sure that Jane mouthed to Ulysses, "*No trouble*," before we launched into, "Cochton, Cochton we love you. Cochton, Cochton, we'll be true. Corn grows, manure flows, everybody knows, to get along, we'll stand strong."

After a heavy meal of ham balls, which had an aftertaste even when smothered in sweet sauce, the band began. Old songs of course. The first song they played was "If I was a Rich Man," which had been high school Rex's favorite oldie. He played it on his iPad that hour after school in his bed before his mother got home from working at a clothing store. He changed the lyrics as he sang along to say that he'd have all the time in the world to sit before a computer and play instead of saying he'd sit in the synagogue and pray. This was before I was truly a smart girl, although I was toying with the idea, deciding if it was worth the struggle and an identity I could grow into. The memory was too much for me. I'd been so stupid about men all my life, selling myself short with the shallow ones.

I excused myself, grabbed my clutch purse, and went to the bathroom. Jane followed and caught me as I surveyed myself in the mirror. I loved my dress. It was out of character, but it honored a part of me I hadn't dared to explore. I fluffed up my hair, then dug into my purse for lipstick. I had some that changed color to complement the wearer's skin tone and personality. Mine was definitely plum. I squinted at the code on the side of the tube: *independent, reliable, and ambitious.* That was me in a nutshell. Jane came up behind me with a comb. Her lips were pinkly sweet and sociable.

"Want a tease?"

I thought maybe she was flirting with me, but she grabbed my hair and back-combed it.

"A little more height looks good with your low-cut dress." She bit her lip and stared at me in the mirror. "How'd you meet Ulysses? He's a looker."

"I...I just ran into him one rainy day at Union Station." I sounded naïve, even to myself. He must pick up women all the time in his profession.

"However did you get him on New Year's Eve? Does the necklace tell the story?"

I saw no point in lying about how I got him here, since I was a horrible liar. I applied lipstick and smooched my lips together to even it out. "It's from him, since you're asking. Is it illegal?"

"Oh, sweetie, yes. And if you love him, the Heartbreaksville Express is coming. Bernadette snaps her fingers and he runs. You do know about her, don't you?"

She might as well have kicked me in the stomach. How did this sweet girl know so much about him? Oh, I was being too paranoid. Everyone knew bartenders.

"I do and I've met her. Now you tell me, how did *you* meet Jester Rana, and what are your intentions with him?" I straightened my necklace, trying to keep my composure.

"At a malt shop. I was with friends, and he looked forlorn, so I flirted with him. He seems nice and nerdy. Sort of oddball."

"Not for a scientist."

"He's out of character for me. We both want something new, don't we, you and I? What do you think? Is Jester a keeper despite his name and his parents?" I had to admit she was cute with her heart-shaped face and big eyes. I had no idea what she meant about his parents.

"I'll clue you in. He's only going to marry a virgin."

She took the comb to her hair. "That's what they all say here. They have to." She put it in her purse. "Want some free advice?" She put her index finger on my ear and her thumb on my chin, appraising me. "You'd look good in short hair, too. You can go either way. You've got that going for you. Glad you had a condom."

"I don't know what that is," I said, closing my clutch purse, trying not to show how much she was rattling me.

"Me neither," she said, avoiding eye contact and holding the door open.

Ulysses and I danced. The music had evolved while I'd been in the bathroom. The band played something sad with a tint of gospel called "I Can't Stop Loving You." Ulysses rested his fingers on my bare back, steadying me in my pin-up pumps.

"You okay? You're shaking."

"I had a strange conversation in the ladies' room."

"Don't let her intimidate you. You look beautiful. You got the best legs here," he said. "Probably nobody else is as sweet in bed either."

"Thanks for being flexible and coming with me tonight," I said. "Tell me one thing about this place. How can it be against art but allow music and dancing?"

"There's nothing new allowed. Creating art is seen as a waste of resources. Only old show tunes and archaic pop music are allowed. They want us to touch, be tempted, and then marry hastily, as in Victorian times and the 1950s. Cochtonville has more purity laws than a Bavarian brewery. The goal is a lack of citizen independence. Shit, I admit it. This place makes no sense. I've got no place else to go, but you, I keep wondering why you're here and how long you'll stay."

"As long as there are beans to study."

"You're lucky to love a field that appreciated."

But it's not all there is to life, and without creativity it dies.

Jane came up behind me and tapped my shoulder. We switched partners with Jane and Jester. As I watched Ulysses dance with Jane, I foolishly wanted him even though I'd had plenty of warnings.

He moved skillfully, looking into her eyes, yet there something he wasn't doing—he wasn't talking to her. He was saving it for me. I had a chance, a chance to hang on to him even if I did drag him here to his discomfort. I knew I did.

As Jane stared openmouthed at Ulysses, Jester said to me, "You're going to get both of us in trouble. If he looks at Jane with those puppy eyes much longer, I'm going to give him a knuckle sandwich."

"He does have big eyes, doesn't he?"

"A real dreamboat," he said sarcastically. "She's swooning at the sight of him. Why doesn't she do that with me?"

"She's making you jealous. You're giving mixed signals. She won't put up with them. Plus, he's handsome. We have attractive dates, both of us."

"Earth to Catrina. Good-looking people can be self-absorbed jackasses. I'm giving mixed signals because I'm mixed up. Pretty necklace. Did *he* give it to you?"

"He did."

"You must be putting out something fierce."

"Jester, do you like it when I slap you?"

"I like—"

We were interrupted by Mike, who was in a black smoking jacket with a gold collar as if he was too cool to dress formally. "Glad you could make the scene. Lookin' good. Great bash, isn't it?" he said with a wink. "Be sure to stay for the treat—the greeting from the Cochtons on the big screen at midnight."

"How wonderful," I said, putting my fingers to my temple. "Too bad I sense a headache coming on."

He ribbed Jester. The band broke into "Why Do Fools Fall in Love?" As couples began to four-step, Jester and I shared the panicked looks of the uncoordinated. Ulysses came to my rescue, spinning Jane into Jester's arms and grabbing my hand. Mike caught my eye, and he looked at the clock as Ulysses pulled me toward the cloakroom and I fetched my coat from the checker. We rushed to the door.

We stood in the lobby, which was sparsely furnished with urethane-upholstered dark couches and glass-and-metal end tables.

"Discreetly put your hand in my pocket," he said as he looked toward the street.

I slipped my hand into his wool pants. I felt the crinkle of a condom. My eyes widened as I met his.

"What I promised. The beanstalk. They're selling like hotcakes this week, a little behind the exploding fireworks and party horns."

For a fraction of a second, I was uneasy. "How did you get it made so quickly?"

"It's my secret. Are you up for it?"

"That's your responsibility."

He took my hand, and we ran for the taxi pulling up in the drive.

Behind the bar, Bernadette was wearing a Minnie Mouse costume, low-cut to show her cleavage.

"About time. There's a mess in the men's room waiting for you," she said when we came through the door. A DJ was playing "My Favorite Things" from *The Sound of Music*. People were dancing, shooting pool, and those in the booths were playing checkers and Mr. Potato Head. Ulysses tossed Ernie Ray from a barstool.

"Sit here," he said to me. "I'm going to be busy." He drew a Rainy Day, poured a glass of water, and put them both in front of me. "I've had a wonderful evening already," he said, taking off his coat and rolling up his sleeves. "But it's going to be a long night."

"I hope so," I said before taking a sip of the ale.

Ernie Ray, in his newsboy cap, leaned on the bar next to me.

"Let's get this party started," he said. "How about a dance?"

"No."

"How 'bout Twister?"

"I don't do Santa Claus," I said, sick at the sight of him.

"No harm, no foul," he said, his eyes bugging. "I wanted to have a spoof on Ulysses, see if I could make him jealous. Bernadette hurts him real bad with her words. I wanted to make him forget about her and want you."

"Leave that up to me," I said, looking at my gorgeous bartender returning from his task in the men's room. In reality, I wasn't sure how I could keep a man like him. The DJ played "Tonight" from *West Side Story*. I felt swept up in sentiment. Maybe tonight would be enough to leave me with a heart full of memories.

Ernie Ray put a hand on my shoulder. "Berni told him he lacked athleticism and that she needed more size. She says she's the Grand Canyon."

"Not me." I brushed his hand away, trying to keep from slapping him.

"Got a big clit too, from what I hear. Almost looks like a dick." His breath smelled like licorice and beer.

I looked for Ulysses to save me. He was headed to the men's room again.

"Too much information, Ernie Ray." I pushed him away with my hand on his chest, which made him inch closer.

"She can make a man believe he can do anything. Hard to imagine that little guy she's got here tonight has more size. His feet ain't even big. They still live together, Ulysses and Bernadette. They own the place and neither will move out. Take turns sleeping in the bed. Maybe he thinks he can get her back in a week or two. He'll go back if she asks."

"PS, I don't want to hear one more word about Bernadette." I spun away from him before I caused trouble.

"Point taken. Oh boy. Don't turn around," he said nervously.

"Why?"

"Vice Patrol."

In the mirror behind the bar, I watched the two Washers I'd seen in the theater, fat and thin, come through the door. They halted there, belts bursting with black rectangles of weapons and devices for communication. Snow twinkled on the fur collars of their bulky jackets. The fatter one held one of those big guns. If they'd been jars of chemicals, I'd have backed away slowly.

The DJ stopped the music and announced, "And now, for your safety and enjoyment, let me introduce our favorite Vice Washers, Barnabus Smith and someone new and eager. Introduce yourself."

The well-built man waved to the crowd. "Axel Whitehead, born on the streets of Chicago. Honored to be with you tonight as a proud citizen of Cochtonville. Always a pleasure to be in on the inception of a great empire." He was telling the truth—he *was* from Chi-caa-go, as he pronounced it with emphasis on the *a*—a tough-guy accent like a mobster in a black-and-white movie. I hadn't noticed it when I'd first met him because I, too, was from the Great Lakes region. This guy was an experienced outsider, brought in to show the Vice Patrol how to crack down on unruly natives. It must have seemed like a piece-of-cake assignment—this place where condoms and art were crimes.

The bar patrons lifted their glasses politely as the Washers bowed. Ernie Ray walked quietly to the restroom. I put a hand over my eyes and studied my phone.

"We're doing a check for deviants. Seen any tonight?" asked Barnabus, the husky one with the big gun.

"We got cards to hand out," Axel said. "Our beloved city manager sends these tokens and her best, unless you're a leech on the state. Remember—food rations cut as of midnight tonight. None of you are parasites of the state, are you?"

Bernadette walked from behind the bar, straight up to the Washers as if she wore a hazmat suit. "Nothin' here but show tunes and clean-cut hetero kids. Everyone, tell these guys your favorite Cochton motto."

The crowd shouted out a jumble of words.

Her boobs were right in Axel's face. "Are you happy? That was strictly New Capitalism." She licked her red, pouty lips.

"Very happy," he said.

"Obviously all we're serving is beer and water with plenty of snacks. We have wholesome entertainment. Do you approve of what you see?" She was tall with a slender waist and the ability to handle danger.

"Yes, ma'am, I do."

She embraced him and cooed like a lonely dove. "Oooh, me toooo. I like you. You're the understanding type, and loook at your muscles. Do you enjoy games?"

"What kind of games?"

"Have your friend put down his Smith and Wesson. Grab a booth. I challenge you both to a round of Cootie." She batted her eyelashes.

Axel looked like he might oblige until Barnabus said, "Nah. We got lots of stops tonight. New Year's Eve is Halloween for the predators, you know."

The Washers waved to the patrons. Barnabus said, "Night all! Be good now."

"Thanks for checking up on us. Thank you so much for your expert protection," Bernadette said as she opened the door for them and closed it firmly after they'd left.

She joined Ulysses, who was back at the bar.

"You handled that with style," he said.

"It's always up to me," she said to him as she took a bottle of gin from a cabinet beneath the bar. "Every fucking bit of trouble."

Ulysses poured a beer and gave it to Maven, who'd appeared the moment the Vice Patrol left. "I had to lay low. They saw me at the theater last week. I didn't want to jog their memories."

"WTF, how did that happen? Did you hang around there and masturbate?" Bernadette slapped him on the back. It was obvious they still shared attachment chemicals.

"It was just the timing of it all."

"Timing? Newsflash, buster. Your timing has been off for a year."

"I'm getting my rhythm back." He gave me a soft look.

"Customers need new ideas, not excuses. What do you got in the pipeline for me for Valentine's Day? We need something in the works next week, and I don't mean chocolates. You're not going to get seasonally appropriate ideas going solo or having a one-off with some scientist." She threw me a squint. "What's next? Periodic table vibrators? Condoms with Velma from *Scooby-Doo*?"

Her jabs at me hurt.

Ulysses said, "That would sell as fast as the Pokémon ones. Don't talk about trouble. You shoved your tits in the new Washer's face. I bet that's not the last we see of him."

"You know what? He's cute, with a stable job."

With the Vice Patrol gone, the patrons pushed their games to the side, leaving a litter of cards. The music slowed, and so did the dancing. The clients clutched each other with exquisite grinding. The windows of the bar fogged. Ulysses and Bernadette served mixed drinks. Jealous of the dancers and watching Ulysses measure carefully, not with haste as Bernadette did, made my body ache for him. There's nothing so sexy as a man who understands precision. I lost all caution. Observing him had me quivering all the way from my crotch to my shoulders.

"'Freebird!'" a patron yelled out.

"If I hear that song one more time I'm going to kill someone, probably myself," Ulysses muttered.

Bernadette had been standing back, watching him. She patted his ass. "You know how to make me horny, Ule. You look good all dressed up."

"Hands off, bitch," I blurted. My hand flew to my mouth, but I didn't apologize.

She reached for Ulysses as he dodged her. "Bernie, I promised Catrina a date tonight and three's a crowd."

"Enjoy your one-off," she said to me with a grimace. One Minnie ear was folded over from the stress of the evening.

"It'll be a two-off." I grinned and pretended to watch the crowd. Of course, I longed for more than a two-off, yet barely dared to admit it to myself.

She grabbed a handful of my hair. "Want to get deported? It can be arranged."

I yelped. Having a girl fight flashed through my mind. I didn't want to ruin my dress or call the Washers back, and this left me twisting in her grasp.

Ulysses shoved her hand away. "Dream on. Cochtonville won't deport a scientist. Or anybody."

Her face was she-devil red. "You're going to wish she was deported, both of you. Don't mess with me."

The DJ called out, "We're ten minutes away from midnight!"

"Holy shit," Bernadette said. "I can't work with this distraction." She pulled bottles from the cooler. "Get your hands out of your pants and help me here."

Ulysses lined up plastic glasses on the wooden bar, uncorked a bottle of sparkling wine, and poured it. Bernadette served it to the rowdy crowd.

"May I?" I asked, grabbing another bottle and pouring, filling each glass a third full as Ulysses had done.

"Don't give too much," Bernadette said as she rushed off with a tray of the drinks.

"She's got it, Bern. She's got it," Ulysses said, more to me than to anybody. "If the Cochtons fire you, you've got a job here."

Bernadette hurried off with another tray and then another while I enjoyed the familiar sensation of dispensing precise amounts of liquid. When it was finished, Ulysses leaned over the bar and kissed me, putting a hand to the side of my face as our tongues found each other.

The DJ stopped the music and announced, "In celebration of the New Year, I give you the much-requested poet laureate of Union Station, Ernie Ray!"

The patrons clapped as Ernie Ray took the microphone in one hand and removed his cap with the other. Ulysses came from behind the bar and put his arm around me as the crowd focused on Ernie Ray.

"I got a dangerous poem in honor of all those in love or who hope to be so. This is for all of you struggling with the shit life's tossed you and getting up again. It's called 'What No One Can Take.'

"I'll tell you now
There's nothing they'll take from me
Cuz there's nothing in my pocket, man,
Not even my hand
They chopped it off
Along with my dick
My dynamo beneath a boxcar
Copulation before the fates
What are they snipping, my love?
What strings come with you?
Eight hours of no good.
Rat race rat race rat race
Come be with me.
Be my home in madness
American Gothic in a sewage lagoon
Ashes ashes we all fall down
And yet, before my eyes, shattered fragments reassemble."

As the applause swelled, Ulysses held me tight and kissed me until I turned inside out.

"Thank you, Ernie Ray. Let's start the countdown folks!" The patrons, some dressed up, others in overalls and caps, joined the DJ as he counted. "Ten, nine, eight, seven, six, five, four, three, two, one—lift off! Happy New Year!"

As cheers and chaos erupted, Ulysses and I took each other in. His eyes held the jungle of another human being, tangled, and yet, a refuge.

"I'm in the eye of a hurricane," he said. I replied with a sigh that was more like a purr.

"Barf! Take it upstairs why don't ya?" Bernadette said. She had her arms around a blond man wearing small wing tips. Her breasts were popping out of Minnie.

"Berni, the balcony is crowded, so I'll accept your offer." He gave me a bedroom glance. "That is, if you'd be alone with me."

"I thought you'd never ask." I undid his bow tie.

Bernadette licked her lips. "You've got the bed for ninety minutes. Then get back down here and help me pick up the mess."

We grabbed hands and slipped upstairs to the apartment. As soon as we crossed the threshold, he locked the door behind us. He unzipped my dress and pulled it over my head. He put it and his jacket on the futon. I unbuttoned his shirt and said, "Yum. You smell like Rainy Day." Rational thoughts were blowing away like milkweed seeds. Ulysses tossed open the bedcovers. His hands were shaking. The sheets were littered with used condoms of various colors.

He breathed heavily. "Bernadette likes to taunt me with her antics. Let me change this." He pulled the sheets to the floor, went to the closet, and grabbed a fresh set. He made the bed with quick precision.

"This is all we've got, I'm afraid," he said. "Barbie and her Dream House sheets. Maybe we should wait. I hate quickies."

I flopped naked on the bed and put my hands behind my head, letting my hair spread across the sheets. I'd always wanted a dream house.

"Now and later," I said. "Promise me you'll see me again."

He leaned over me. "I'm a man of my word, and I give you that. Do you dare meet my mom on Sunday?"

I laughed. "I've never had a man with an erection ask me to meet his mom before, but I dare. She won't bring up grandchildren, will she?"

"No promises. You need to know, my life is complicated."

"Complicated things interest me," I said. "Let me see the beanstalk condom. I need to check it for accuracy."

"It's art," he said, taking one from his pocket, unwrapping it, trying it on to show bright green leaves and intertwined tendrils, giving the appearance of great length.

"You're right. Never have I been so inspired."

I flickered and sparked as the intensity mounted between us. He listened to me, hearing my breath and voice, the jagged sounds of climax, sensing it, and only then did he shift into selfishness, the deliberate carnal breathing that came as he took at last what he'd come for, and this in itself excited me further. Tree-like nerves sprouted between us.

As we lay together in the glow of us, we talked as we watched the clock. Downstairs was a chaos of laughter, shouts, and music. Up here, everything fell into place. I didn't need him, but I wanted him. It was sex, chemical attraction, not love, yet it felt so good. It was like being in a lab, where nature writes the results and a scientist merely observes.

He entwined his smooth fingers in mine. "Do you think there can be things no one can take?"

"I didn't really understand the poem."

"I'd like to think no one can take us from each other."

I didn't dare bring up the B word and the conversation I'd had with Jane in the bathroom. It seemed like it could be a male trick —to pretend that no one is good enough to break you from your ex in order to inspire women to try. I changed the subject.

"Am I in the rat race?" I said.

"How do you feel at work each day?" he said, tracing my breast with our fingers.

"I'm playing. It's like Newton said, picking up shells and pebbles tossed from the majestic sea of truth. It's why I love being a scientist. So close to the truth and on the shoulders of giants."

"No, you're not in the rat race. A rat race is a maze. You don't know where you're going. Every turn is a dead end."

"I'm going places. Coming with me?"

"I think I've answered that. We have a chance at what no one can take, don't you think?"

I wasn't sure how comfortable I felt. Yes, I was falling for him even though the future, I couldn't see it. And I couldn't not see it. The evidence wasn't all in. There was Bernadette, after all.

He said, "Let's say yes. Us against the world. For tonight just us. Just us. It sounds like the party downstairs is winding down."

I stroked his new erection. "You're not. The General is ready to charge again. Do you think there's time?"

"General?"

"U.S. Grant here. I mean, you're named Ulysses."

His teeth flashed a smile in the dim light of the bedroom. "And my penis needs a name too? You are just flowing with ideas. I can see it now. A series of Famous General condoms."

"It's not only the ideas that are flowing."

We embraced again and became one as only lovers can. It didn't take long this time until we were both a mixture of relaxation and warmth. We held each other for one last minute. On the street, cars were passing and people were saying their goodbyes. I drifted, wondering what would happen if we broke Bernadette's deadline.

"I'm scared to go down there," I confessed. I didn't want to knock his ex, but Bernadette was as volatile as a thirty-year-old bottle of ether in a meth lab.

He said, "Before we go, Little Honey, there's something we've got to talk about with the condoms."

My mind was jarred by this urgent business. I could only imagine the worst. Then came the metallic scrape of a key in a lock.

CHAPTER EIGHT

Latex is a milky-white substance that occurs in some plants and acts as an insect repellent. It's a mixture of alkaloids (steroids with a bitter taste), proteins, and other substances. It's an emulsion, a frothy combination of two liquids that don't mix. Latex is a common material for condoms.

"Oh shit," Ulysses said as a door creaked and a heavy footfall came across the wood floor of the apartment. "Be cool. I'll take care of it."

The door opened and Axel and Barnabus came into the bedroom. Axel snapped pictures of us together, naked. Barnabus held the automatic rifle to Ulysses's chest while Axel took shots of the condom-littered floor.

"Fornication, clearly," said Axel. He gawked as I pulled the covers over myself, praying he wouldn't recognize me from the theater. Fortunately, he was staring at my body.

"Damn, Berni. She called this in, didn't she?" Ulysses said.

"Don't blame her," Axel said. "We came back to see if you needed help closing up and the ceiling of your establishment was rocking and rolling."

"It begged us to investigate what was happening up here," said Barnabus.

Axel said, "She didn't have to say a thing. Being a loyal citizen of the Empire, she gave me the key to save the door. Deviance is disrespect for Cochton's moral code. Care to explain?"

Barnabus pointed the gun at us. "Identification."

I was sick at the thought of Cochton Enterprises finding out anything about this and frightened by the gun pointed at Ulysses.

Axel held out a tablet and said, "Fingerprints. Or do you confess to the obvious?"

"No need for prints," Ulysses said. "We admit to everything."

"We do," I said. "Just put the gun down. Is there a fine?" I couldn't afford this. Was I going to be forever lower-middle class?

"Jail time," Axel said. "Six months or more, depending."

My stomach twisted. "I'm a scientist. I have an important job with Cochton Enterprises." I hoped that just tossing out the name of my employer would give us some leniency.

"Not anymore." Barnabus had a scratchy laugh. "They don't like deviants."

Ulysses sat up in bed. "We don't want trouble. If you please, we're not deviants. We're not dirty. Just two people in love who can't wait. The world is spinning so fast. There's an urgency to love, an abandon, don't you agree?"

Axel said, "Where are you going with this, besides to hell?"

"I was about to propose. That will put this right in the eyes of the state, won't it? So if you'll excuse me."

Axel said, "Propose? That'll get you halfway to respectability. Let's see the ring."

Ulysses opened the drawer of the nightstand, fumbled through a pile of socks, and took out a box. "I have it here. This isn't very romantic with you two and the weapons. Could you step outside, please? Give us some privacy." He winked at me. How much of a joke was this? I didn't find being a pawn in this Cochtonville cat-and-mouse game funny.

Axel said, "If we go out and come back in, we'll search this place. I estimate you're one condom short of years in prison. Do I need to spell it out to you? If I find one more thing in this apartment, you're gone."

Ulysses's mouth twisted up. He looked panicked. "You're kidding me. She has to make a decision with the two of you standing there?"

"If you're so in love, it won't be a hard choice," Axel said.

I pulled the covers up to my chin. Jail would ruin my career and my life. The most shocking thing of all was this—I didn't need that much time to make a decision. If he was serious, I'd marry him.

When people think of a scientist, they imagine someone who stands strong against social pressure. But Darwin didn't *want* to buck society. He published his theory after much hesitation because he was bursting with evidence and thought someone was going to scoop him. Galileo capitulated to the church, perhaps muttering under his breath that the Earth went around the sun, but publicly declaring what the authorities wanted him to say—the Earth was the center of it all and thus in God's direct eye. Einstein, Fermi, Feynman all worked on the bomb. Lise Meitner was one of the few nuclear chemists who refused to collaborate on such a weapon. She was the tough one. It's why she has an element named after her. She still felt the sting of the outsider, saying that being a woman in science was "half a crime."

Being an outsider here in Cochtonville was destabilizing enough. Don't think less of me when I say I was almost eager to give in. I was curious. I wanted to experience married life. I imagined it was that missing component I'd been longing to find. Besides, the Washers had guns. However, the missing part was not marriage, not a man. It was not the baby I hoped to have. It was more elusive than that.

Naked, utterly handsome to my hormone-infused brain, Ulysses got down on one knee at the edge of the bed. "Catrina, I mean this truly, will you marry me? As God and these two goons be my witness, I'd like nothing more at this moment than to be your husband."

Scientists don't take foolish risks, but they are ever optimistic, seeing the future as a home where progress lives, a place of greater knowledge. I was hopeful and in the mood for adventure. Even more important, this would keep me from getting in trouble at work, keep Ulysses from being shot, and I didn't have time to think about it.

I said, "I do."

"You're sure?" he said.

Of course I wasn't sure. "I want to experience all of life. And I don't want trouble."

Ulysses slipped a ring on my finger. It fit, wasn't so big as to get caught on lab equipment, and matched my comet necklace.

Barnabus said, "I'll be damned. It's true."

Axel said, "We'll get it all taken care of for you. Considering the circumstances, sooner rather than later." He entered data into his tablet. "Church or courthouse?"

"Courthouse," we said together. We were already a unit! I threw my arms around him and covered his cheek with kisses.

"Glad you're doing the right thing." Axel held out a tablet and stylus, and we signed an intent form.

Axel pushed a button, and a hollow cube popped out of the tablet. "Put your fingers here. Ladies first. We got all the time in the world."

Barnabus explained, "We get time-and-a-half tonight."

Axel said, "Let's get the blood scans over with. We're checking for diseases."

I put my finger into the device and felt a prick. More than blood was drawn at that moment. An idea assembled in my mind. This test could be done so much better—cleaner, safer, cheaper, more painlessly, maybe even faster and with an even more stupid operator. I could make it happen.

Axel reviewed the data on the screen. "You're both as clean as the driven snow. I've got you down for a ceremony on the second of January at noon. Hope that's easy enough to remember. Now, miss, my partner will take you home. No more frisking about with this guy until he's your husband. I'm staying put and keeping an eye on this place. Get yourself dressed and presentable."

———————

I walked through the bar, stepping over scattered Twister mats and a Mr. Potato Head as Barnabus clutched my arm. The ceiling lights were on and the customers had scattered. Ernie Ray and Maven remained, playing pool with a big, dumb-looking kid with flaring acne. Bernadette, her date nowhere to be seen, was filling salt shakers.

Ernie Ray put down the pool cue. "What's buzzin', cuzin? The new girl and the Washers? No way!"

"Outsmarted herself," Bernadette said.

Maven said, "Hauled off by the Washers. That bites. Bernadette, you got something to do with this, don't you?"

"Cut the sympathy. It could be you, Maven."

Maven smoothed her hair over one eye. "Won't you ever let Ulysses be happy? Anytime he tries to find love, you stick your finger in it. Why?"

Bernadette plunked the shaker on the table. "Because I can. The man's not disciplined. One way or another, he's never going to stop thinking about me and how I'm right about everything."

Barnabus spoke up. "Cool your jets, everybody. Nothin' more than a free ride in the paddy wagon for the bride-to-be."

Axel came down the stairs and made a beeline to Bernadette, crunching over Cootie legs and antennae as he jogged to where she filled salt shakers at a table. There was no trace of her date, with whom she'd produced all those used condoms I'd been blamed for. It didn't matter. Ulysses was safe and safely mine for better or worse. Bernadette had a glint in her eye, or perhaps it was the Tiffany lights that shined above the bar.

"Can I give you a lift, away from that criminal, beautiful?"

Clearly, he was a good-looking guy with a world of confidence.

Bernadette put her arm to her forehead, sobbed, and collapsed in his arms.

"Don't worry, baby. Big Daddy is here," Axel said, gathering her up and peeking down her polka-dotted dress.

The heavy door of Union Station closed behind me.

CHAPTER NINE

Caffeine is used by plants to kill predators and to give a brain buzz to pollinating insects, which return to the plant to get another fix. It may damage the heart and cause excess gastric acid production. It stimulates the central nervous system. It's the most widely consumed human (and perhaps insect) psychoactive compound.

I broke the news to Jester, and not very delicately.

"I'm getting married today. Will you help me? I need a ride to the courthouse over lunch."

He jerked his head from the fume hood. "Married? To that guy at the dance? No!"

"Do you know him?" If Jester had something bad to say, I might call the wedding off.

"No. *You* barely know him."

"It's marriage or a notification sent to Cochton. I didn't want to lose my job. I might've even ended up in jail or been shot."

"You got caught *in flagrante delicto?*"

"Yes. Those Washers are terrifying."

"Washers? Is that some sort of street lingo?" His eyes bugged behind his safety glasses and his mouth fell open. His amphibious look and unfamiliarity with the term sent my heart racing. There were two worlds in Cochtonville, and I'd stumbled upon the dangerous one. Even worse, I fit in there and was soon to be wed to it, forever mixed. Like dissolves like. I'd found my tribe. Unfortunately.

"The...the Vice Patrol. They're everywhere. You must have run into them. The guns-and-black-jacket guys."

"Never in person. You've been in the wrong places. Didn't I warn you? You were too obvious with that necklace and fella of yours. You're lucky they didn't shoot you. Everybody knows once they spot you, they keep coming back like a whoopee cat after a dame."

"We're both clean," I said, grasping for the silver lining. "The Washers have an add-on that gives you the whole premarital blood screening right on the spot. How can they have such technology yet the buses still break down?"

"You're too old to be such a babe in the woods. The state cares if you're deviant. They don't care if buses break down. Only people on the skids ride buses. Same for phones. Who cares if you can't talk to Grandma? Clean water? Who needs it? Geez. You're in a heap of trouble, sister."

"Will you help me, please?" What was I going to ask? Help me get out of here? Help me get married? I thought about running, heading for the airport. But I couldn't just ditch Ulysses. Who knows what would happen to him if he was left at the altar. The bonding chemicals were already mixed in me, like an addiction. "I've only got an hour to get there, get married, and rush back to work. And will you be my best man?"

"I don't want to be an accomplice to this. You're scaring me."

"Please, you'll be there anyway since you're driving."

"Just this once, if you promise to come to me if anything goes wrong."

"I will."

"Another thing. Don't complain. I'll be driving you there in a hearse. My dad's a retired mortician, and it's my only wheels."

Considering how much Cochtonville pushed marriage, they didn't make it cheap. The license fees cost a fortune—$1,000. Or maybe this was just the fee for us. The fines were as individual as the punishments. Ulysses and I each chipped in half. So much for a honeymoon. We had to work.

Before the ceremony, Ulysses slipped me a note as I went to the bathroom to change into my dress. *If you're asked to pledge to something you don't agree with, squeeze my hand and I won't hold you to it. I'll do the same. All my love.*

There was that overused word—*love*. I'd said I loved science, my dress, the beer, yet not him. We'd never said it. It was looking me in the face with all seriousness. I ripped the note into small pieces and flushed it so no one else would see it. I met him outside in the hall and took his hand. I squeezed it and said, "This is a test."

He'd shaved his mustache and looked downright wholesome. "Here we go. Scared?"

"No. Should I be? Are you?"

"Kind of."

The city manager, Frani Foil, a horse-toothed woman with stiff, sprayed hair, known to me from the cards she had the Washers hand out, officiated the ceremony in the dark-paneled room of the courthouse. Ulysses and I joined hands and faced each other. We were both in the same clothes we'd been in two nights before. A security guard, dressed in a green-and-gold getup that resembled a band uniform, stood behind her. To the average Cochtonvillian, this place presented a cheerful face of compliance.

Much to our chagrin, all we could manage to get for witnesses on such short notice and during the holiday season were Jester in a Cochton polo and Bernadette dressed like Elsa from *Frozen*.

Frani Foil spoke through her nose. "Dearly beloved, we are here because this shameful couple got caught by the Vice Patrol." We squeezed hands as Bernadette snickered and Jester stood stone-faced.

"Are you both in agreement that you wish to be wed?"

"We are." I was high with excitement. I was going through with this!

"Do you agree to be fertile and multiply?" Why was this complicated issue part of the wedding vows? I wasn't sure if I should press Ulysses's hand or not. The question wasn't quantitative. Multiply how much? A *couple of kids* would dip my toes into the sea of life without drowning me. I was okay with it. I had no idea if we were a fertile couple or not. How could I pledge when I hadn't enough information? Ulysses searched my face for the indication of a response.

"How can one know if they are fertile until they try it?" I said.

"I feel sorry for you," Frani said to Ulysses.

"She's only being up front," Jester said loyally.

"He's never going to be a father," scoffed Bernadette.

"I sense some fines coming up," said Frani Foil with irritation. She looked over her shoulder at the cheerfully dressed guard. "Or maybe we'll simply shoot the witnesses."

Jester clamped his mouth shut and avoided the watchful stare of the security guard, but Bernadette pointed a finger at Ulysses and pretended to pull the trigger.

"We do," Ulysses said. "We will. We'll give it our best. Can we get on with this?" We didn't squeeze hands, but of course, being fertile and multiplying would make my job as difficult as it would make it exciting.

"Catrina, do you promise to obey Ulysses and take his name?"

Oh, how outdated was this place? I had to change my name? I was Dr. Van Dingle. It said so on my diploma. Bernadette rolled her eyes. I could see why she didn't want to get married. I almost respected her for it.

Ulysses squeezed my hand. I squeezed his. "I do."

"Ulysses, do you agree to sufficiently control Catrina? I sense it won't be easy."

Our hands turned white from squeezing. "I do."

"Do you agree to obey the laws of Cochtonville?"

How could I when they were so nebulous? Squeeze.

"We do."

"If you have rings, exchange them now."

Ulysses fished in his pocket and drew out two bands. I was grateful for his resourcefulness. He'd gone back to the department store for a matching set this morning. All I'd done was wash my underwear.

City Manager Foil said, "I now proclaim you respectable citizens of the Cochtonville city-state. What Cochtonville has joined, let no man separate. You may kiss each other as husband and wife."

I was sure we'd be happy. He was handsome and kind with an interesting dark side that would keep me from getting bored. Plus, he was good in bed, which at this time in my life brought a missing piece to my puzzle. As our lips met, he jumped. Bernadette had pinched him on the butt.

After the ceremony, we signed the marriage certificate. I saw the full name of the man I'd wed: Ulysses S. Butz.

"Butz?" I said quietly. "My name is Catrina Pandora Van Dingle Butz now?"

"Looks like it," Jester said, putting a sympathetic hand on my shoulder.

"Half of why I didn't marry him," Bernadette said. "Where's the incentive? Who wants to be Bernie Brown Butz?"

"It's a fine name, once held by a secretary of agriculture," Ulysses said.

"It suits a chemist who studies plants," I said.

Ulysses scratched his head. "Of course, he was kind of an ass and started corporate agriculture. No relation to me."

I took his arm. "I'm proud to carry it."

We hadn't much time. My lunch hour was sneaking away, and another couple was ushered into the room. Jester snapped a quick photo of Ulysses and me. We looked scared and hopeful, like every bride and groom since the beginning of time. We tossed on our coats and kissed goodbye.

"Where are we living?" he asked as he helped me to the front steps.

"At the inn, I guess." I climbed into the hearse with Jester. I sent the photo to my parents and almost immediately got their shocked reply. I forwarded it to Hans too and made arrangements to pay the extra rent. I wasn't going to let anything ruin this day. Being a scientist, especially a young one, gives a person tremendous confidence that anything can be solved with the right application of diligence and intelligence. My marriage was no exception. I studied the small platinum band signifying my new social status. It began to snow. I shivered.

"If you had a long white dress your legs would be covered," Jester said.

"There was no time to shop," I said. "And I like this one. It holds a good memory."

"'Memory' as in singular. You got married after some half-baked week-long romance. What's the rush? Are you knocked up already?" asked Jester sullenly.

"What kind of person do you think I am? No!"

"Should I give you a medal? You can have deluxe sex whenever you want now."

He was right. Sitting there thinking about Ulysses had me rippling. At last I finally had the prospect of a decent sex life with a man. This whole week had me in a near faint like those little goats that tip over when panicked.

"I will," I said firmly.

"For all you know, the man could be a pervert."

I smoothed down my dress. "He's not. I did what society wanted, and obviously in your opinion it was stupid. Society gave me a choice—deviance or foolishness. What's so wrong with being foolish?"

"It isn't very scientific. You've got nothing in common. A person can pretend during courtship. There's a saying in Cochtonville: 'Everybody's hiding something.' In a few months, you'll know the real man."

That night back at the inn, I put my hand on the doorknob. I had cold feet. This wasn't a fling now. When Ulysses got off work, he'd come here and he'd be my husband. I'd said I loved him during the ceremony. Or had I said that? Love and marriage didn't always go together. I had no idea what I was doing. I studied the message from my mom on my phone.

Congratulations, Mrs. Butz! Can't wait to meet him. He's not a scientist? :(

A frowny face! Some wedding night. At least I wouldn't be alone with Whisper Whizard. I opened the door to my room.

Candles glistened by the bed. Roses were on the nightstand. Ulysses sat at the table in his wedding finest, wine and a bag of carry-out from Panda Palace in front of him.

"Welcome home. Come sit on my lap, Mrs. Butz."

"That's *Dr.* Butz, if you please." I said it gently, yet it had meaning for me. Being married didn't mean throwing away all I'd worked for. Seeing Ulysses had my heart leaping. Maybe this wasn't stupid. "One moment, please."

I put my purse and wedding dress on a chair. I took off my work clothes and left them in a smelly pile on the floor. I didn't want one shred of work clinging to me. I walked to the dining table in my bra and panties. I was wearing my bra decorated with Frida Kahlo poking her head provocatively from mountains of fruit and flowers along the left pectoral. I sat on his firm lap. He cupped my breast. "Oh, I do love art."

"It's all about love, you know—art."

"Isn't everything?"

We kissed and all of the bounties of life poured forth. We were running our hands through it. He was the pebble on the beach, the truth I'd ached for. The ocean of truth was love and its waves rocked us. At last, we stopped for air and gave each other shy, sweaty smiles.

"I hear you like Chinese food," he said.

"If it comes with a handsome man, I'll eat anything," I said, smiling.

"I'll hold you to that, if I'm the man."

He poured plum wine into a single glass, and we took turns drinking to our future together. People were meant to be together, to communicate with their bodies. Oh, those eyes of his. They were cenotes, so deep and blue with a current a hundred feet below the surface.

"Are you hungry?" he asked.

"Famished."

"I brought carry-out."

He picked up peanut chicken with chopsticks and fed it to me. With each bite, I felt him quivering. With my fingers, I lifted a fried oyster to his lips, then another, and another as peanut oil ran down my arm. We opened the one fortune cookie, for now, our future was a singularity.

You will live happily ever after.

I laughed with delight.

He said, "I admit, I had it made special order."

I put my arms around him. Ulysses had that unique loneliness of a man who worked for himself and scrambled to make a living. I intended to solve that loneliness and banish that scrambling. "I need a shower. Come with me."

He carried me to the bathroom. We undressed each other, then stepped into the steamy spray. He lathered me with soap. I did the same to him, running my hands over his body. I leaned into his arms, feeling his firm body behind me.

"The backside attack should work best here," I said, my slippery skin sliding against him. He looked surprised, sexy, wet.

"It's a chemistry term, but you get what I mean. We'll have to be quick about it," I said. "There's not a lot of hot water."

"Just this once," he said, grabbing me and laughing. "I'll owe you more time."

"A lifetime," I said.

We laughed as we tumbled out of the shower afterward and dried each other. He wiped the foggy glass, and we looked at ourselves in the bathroom mirror. We both took deep breaths. This was real. We were married and possibly fools. Ulysses stood behind me and cupped his hands over my breasts—a gesture that came across as protective.

"We'll make this work," he said.

Wrapped in my towels left over from college, we sat at the table and fed each other chocolates. After licking the candy from each other's lips, he picked me up and brought me to the bed. We stretched out, held hands, and put our heads together.

"I never thought I'd be this ecstatic to tie the knot," he sighed. "What a day."

"It's not over yet."

He stroked my breasts as he recovered from our time in the shower. "Would you like to feel my skin inside you, wife?"

A chill ran down my spine. "You mean as in no condom? Already?"

"Just wondering. I've never had married-person sex before. We didn't squeeze hands."

"No, I want you all to myself for a while. Besides, your products are so pleasurable, like nothing at all." In truth, I'd never had sex without a condom. His felt much nicer, or maybe it was the man. As tempting as it was, we couldn't afford the career ding that came with a baby yet.

He reached for one of the many condoms he'd placed on the nightstand. "In that case, the general is ready for another charge. I've got George Washington, U.S. Grant, Julius Caesar, Cryptor, and Pancho Villa. Should we start with Grant?"

"Yes, he's always been my favorite." It was a relief that he'd come prepared.

He lay upon me and loved me so perfectly. Waves of pleasure passed through me until at last I sat up with a jolt and began to cry with joy and release. He kissed my neck and finished himself. I loved every twitch of his body. Yes, it was love. It had to be.

Beautifully complicated love. We basked in the afterglow. He put his arms around me and snuggled his cheek to mine.

"You dried my hair," I said.

"This marriage idea is genius," he said.

"Were you really going to propose so soon?" I asked.

"Of course not. I bought the ring along with Ma's necklace. I was going to launch a campaign and court you as fiercely as I could. As I said, that gun to my head at the theater told me that my single life wasn't making me happy, and your contact lens story ambushed me. Most young women in Cochtonville, even ones otherwise scornful of its rules, have devolved into juvenile behavior since little is expected from them beyond their appearance. They are afraid to grow old and grow up. You're a breath of fresh outside air in a stuffy room. Would you have said yes if the Washers hadn't threatened us?"

"I might have if that's the only way to have safe sex here, but the truth is that it takes a while to form a healthy attachment." His use of the word *devolved* had me melting in his arms. He was as intellectual as he was handsome.

"It's efficient this way," he said. *Efficient.* A thermodynamic term. I was luckier than I'd imagined.

"Efficiency is always good," I agreed. "Less waste, like a chemical reaction with a high quantum yield, or a reaction that produces a low waste volume because it has atom economy, the second principle of the twelve principles of green chemistry," I added as we snuggled together.

"Mmmm." He pulled me closer and heat radiated from him.

"Speaking of efficient, how did you get them made so fast?"

He jumped. "What?" He'd almost been lulled to sleep from my chemistry chatter.

"The Generals. We spoke of it only a few days ago, and here is a whole series."

He ran his fingers through my tangled hair. "I'm a sort of artist, I guess."

"The design and construction of them all came so quickly. Do you have a condom factory hidden away somewhere?"

"Yes."

"Yes?"

He took a deep breath. "Here's the deal. I make them myself. I'm what's called a Printer. I design them; Berni sets up the program. We even construct the cartridges. We can print them ourselves, as I did in this case. We have a 3-D printer in the apartment. It's why I didn't want to be searched. We sell condoms under the table. For vibrators we sell a print package to other entrepreneurs. Been to a Just Be You party? Those people print their own using our supplies and programs. We take care of Cochtonville's needs."

"Yes," I said slowly, putting all the pieces together and wondering where the printer was at the Brownstone.

"I thought so. Just Be You is B. U. That's us—Bernadette and Ulysses. Totally illegal, and totally profitable to make her happy. A service industry to give me a sense of purpose. We pay the bills. Sometimes we trade condoms for seeds and pass those out to clandestine gardeners. That's a risky thing, gardening. Needs to be done in a closet with grow lights or in a rarely traveled public space."

"The bar is mostly a cover?" My scalp was tingling. I was comfortable with selling a condom here or there, but a whole business supplying everyone in Cochtonville was ominous. I was uncomfortable with marriage to a secret this large.

"How better to hide a cash-only business than with a bar where people are in and out all day and night? We can fold the cash for the condoms and print supplies in with the rest. I've got money taped behind Grant too, if you ever get in a pinch."

"You and Bernadette are business partners? That's your relationship now?"

"Yes. She thinks you're a genius with your ideas. Beanstalk and the generals are best sellers. As for her and me, we're fighting partners for a lot of reasons. We can't agree on where to expand next. She wants to cut corners on materials and get into more kinky stuff. I don't want a baby named after me, and I don't want to escalate things and get the electric chair. There's a fine line between getting in trouble for a vibrator or condom and getting offed by the state for overwhelming deviance. The risk isn't worth it.

"I'm sorry to drop this on you after the wedding, but a wife can't testify against her husband and you're my wife now."

His confession had me frozen. This was even more serious than I'd imagined. Yet I wasn't one to give up. I'd chosen this path, and I would make the best of it. Yes, I'd adapt, I'd stick with him and this city-state because a chemist can make anything work.

"Please don't look at me like that. Say something," he said.

"You're telling me that you're more than a petty criminal selling condoms. You have a whole business in the sex toy and condom industry and you distribute seeds. Could you be put away for life?"

"Or shot by a Washer, yes. They'd probably kill me on the spot. I'm not going to lie. It's a dangerous business. I'm sorry if this is a shock. Please believe me. I honestly love you. I vow to be a loyal husband to you. If I get caught, we'll get an annulment so you won't be incriminated. Please say you forgive me for withholding. This marriage happened so fast, and I didn't dare tell you before. Say something. Anything."

My mind went flying, soaring, fumbling through books of possibilities, anything to make this situation better and to find a way and render these products more innocent in appearance.

"How about a series of color-change vibrators, sensitive to heat and pressure? We could say they're diagnostic tools. A woman needs to keep that area strong, you know. We could call it Dipstick Vaginal Monitor. I'm sure the technology could be used in condoms too. You'll want to make some color-change mugs. Maybe changing koozies with *Union Station* printed on them to keep away suspicion about the materials. It'll be good advertising."

I let my fingers move across his chest. He was too skinny. He needed feeding. All those ancient stereotypes flooded through me.

I would take care of him. He'd take care of me. We'd be so happy even if he was a criminal. I worked for Cochton Enterprises, the company funding this crazy city-state, so I wasn't blameless either.

"Well," I said, "I hope I'm not being too bossy. What do you think?"

"I think I'm the luckiest man alive."

I never could have imagined what was to come.

CHAPTER TEN

Flavonoids are made from fifteen carbons arranged in three rings, one containing oxygen. They are found in most plants, especially tea, fruits, and soybeans. They are believed to have health benefits such as anti-cancer and anti-inflammatory properties. Some may produce hair growth.

At work I was a fountainhead of ideas. I explained my brainstorm to Mike as I sat in his office. The appeal of being involved with a bad boy, protected by being married, was evident. Suddenly, I was given permission to buck conformity. I had no earnest man looking over me, wanting me to behave myself. I was flying, sky-high with new ideas.

"Thanks, that's enough, Rhonda," Mike said to the furrowed-browed office manager who was giving him a shoulder rub. "Catrina, Dr. Dingle, oh hell, can I call you Cat?"

"No, you may not. It's Dr. Butz," I said with my newfound confidence.

"Rhonda, Dr. Butz and I need to be alone. Fetch us coffee."

Rhonda left, her frustrated heels clicking like a cowbell on the cement floor of the hallway. I had laid out my plans for a fantastic device a person could use to screen potential sex partners.

Mike leaned on his executive desk while I sat perched next to him on the uncomfortable visitor's chair.

"I'm making a suggestion, that's all," I said.

"If you don't watch it, I'm going to put a note in your file that you question everything. Dingle, we hired you to study these damn beans, not to think about sex. You're fucking that rogue and now you came up with this idea—a touch-screen STI test."

"He's my husband, not some rogue. I thought I was being compliant with Cochtonville's customs by marrying."

"I need you to be a chemist first and a citizen of Cochtonville second."

This place confused me. It was like a person who was never satisfied. "My idea uses newer technology, at least for this country, but ideas in the public domain."

"'Public'? That word is banned. We can't have swearing here," Mike said nervously.

He was right. My confidence had pushed me too far. I couldn't draw attention to myself or my husband.

"Have you ever been tested, Dr. Watson?"

"Can't say that I have."

"I got tested before I got married."

He grimaced. "I've never had the pleasure. Women are all gold diggers."

His personality was becoming clear. High androgens, low neuropeptides. With his biochemistry, he was lucky to be a man— hard to get, a player. A woman with this chemical balance would be called a slut. I leaned forward in my chair and put my hand on his arm. "Well, let me enlighten you. Currently, to get tested, you need a finger prick. It's unwieldy. It's not too far of a stretch to work out a touch-screen device. If we added a sensor for fertility, people could use it before sex with a new partner or anytime they wanted to make sure it was safe. It's not that difficult to turn a device into a spectrometer. Scheeline *et all* did it with a phone in the early teens. Google has it in a watch. With the laser-bubble technology, we could swing this. Every invader leaves its signature on the host."

He rubbed his hands together. "We'll have to spin it right."

"That's what marketing is for. For us, it's simply a matter of utilizing standard tests in a new delivery system."

"I'll think on it. Missy, keep in mind this isn't one of those women's rights countries. You work here at my pleasure, foreigner, no matter how creative you are."

"I'm married to a citizen now. I'm loyal to Cochtonville and Cochton Enterprises. Listen to me on this. My device is a winner. It can be called No Regrets."

He stroked his chin. "It would be assigned to the Cochton National Security Health Division, but our group can consult. You and Rana would look good at a press conference. You're both young and for scientists, decent-looking. People like that. I'll let you know, Dingle."

I put my hands in my lap. Men like Mike were always a problem for smart women who couldn't give him the sweet-and-dumb act he best responded to. "Thank you for understanding," I said as pleasantly as I could. "I knew I could depend on you."

He stood and came toward me. His face was red and his hands grasping, like raptor claws, pouncing on the back of my chair. "Take my advice, married woman. You get pregnant, you become a security risk. You have a miscarriage, that brings a whole investigation. You can't afford it. Catch my drift? Anything you do when pregnant might be examined. Every aspect of your life will be investigated. You could get put under house arrest for any subsequent pregnancies. We'd lose your expertise. We need your expertise." He rested a hand on my leg. "We need you."

Why hadn't I taken more psychology courses? I might know how to deal with this. "Birth control is illegal, sir. So let's hurry and make this device. Give the rhythm method a boost."

He put his hands in his pockets. "Hmm. Think about it. That's all I'm saying. I'd hate to be without you. If you're longing for kids, freeze your eggs for later. There'll be plenty of time in retirement."

That Sunday, his only day off thanks to the laws in Cochtonville, Ulysses and I caught a taxi and went to meet his mom. As we swept through the arched front door into the warm living room, I could see immediately that his attraction to me hadn't been a coincidence. She was petite and, like me, had large eyes and long, wispy hair, although hers was gray. She wore an old sweater over a batik shirt and jeans. Her house was filled with candles. A photo of Ulysses's dad, a principal who had been killed in a school shooting, was on the crowded shelf in the living room along with bits of amethyst, rose quartz, and bound books. Ulysses hadn't told his mother he had married, keeping it for a surprise to be revealed in person.

He put his arm around me as we stood in the living room together. "Ma, I got someone for you to meet. My wife, Catrina. Catrina, this is Blossom."

"'Wife?' Did you say wife?" She nearly fainted onto a leather couch and put her hand to her heart.

"Yes, Ma, I did."

"Oh my! When did this happen?"

"Last Friday. It was sudden. We married over her lunch hour. I would've come earlier, but we've been working and honeymooning and I wanted to tell you face-to-face."

Blossom was a shimmer of emotions, and tears wetted her eyes. "Oh my, look at her. She's so young and precious. So tiny. Such small hips." She rushed to hug me and kissed my cheeks. "What a surprise! I don't believe it."

"I've got a photo." He took his phone from his coat. "I just sent it to you. Sorry there's nothing more formal."

She put her hands to her face. "I'm in shock. Did you get caught together?"

"We did, Ma, but we love each other."

"What ever happened to Bernadette?"

Ulysses took my hand. "She dumped me last fall, Ma. Remember? It's for the best. We were never gonna tie the knot. I love Catrina for herself, not for business. We live in different worlds by day, so we won't be fighting about the rat race."

Blossom kissed her son and gave him a smile filled with joy and confusion. "You two look so beautiful. I thought this day would never come. Take off your coats. Let me make some tea." She hurried to the small galley kitchen. Even across the room, I could clearly see her remove photos from the refrigerator. They were of Ulysses and Bernadette. It had to be her. Who else had a figure like that? Blossom paused and stared at each one before putting it on the counter.

"How long were you and Bernadette together?" I asked Ulysses as we sat in overstuffed chairs crammed into the small living room.

Ulysses grabbed an arm of my coat and helped me wiggle out of it. Blossom took scissors from a drawer and cut a photo in half. "We've been in business together for six years, but I knew her before that. We weren't together, really, but just in contact. Yeah, in contact. That's about it. Want me to show you around?" He grabbed my hand, jumped up, and pulled me into his arms, diverting my eyes from the kitchen, where the garbage disposal was grinding.

The two-bedroom cottage was small but warm, with plaster walls with a vine pattern around the doors and woodwork throughout. His bedroom, untouched since his youth, contained track ribbons, taekwondo certificates, building kits of all kinds, and bunk beds with batik spreads. His art covered the walls with landscapes featuring farms and rivers along with one of a naked woman who looked a lot like Bernadette.

"You must enjoy the outdoors," I said, ignoring the watercolor breasts.

"It's beautiful out there. Someday let's move to the country and get off the grid." He took down the portrait of the woman and tossed it into a metal wastebasket.

"Not many chemistry labs off the grid," I said. "What will I do with my time? Pop out babies? That seems so mundane."

"You can do whatever your heart desires. Start your own lab."

He pulled me close and kissed me. "I used to dream of this when I was a kid—a woman in my bedroom. I have General Cryptor in my pocket. Want to give him a try? He's a hothead."

I unbuttoned his jeans. "Hot enough to warm me up, I hope. Which bed is yours?"

"Hiram was always on top. He's my brother and was named after my dad. He's a geologist." He pulled me onto the soft mattress of the bottom bunk.

"How many other girls did you sneak into this bed?"

"Just one, just once. Sophia. She helped me with calculus and women. She ended up at MIT. There's the danger with smart girls. They're always one step ahead with one foot out the door. They don't need you. Tell me again that you don't want a one-off. I find it sexy to be in for the long haul." He was doing it to me—putting his knee between my legs, parting them with a nudge.

"I want to linger with you forever. But I'll take a quickie." I laughed. I had to admit to myself that contentment was rapidly becoming familiar. Discovering Ulysses was as lucky as finding penicillin in a moldy petri dish.

"Hurry," I said. "Let's beat the teakettle."

Blossom poured the tea into moon-and-star cups. A warm peach fragrance rose up. Relaxed and flushed, we sat at a table covered with a paisley cloth and drank from china in the warm house.

"Children on the way? I'm not one to judge."

Ulysses gazed at me over his teacup. "Not yet, Ma. We're saving. Catrina's a scientist and quite the innovator."

"A scientist. Ulysses always goes for 'numbers' girls. Says that the kids would be well balanced. How did you end up here?"

"I work for Cochton Enterprises," I said.

Blossom made a face. "Oh, such a nasty lot."

Ulysses put his hand on hers. "Try to stay positive, Ma."

"What do you do for them?"

"I'm an analytical chemist, so I have my hand in about everything. Plants are my specialty. My thesis concerned natural plant remedies for snakebites, but I've got several projects going. That's why a baby is on hold. Someday, when we're settled."

Blossom said, "Life goes by so fast. There's not a lot of wiggle room."

"You just want grandkids, Ma. Give us time," Ulysses said. In my head I calculated. Blossom was right. There wasn't that much time. Kids in college and retirement plans would overlap if we didn't get started, not to mention that each year that went by would increase Ulysses's percentage of damaged sperm. Life was tossing me plenty, all at one time.

"I'm wondering," said Blossom. "How's Bernadette taking all of this?"

———

Jester came to my lab with a new venture to discuss. He wore a big T-shirt that featured a thermometer breaking and the slogan, *There's No Limit to Big Yields*.

"Mike says you might be able to help with this new project. It's a plastic immobilized antibody test he came up with, kind of like you were telling me about after you got married." He showed me the proposal. My eyes widened as I read it. This was *all* my idea!

"Mike says he came up with this? Hard to believe. I hear he can barely synthesize benzocaine. Maybe it's really *my* idea, don't you think?"

"It's true. We need your help, of course, and you'll be in on the patent. You'll have to be. You'll be the one deciding if this works. I'll be interfacing with the biochem division to come up with the materials and with you on evaluation. Not sure about the fertility test. We'll add a pregnancy test instead. The state would prefer it. People don't need to be dodging the bullet. Mike wants it ready for clinical trials before the next quarter."

"Wow. That's rushing things."

"That's the way we work at Cochton Enterprises. Speaking of rushing, how's married life?" He winked.

I adjusted the wedding photo on my desk. "Connubial bliss, although we're on different schedules. How's dating?"

"I'm working at my own pace. I'm just not sure. It's me. I'm scared. He's good to you? Things are going the way they should for married folks?"

"We've got a healthy sex life." I could feel my stupid grin.

He clasped his hands together and twiddled his thumbs nervously. "I wouldn't know a healthy sex life if I read about it in a textbook. He's kind to you in other ways?"

"So far."

"Sometimes an older guy will go for a younger woman so he can retire and live off her. Happened to Rhonda, the office manager. Her husband worked in production here, but he retired early and goes fishing every day now while she's stuck doing Mike's bidding."

"Ulysses has never once mentioned fishing and he's only a few years older."

"Promise me you won't stay in a bad relationship."

"I won't. That's the beauty of having a good job. Stop worrying about me. Let's get on it now and start this project."

Jester and I put our heads together and worked out the details of our collaboration. I couldn't wait to get started on my device. Yes, my brainstorm had been stolen, but I was still able to work on it. The project wasn't all mine but it was alive.

I told Natharie about my idea and how the decision had been made without me.

"I have a Ph.D., just as the men do, and was hired at nearly the same time as Jester. Why are only they making these decisions, and when?"

"Poker," said Natharie. "The men play poker and work out what projects will get funded."

"How do you know this?"

She unclipped her long, black hair. "I hear them talk. They go to Mike's house, play cards, and discuss what projects he should favor."

I unclipped my hair and fluffed it.

"Even Jester?"

"Even him."

"He seems so pure and innocent."

"He's not. None of them are. Men aren't innocent." She refastened her hair behind her head.

———

During those first few months of marriage, Ulysses worked until two a.m. He got cleanup duty more often than not. Since the buses stopped at eleven and taxis were expensive, he walked the two miles home on the crumbling sidewalks of Cochtonville. Two miles isn't far, a half hour walk or less if you're driven by desire. He'd sweep me into his beery arms, and I didn't even shake off my dreams as our tired bodies moved together in what, in retrospect, was such a luxury. Some mornings I cupped my body over his in a twinkling mess of affection. He always had a condom, and the condoms were well made. It made me a little sad. It was unlike a chemist to wish for an accident.

One Sunday night in late winter as we curled together in bed, we made the mistake of watching the State of the City Address in front of the television. The mayor, General Stone Berke, who had a large chin and straight-ahead gaze, spoke. He said productivity was down in Cochtonville.

"It doesn't take a genius to know people don't want to live here," Ulysses said, his face scratchy with the luxury of a day off from work.

"There are several root causes," the mayor said. He took a drink of water from a clear glass.

"It smells bad," Ulysses said.

"Too many prudes," I said. In our time together, the secret

between us had bonded me to him. I was in his corner now on all matters legal and illegal.

The mayor said, "According to my advisers, solo sex is interfering with the efficiency of our citizens. To compensate, there will be additional penalties on devices of sexual pleasure. Likewise, the sanctity of life will be protected with registration and monitoring of all pregnancies. The death penalty will be strictly enforced as a deterrent to crime."

I said, "There's nothing evil about checking your pressure. Dipstick's a health device." The radiators in the old inn rattled.

Ulysses said, "Wouldn't it be made by Cochton Health in that case? This has me worried."

A rap on the door shook us to the bone.

Ulysses held me tight. "If they're coming for me, just let me go. No heroics. I don't want you mixed up in this. Pretend to know nothing about it."

"I won't let them take you," I said desperately.

The knock was more insistent. "Hide in the tub. I'll tell them you're not here," I said.

"It won't work. They'll search the place," he said, jumping from the bed and rushing to open the door before I could try to save him.

It was Wilma in tight, red pajamas with a dragon pattern, her silver hair streaming down her shoulders like steam. "Did you see the news? People will be stockpiling them. We need more materials. The Dipstick ingredients in particular. I need a cartridge ASAP."

Ulysses standing there in sweatpants and no shirt, as handsome as the first time I'd seen him like that, said, "There's a holdup on my end. A Washer's been hanging around. I'll do my best, but I don't live at the bar anymore and my partner in crime isn't feeling the love these days, at least not for me."

"Think of something. People are depending on you," Wilma said, peeking past him to me in bed.

"I'll try," he said. "I'll try."

"Some of us fly solo and others need protection."

"I know that. I share your concern for all citizens."

"Goodnight then." She pulled the door shut.

Ulysses came to bed and put his head on my chest. "I need to get out of this. It's too dangerous. I'm a married man. I have you to think about."

"We'll keep our noses clean and nobody will be the wiser," I said. "I'm independent. You don't need to take care of me except to keep my fire going."

He laid his head in my lap. "Am I a horny rotter or did Wilma look pretty good?"

"She's in great shape. See, she's right. People need your products."

CHAPTER ELEVEN

Serotonin (5-hydroxytryptamine) is such a studied molecule that it even has its own club, headquartered in Sydney. Present in the brain, immune system, and bowels, it regulates mood (including libido and aggression), sleep, pain sensation, bone growth, blood clotting, and gastrointestinal function. It is a neurotransmitter regarded by some scientists as a hormone.

We'd tiptoed as quietly into marriage as we could. There was no reason to panic the customers. Ulysses was a familiar figure among the locals, so the word was out. He'd caved in to the pressures of the state and taken a bride in a rush. Shockingly, she worked for Cochton Enterprises. Something needed to be done to ease the tension, to show the citizens that Just Be You was still intact and unafraid of the Vice Patrol. Even if it wasn't one hundred percent true.

When spring came and indications were that we'd be happy together, Ulysses and I planned a wedding reception to acknowledge and celebrate the whole matter. My family couldn't get permits to come for the event since they weren't agents of commerce. We held it at Union Station sans my family. Bernadette was surprisingly accommodating, seeing it as advertising. I was too tempted by the idea of a white dress. I didn't want to miss out on the tradition, so I bought one that was flowing and deceptively innocent with petal sleeves and a neckline low enough to show off my comet. We decorated the bar with LED strings and fake birds, hired a DJ, and invited guests who showed up in spades and brought dates. Ulysses's brother Hiram spent time at the bar chatting up Bernadette while his pretty wife begrudgingly hunted for their children as they played hide-and-seek among the tables.

I couldn't help noticing Blossom sprung tears when she saw Bernadette working the bar and serving drinks wearing a scarlet cowgirl outfit with a toy six-shooter in a holster. Blossom was sporting the bracelet Ulysses had bought Christmas Eve—the same night he bought my comet necklace and the engagement ring on speculation. Blossom was still concerned that her son had hurriedly married someone from The Company instead of his business partner who couldn't betray him without betraying herself. I'd prove I was no mistake.

The cake was tall, phallic, and decorated with birds and bees—my idea and our next condom design—which we cut and served to our guests as they drifted over and shared words with us as music played. Hans and Jan felt free to dance together and with Wilma.

"Congratulations, Sailor Moon," Bernadette said to me as she took a thin slice of penis cake. "It's the look you're going for, right? Very traditional and sweet."

"You have such an eye for costumes," I said, not wanting to argue with her. Ulysses still needed to work with her, and she and I needed to be friendly for the sake of the business.

She laughed. "You might save the world, but you didn't get much of a prince. Sloppy seconds. And I do mean sloppy."

Upon hearing the word *sloppy*, I looked around for Jester and was disappointed to see he hadn't come.

"Hey," Ernie Ray said. He was wearing what might have in a previous era been called a maroon leisure suit—pull-on pants and a jacket with stitched front pockets.

"Move on," Ulysses said, reaching for Wilma's hand as she stood with Ernie Ray.

"Not 'til I give my regards to the missus." He hugged me, put his cheek on mine, and said, "Best of luck to you. Newsflash: Bernadette's dating that cop. Crying on his shoulder. Has there been any fallout?"

Ulysses shoved him away. "I didn't hire you to touch my wife or to be a damn Greek chorus."

"Hey, man, don't shoot the messenger," Ernie Ray said. "Gonna be a long summer without your goods."

I couldn't enjoy a father-daughter dance for real, but I called my dad and danced with the phone.

He said, "Studies show people who marry after a rushed hookup are more likely to be unhappy. The man never met us or asked our permission. We had this dream of you and a man in a white coat."

Ulysses cut in, grabbed me, and put the phone on a table.

"Whew, thanks for the rescue. I was just about to be declared a failure." I grabbed his butt and pulled him close. The crowd whistled. My dad was wrong. We were beautiful together, especially at this moment. Bernadette watched, one hand on her pistol, her mouth a line straight across. She still loved Ulysses.

"You look so fetching tonight," he said as he held me in his arms.

"And you, ruggedly handsome."

"Remember, though, I fell in love with you when you were drenched and wearing your Cochton costume."

"And you were a harried bartender."

"I'm sorry I'm not just a harried bartender. Maybe someday. Breaking the law gets old."

The DJ stopped the music abruptly. All heads turned to the door. There was Axel in his uniform.

"We're pleased to welcome the new Vice Commissioner, Axel Whitehead," the DJ announced.

Axel waved to the wedding guests. "Pleased to be here." He went behind the bar and pulled Bernadette to the dance floor.

I put my arms around my husband and whispered in his ear. "Was Ernie Ray right? Are they together?"

He faked a smile as Blossom took our picture. "She told me an hour ago, and she's stopped all printing except heat-sensitive koozies." We had a stack of them to give away as wedding reception favors. If only they'd been condoms.

"What about our new condom idea—birds and bees?"

"On hold until she comes to her senses."

We smiled as others snapped us, but I knew what this meant. No condoms and much less money, and for the people of Cochtonville—disaster.

"I've got some stashed away for us," he said. "And plenty to sell and trade too."

The DJ stopped the music and said, "Beautiful night. Beautiful couple. So filled with hopes and dreams. Now let's pause the tunes long enough for some original words by our resident poet and dreamer, Ernie Ray." Ernie Ray climbed onto the bar and stood there with a duffle bag. He pulled out a triangle. He tapped the one side of it and rushed the striker across the opposite side, creating sharp pings. His eyes bugged out as he recited.

"I call this poem 'Fresh Love.'

Conformity *ping*

Interrogation *ping*

Lost Middle Class *ping*

The Flock is in the Streets."

At this he ran the striker through the inside of the triangle, making a sparkling sound.

"They've taken the truth serum *ping*

The revolution is victorious

No one knows what they want. *ping*

Let it not be said

Easy come, easy go

Come and come again, a cock and a hen with a nest, like skaters over ice, hot as the planet

They are not pros

They believe we aren't alone

They stroke ideals."

He reached inside the duffle bag and took out a rainstick. He turned it carefully and it made what could be imagined as a sizzle.

"Now you're cooking with gas."

The DJ said, "A tribute to our newest couple. May you live long and prosper!"

Everyone held up their glasses and toasted us. The DJ played a lively Spanish guitar tune. Berni and Axel burst into a flamenco—beautiful and foot-stompingly passionate. The climax was Bernadette falling backward into Axel's arms, her breasts more majestic in their thrusting than the Tetons.

"Satisfying," Ernie Ray said loudly as everyone else stood in awe.

A siren shattered the stunned silence of the crowd.

Axel helped Bernadette regain vertical posture. "Duck and cover, everyone," he shouted. "It's an air raid."

Maven grabbed her plus-one, a teddy-bearish bus driver named Maurice.

"Who would attack?" she said from under the table.

"Someone who wants dirty water and hogs," said Natharie sarcastically as she ducked beneath the pool table with Ernie Ray and Wilma.

Ulysses said, "Ignore it, people. It's fake."

The DJ announced, "The groom says it's fake."

Bernadette said, "You're being reckless, Mr. Newlywed. The Vice Commissioner outranks you."

The DJ declared, "It might be the big one this time, folks."

Axel said, "Not so fast, Butz. You've committed a Crime of Disagreement. If there's an air raid, it's not up to you to question. I'll let you off with a warning this time, Shorty. Everybody, get under something, or I'll take you to the pokey. I have it on authority there might be a war brewing."

The DJ shouted, "War and rumors of war. Duck and cover. Squat down. Hands over heads."

CHAPTER TWELVE

Cyanide is considered a chemical warfare agent. It suffocates any creature that needs hemoglobin to transport oxygen because cyanide blocks the link between the blood's iron and oxygen. This is a toxic breakup. Some say cyanide smells like sweaty athletic shoes. It's slightly less dangerous as a salt, although a fifth of a teaspoon can kill a person. It's found naturally in some fruits and vegetables, including cherry pits, bamboo shoots, and apple seeds.

Of course there was no actual air raid. Natharie had been right. Who would blow up a place with more hogs than people?

As we worked together on the plant analysis project, I told her about isolating a molecule with psychoactive properties from Mother. My phone flashed and the face of the security guard came on the screen.

"Visitor waiting in the lobby for Dr. Catrina Van Dingle," he said.

"That's not my name," I said. "Ask them what they want."

"A man from In-Sight Optics."

Tudor's white-toothed face appeared on the screen.

"Hi, Cat, it's me."

I was shocked, facing what I'd tried to forget—that married ex who'd left me so full of doubt about myself and men.

"Would you like to have lunch?" he said cheerfully.

"I don't have much time," I said. I was blindsided. I didn't expect or want to confront my past now that my present was so happy. My pride didn't allow me to walk away. I wanted to let him know how well I'd done without him. "But sure."

"See you after lunch," I told Natharie.

"Is everything all right?" she asked.

"No." As I walked to the elevator, Mike glanced at the clock.

The elevator doors opened and there was Tudor, in an expensive wool suit the color of a feral pigeon's wings, examining Aiyn Cochton's statue. I went to him, bravely, I imagined, and said hello. He put his hands on my arms. His touch made my skin crawl in what I imagined was culturally induced shame. It was more. I was angry at myself for my naiveté. During our affair his kisses and fingers had been so quick. What I'd always thought was passion was greed, the strongest force in the array of evil forces—the opposite of gravity, which draws things together. What I'd taken as his prudence was simply a carefully hidden family.

"I'm here for business," he explained. "Not here. Close to here at Silent But Deadly Manufacturing. I knew you'd taken a job with Cochton and looked you up. I hope you don't mind seeing an old friend. You look good. You're all into Cochton with that uniform."

We went to the company cafeteria. We balanced our plates and glasses carefully on plastic trays as we found a table in a corner. We settled into the yellow plastic chairs and pretended to be old chemist friends as we each bragged about the molecules we studied. It seemed funny that Tudor could come to my place of work and have lunch with me while Ulysses, since he wasn't a scientist working for a company, could not. Needless to say he wouldn't want to set foot in Cochton Enterprises anyway.

We sat across from each other. I hoped no one I knew would see us together because I didn't want to explain later. On his tray was a colorful mix of tacos and fruit. He pointed to mine, gemelli pasta with pistachios and green beans. I studied Tudor's face. I was surprised at how much he looked like Ulysses, as if I had a type.

"Have you gone vegetarian?" he asked.

"It's hard to eat meat when the odor is so strong," I said, remembering his kisses that had been more like lip suckings. If ever I appreciated Ulysses, it was now.

"You're right. This place stinks, but that's no reason to give up bacon," he said. He took a careful bite of taco, and I ate a forkful of pasta. We looked at each other.

He said, "Prepare yourself. There might be a war, you know."

"War?"

"We can only hope. Peace never lined a pocket. My company, In-Sight Optics, sells to Silent But Deadly, and they're placing a major order. We don't take sides. We just make the guns and spread rumors of war so countries buy them. I've developed new optics for gun sights. Deadly accurate. The problem is it's temperature sensitive, like the Nernst equation."

"Or the Boltzmann distribution?"

"Exactly. Not enough to rule it out. The shooter needs to be aware." He put a hand on each knee and leaned forward. He was good looking and well employed. Well-endowed too. A catch. Unless you wanted someone trustworthy.

"Isn't it a liability?" I said.

He shrugged, "We sell 'em anyway. They don't work subzero but how many wars are fought in the cold these days?"

A flicker of my missing component, the thing that would make me whole, rose in me. "A gun that doesn't work? Aren't people going to get hurt? Do you ever think that just because we can do something, we shouldn't?" I asked, watching him eat a spoonful of berries. This was no doubt a perfectly normal thought for most people, but for a scientist, indoctrinated with a sense of adventure —do it to prove it could be done—this humanitarian trait hadn't been carefully nurtured in me. I wanted to prove I was smart and a success. I wanted to discover new things but also I now wanted to help people. Tudor was right. That kind of awareness never lined a pocket.

He talked with a full mouth. "No. I'm not rich enough for such luxury, and if I was, I wouldn't be moral enough to worry about it. Rich people aren't moral as a rule."

He tossed his hair. "You're looking good. I've missed you. Believe it or not, I miss having a woman to talk science with."

"I'm very happy now." I took a bite of pasta.

"I'm getting a divorce."

"I'm sorry." I was glad I wasn't responsible for causing it. I didn't like harming other women.

"She wasn't, isn't, smart," said Tudor. "Being smart is the coin of the realm in today's society. Smart woman—smart kids who won't need to mooch off you in your old age. Smart woman—smart income potential. What we had was real." He took another bite of berries. A drip of red bloomed on the corner of his mouth.

"Don't lay all the faults of your failed marriage in her lap, Tudor."

"So much of who you end up with depends on timing."

"It worked out well for me. You've got kids, Tudor, and it looks as if you've been eating them." Anger stirred in me. He must be a terrible father.

He wiped the berry juice from his mouth. "If at first you don't succeed, try again."

I waved a fork at him. "What a terrible thing to say about your kids."

"I mean you and me. Cat, what happened between us wasn't wrong." He looked directly at me. There was that combination, dark hair, blue eyes. Ulysses wore it better. Had I not stumbled upon him, I'd be caving in to Tudor at this moment. I was indebted to the short courtship. It had spared us both so much bullshit. I was going to go home and give Ulysses whatever he secretly fantasized about.

Encouraged by my silence, Tudor was still talking. "We meant so much to each other and we have all of science in common. Our love was the real thing."

"Fortunately, I got new evidence concerning 'real' and 'love.'" I took a big bite of green beans and pretended to be interested in eating. It was true. I loved Ulysses, not just for the sex but because I could depend on him. He inspired me to do my best work. He cared about humanity.

Mike came to the table and stood at attention until I acknowledged him.

"Dr. Tudor Tupenny, this is my boss, Dr. Watson."

Mike saluted Tudor with the one-finger salute of Cochtonville. Tudor returned a one-finger salute.

Mike said, "You've got nice arm action, young man. Military?"

"I work in the firearms business. I'm all about action," Tudor said.

"Although not as much as he thinks," I added.

"Catrina, Dr. Butz as she insists on being called, is one of our prized chemists. Do you have business here?"

Tudor said, "We were discussing optics."

"As in seeing things clearly," I said.

"You're not a headhunter?" said Mike. "They aren't welcome."

"More like a tail chaser," I said.

Mike saluted again. "A trait to be admired. Don't steal her away from me. Carry on."

As Mike walked away, Tudor leaned toward me. "What a character. Why was he calling you Dr. Butts? I always liked your ass, but to put it that way is crude."

"It's my married name. Tudor, I got married three months ago."

"Married? You? No. You're independent. April Fool." He took a bite of his taco.

"No, really. My husband is Ulysses Butz, a fine man." I flashed my left ring finger. How clueless was he?

He swallowed. "You wasted no time."

"The only wasted time was the two years I dated a man who never told me he was married. Of course, I'm glad since I was able to meet my husband and neither of us was encumbered."

"I'm sorry, Cat. I should've known you had some integrity. It'll get you nowhere, but good for you."

Jester came and stood at the table.

"Jester!" I said with relief. "Join us, please." I was grateful to see him. He'd been mysteriously gone for over a week.

Jester eyed our plates. "Aren't you almost done?" He had his plate piled high with berries and tacos. He'd forgotten a tray.

Tudor stood and held out his hand, "I'm Tudor Tupenny, an old flame of Catrina's."

"Flame, as in he burned me," I added, poking at my pasta with my fork.

"Fascinating to meet you." Jester, I could tell, noted my unhappiness. "It's always interesting to know who your friends are attracted to. Psychology isn't as clear-cut as chemistry. What brings you here?"

"Oh," said Tudor cheerfully, hand still extended, "selling arms and getting shot down."

Jester held his plate in one hand and jabbed out the other to shake Tudor's.

As Tudor pumped his hand forcefully, Jester tipped his plate onto Tudor and the dove-colored suit. Now it looked like a dove shot through. Tudor jumped back.

"I'm terribly sorry," Jester said, dabbing at the stain with a napkin. "It's been a heck of a week. I haven't slept." It was true. He had bags under his eyes, and his face looked etched with acid.

To Tudor's credit, he took this better than many men might have. He refused Jester's offer to pay for dry cleaning and ran to his car to change into his spare suit. As he rushed off, I turned to Jester.

"Thanks for the rescue."

I went straight home after work and went to bed, shaken by the ghost of the past. That night, while the printer in Wilma's closet pitter-pattered as it popped out Dipstick Monitors, Ulysses climbed into bed after a long night of serving beer and popcorn. I woke halfway with the grace of the universe upon me. Here was this honorable man, given to me by chance. In almost a dream, I asked him his fantasy.

"You've already granted it by marrying me."

"A new one. Tell me a new one. I love you and want to make you happy."

"Ironically, it's being a father. Not through trickery though. Not through the gun of the state." He was naked except for a pair of boxers, and his breath was on my hair. I glided into his arms like a skater on the ice.

He rested his head on mine. "I know you're an ambitious woman. Fatherhood can wait or never come. You'd better go to sleep now."

"No condoms from now on," I said, my voice soft with slumber. I was longing for connection and all I could think of was creating something with him.

"Are you sure? I thought you wanted to wait longer." His heart was clattering like the night we'd met. I wanted to hold him and a baby to my breast, no matter what the cost.

"It might take a while, so we'd better get started tonight." My mucous was thin and flowing with fertility. This was no random act. It had been flittering through my mind. I was human, after all, and aware of the passage of time. I was filled with the reckless abandon this new love brought. Yes, it was some amines, serotonin in particular; it was real, as chemistry is everything there is.

He was erect now and his eyes were bright in the dark room. "What's your fantasy?"

"On the bar," I replied. "On the bar after closing."

"The blinds aren't the best," he said.

"Never mind that. Tonight, it's your fantasy. Come here, husband, and we'll see if fate is once again kind to us." I didn't offer up prayers easily, in case they were like heartbeats and each person had a limited allotment for a lifetime, but that night, I prayed Ulysses would have his fantasy realized.

Ulysses was a clean man, and every bit of fluid from him smelled fresh and clean. The state had it backward. It shouldn't force people into commitment. With my new potential condition came a deeper appreciation for my husband and what he was doing as a condom outlaw. To be with child and not want it would be a tragedy—violence to me and the child created —inexcusable.

The following night. I went to the inn after work and changed into my green dress. I took the bus to the bar. It was filled with patrons. Spring's abundant optimism shined brighter than the diamonds in my comet necklace. Ulysses and Bernadette – dressed as a French maid – worked the joyous crowd. Wilma was there, probably hoping to pick up a printer's package, but she pretended to be interested in Ernie Ray's performance. He climbed to the bar and addressed the crowd.

"I've got a new poem. It's called 'Trigger Warning.'
You can't unring that bell, you itchy fingered Pavlov
You won't take away the pain as if it was social security
And give everyone a gun instead.
Keep your own words in your mouth my friends
Don't repeat what They say—"

A crash and the sound of breaking glass stopped his recitation. Bernadette had collapsed behind the bar and taken a tray of drinks with her to the floor.

Ulysses rushed to her side. "Oh shit. You all right, Bernie?" He unbuttoned her tight blouse and her beauty spilled out.

She opened her eyes. "Ulysses," she said faintly.

Wilma got down on her knees. "Lift her legs," she said to me.

"I'll do it," said Maurice the bus driver. "I'm stronger." Maven fanned Bernadette with her clutch purse. Bernadette had cut her arm and blood trickled onto the floor. I got the first aid kit from behind the bar and sprayed the cut with blood clotting spray. She coughed.

"Ulysses," she said weakly. "I need something."

"What is it?" he said.

"I need an assistant. I'm all worn out and you've left me."

"We'll get one."

"Can you take over for the rest of the night?"

"Don't worry about a thing."

"Ulysses," she said.

He leaned over. "Bernie. What is it?"

"Fuck you," she cried.

He and Maurice helped her upstairs while I swept up the broken glass.

Ernie Ray said, "She's tuckered from being Axel's one and only and not having Ulysses wrapped around her finger. A hire will eat the profits. It's a way to get back at Ulysses."

"He's as nervous as if he was expecting a litter," Maven said.

Wilma said, "Wouldn't you be if you were a criminal with a Washer banging your ex? He and Bernadette have got more shit on each other than a couple of plumbers. We've got to do something to help him." She went behind the bar and poured a beer for a customer. I slid the broken glass into the dust bin and took a mop to the floor.

Ulysses and Maurice came down the stairs.

Maurice whistled. "Nice digs."

"There's nothing wrong with her. It was a ruse to get me up there. She's got all new furniture," Ulysses said. "New mattress. New silk sheets with plenty of stains."

"It pays to betray," Ernie Ray said.

"It won't wreck our evening," Ulysses said, relieving me of the mop. "Party on."

It was barely spring and the night was star-filled, even with the light pollution of the city, as Ulysses and I stepped from Union Station and prepared to walk back to the inn after closing. The past winter had been warmer than most and the infant spring was following in its footsteps. The wind tossed my hair. The contentment of commitment and the excitement of gambling even more with our futures, so different than we'd envisioned them even a half a year ago, had us teetering. As we kissed outside, daring the universe to blink at our plasmic brilliance, a Washer van pulled up and parked. Ulysses and I broke the kiss and I held our embrace, tempting the Vice Patrol to arrest us for public indecency. It was Axel. He didn't look at us as he unlocked Union Station and closed the door behind him.

Ulysses said, "Here's a perk of being married. Not even the stink eye from the Vice Patrol. God, I'm glad to not be loving on an ad hoc basis."

"But he's got a key to the whole bar," I said. "Let's go back in and make sure the cash drawer is locked."

"With both of them upstairs?"

"We won't be able to make a sound." It was exciting to me. A way to undermine Bernadette.

We needn't have worried. The floor upstairs started rocking nearly the moment we stepped in.

"Bernadette must be feeling better," Ulysses said. He turned to me, "Have I told you how much I love you?"

He fell to his knees and lifted my dress. He pulled down my sparkling tights and I stepped out of them and my shoes. He said, "You've got no shoes and no stockings. You got panties on?" He was shaking, as he had when we first met.

"No," I said.

My cervical mucus was egg white and estrogen filled. He lifted me onto the bar counter, the beautiful wood cool on my naked butt.

Although it had been coerced by the state, I'd made a choice when I married him. Our union meant I would not have total fidelity to science, or perhaps anything. My mind, my love, would be forever split, without the singular devotion required for fame and glory. I was glad. If Cochtonville had taught me anything at this point, it was the foolishness of robotic devotion to one limited idea. I was going to live the multiverse of human experience.

I was greedy for Ulysses and the multifaceted life his erection offered me. My refractory future was in flux, thanks to a fortunate spattering of ice across a crowded street. It was the end of the day, and we both had an undercurrent of sweaty humanness above the spilled popcorn and sweet beery smell of the bar. He climbed next to me.

"I could grab a condom."

"Not tonight. Pull your pants to your ankles and get on your back," I commanded. His eyes widened and he did as he was told. I climbed on top of him. Never had I felt so in control, so confident. My pagan roots, my alchemical spirit, ran through me with this ritual of mutual respect and pleasure. I could see why people gave up all for love. Those who didn't were fools.

Mike was insistent.

"Look here. Cochtons want to do more advertising. Let people know what they do and what their scientists are up to. They're producing a television show, *This Week at Cochtons*. It'll highlight our research. Let the folks see the scientists at work to make us seem less secretive. You two will be on today's show with your gadget."

"Today?" Jester and I both said. We had no idea why we'd been called to his office but hadn't expected this.

"Do I hear an echo? Of course today. City Manager Frani Foil will be doing the interviewing. I need a good impression from you two. I had Rhonda go down to the store and get you some company blazers. We're charging them to your account. Here, go get yourselves presentable," he said, yanking them from the back of his chair and handing them to us.

In my lab I brushed Jester's hair and straightened his collar. He helped me put on the stiff, green blazer. In a circuitous way, I was getting a shred of recognition for my brilliant idea, even if it was a marketing ploy. We walked into the conference room, which was intense with lights. The film crew teetered about like storks. The smell of leather diffused from the chairs. Here was the holy chamber, where triumphs were announced and failures glossed over. I'd never been here before. The camera was rolling. In walked Frani Foil. Her rose perfume inflamed my nose.

"Cochtonville," she said to the camera. "It's here where innovation takes wing. I, your city manager, embrace science and technology. The generosity of the Cochton family and the tax breaks they're given will be rewarded with successful invention."

She saluted Mike, and he saluted her.

"Miss Foil, welcome to Cochton Enterprises."

"So good to be here, Dr. Watson, and I must say, you're looking fit today. The quality of your leadership is evident. What has your chemical division brought forth? I'm all ears."

I noticed with embarrassment that Jester and I were both still wearing safety glasses, giving us the appearance of absentminded nerds as we sat at the conference table with the well-dressed Dr. Mike Watson.

Mike puffed out his chest. "In alignment with our concern about health, we have a device that tests people for sexually transmitted infections and detects pregnancy without the need of one drop of body fluid. It will be a boon to law enforcement, doctors, and pharmacists. It will be available next week. Everyone can get a scan at local Cochmarts as soon as Wednesday. " He held No Regrets in his palm.

"Would you like a demonstration?" he asked, poking the white rectangular device the size of a deck of cards at Frani.

"Should I brace myself for pain?" She set her jaw and gave him a playful flick of the wrist.

"Not at all. Hold out your hand." She did so, and he scanned her skin with No Regrets. A green light appeared.

"You're as pure as the day you were born," he said.

She clapped her hands together. "Of course I am. And I didn't feel a thing!"

"No blood or fluids needed at all. Easy as an ambush. You could even do this without the person knowing it." He swung the device at me. I froze. I didn't want my secret revealed, especially not on television when I hadn't even told Ulysses yet.

"Isn't this a violation of my privacy rights?" I said, trying not to sound alarmed.

"What are those?" asked Mike. He winked at Frani. "Shall I?"

"Oh, by all means," she said with a horse-toothed smile.

He scanned my cheek. The camera zoomed in. A tiny baby icon appeared. Here it was, the first person betrayed by my device was me. I'd envisioned it for private use between potential lovers. This was not how things would be. We all have things to lose, don't we? I'd lost my own invention. Whatever it was I was missing inside of me, the half that would make me whole, was rolling away like a dropped quarter. No matter. I was a success.

"Congratulations," Mike stammered. Jester smiled weakly at me.

Frani looked down her nose. "You're married?"

I tried to discern her tone. What exactly did she mean by this? Was I not supposed to be, since I worked for Cochton and needed to show the ultimate loyalty to the company, or was she making a comment about my being a scientist? In any case, it was a relief that she didn't recognize me from the wedding she'd performed not that long ago. The last thing a condom outlaw needed was his wife attracting the attention of a city official.

Jester came to my defense. "Of course she is. Smart is the new sexy."

I tried to kick him under the table. If he was too complimentary to me, Jane might get jealous.

Frani took note of the kick. "Is this your husband?" she asked, pointing to Jester.

"No, her husband owns a bar," Jester blurted.

"How interesting," said Frani. "A case of opposites attract, I suppose. Did you plan this pregnancy as part of the product roll out?"

Mike was scowling. Jester retained his a plaster smile. My head was expanding and contracting—ready to crack. I'd planned to approach this carefully with a clever announcement to Ulysses such as a name-the-baby book under his pillow and later a private chat with Mike about maternity leave. Now it was dropping like a bomb.

I stammered, "A fortunate coincidence."

"It's certainly made an impression as to the value of your

creation. Now you can be monitored even earlier. Introduce yourself to the audience," said Frani, her eyes drilling into me, her teeth looming large. "You're a star now. What's your name?"

"Speak up," Mike demanded.

I was on the spot. I couldn't look guilty and arouse suspicion. I had to run with it as if this was acceptable.

"I'm Dr. Catrina Butz," I said, removing my safety glasses and addressing the camera.

Frani said, "Butz! There's a name with a deep history. Aren't you proud of her, Dr. Watson?"

"Nearly as proud as I am of you," said Mike, giving her a wink.

She winked back at him. "No flirting now, doctor."

I walked out of the meeting with Jester and with rising indignity.

"Why did Mike scan me before I even told Ulysses? Now the whole country knows. I wanted it to be intimate, not some grand pronouncement."

"He's going to wonder why you kept it from him," Jester said, trying to catch up with me as I strode to the parking lot. I was leaving, racing to Union Station before Ulysses saw the announcement on television.

CHAPTER THIRTEEN

Cortisol, the stress hormone, is secreted by the adrenal gland. It can reduce inflammation and boost metabolism and alertness. Sustained high levels can harm the immune system, thyroid, and bones. It can be lowered by good sex, laughter, music, and positive social interaction.

I got off the bus at Union Station, my world upside down. As I walked into the bar, everyone turned to look at me. They clapped.

"A cat-eating canary," Ernie Ray said. "Making such an invention and not even telling us."

"And pregnant," Maven said. "Unreal. Bad business move for Ulysses. Who can trust his stuff now?" She and Maurice exchanged worried looks.

"Who can get his stuff now?" Ernie Ray said. "Not that he's to blame."

I went behind the bar and hugged Ulysses. "Did you see it? Surprise," I said weakly.

"It certainly was." He gave me a nervous kiss. "Free advertising too. Your name. Your bar-owner husband."

"Look on the bright side—you won't be suspected of condoms," Ernie Ray said.

"He's in shock," Bernadette said.

"Gone from renegade to father," Maven added.

"Think of the publicity. The bar on Cochton Enterprises' street view," Ernie Ray said. "Washers peeking in to make sure you're not drinking, Catrina."

"Exactly," Ulysses said.

"Scaredy cat," Bernadette said, slapping him on the butt with a towel.

"Don't interfere with this, Bernadette," he said, closing the drawer. "Keep your Washer friend's nose out of our business."

Shockingly, Bernadette came over to me and gave me a hug. "Now you're going to have two babies on your hands."

"You could be next from what I hear," Maven said. "With the baby, I mean."

"With an *ambitious* man," she said.

"They're married, you know," Ernie Ray said, pointing to Bernadette. "Axel can't be violating purity laws."

"You married that bum?" asked Ulysses. He wiped the bar and threw the towel on the floor.

"Yeah. It's true. I don't wear my rock to this dive. I've got one though. Two thirds of a carat. Band with sapphires. The works. Sorry I forgot to tell you, Ulysses. You're an easy man to get over." She addressed me. "I'd have loved to have you at the wedding, Catrina. Too bad your husband makes mine surly."

Ulysses put his hands on the bar and frowned at Bernadette. "Are you living with him?"

"Married people are known to do that."

"Upstairs?"

"Of course. You took your toothbrush, so I didn't figure you'd be back."

"You put our lives in jeopardy."

"I knew you'd overreact. That's why I kept it from you. I told him your junk was locked in the closet. I keep him too busy to care."

Ulysses's phone rang. "Yeah, Ma. It's a welcome surprise. She's doing great."

I called my parents and told them the news, qualifying that it was early along and not a sure thing. Mom sounded ready to cry with joy, but of course Dad made certain we weren't too happy.

"Wow," he said. "The purpose of life is not to increase its speed. How's your health insurance?"

"They don't have it in Cochtonville, Dad."

It was late when we left the bar. For a man who'd realized his wildest fantasy, Ulysses was unreasonably nervous. He crammed his hands in his jacket pockets, and his mouth was a dark slash on his pale skin. I wasn't getting a glimpse of teeth. The smell of dead fish and manure was strong on the river. What looked like white plastic bags were scattered on the bank. It was birds, pelicans, heads under wings. My mind's eye was seeing ugly where beautiful was. I rubbed my eyes. There was nothing sexy about a sullen man.

"You'll not get enough sleep tonight," he said as we walked the dark spring sidewalks of Cochtonville. "We've got to be careful. I'm happy, but the announcement was more of an ambush. We don't need publicity."

Frogs on the river were croaking, oblivious to my troubles. I spoke loudly to be heard over them. "I didn't know until minutes before that I was going to be on that show, and I didn't expect Mike to sample me on television. I wanted to surprise you."

"I planned that if we got so lucky, I'd keep it from Bernadette as long as I could." He was walking faster now. "One of our sore points was that she never wanted kids."

"And the other sore points?"

"I misunderstood our relationship and took her for granted."

"What happened?"

"I cheated on her. I never should've done it. I'll tell you the whole story. Bernadette and I met at community college when there was such a thing, and from the very beginning, she told me we'd be a one-off, a one-night stand. She didn't believe in forced sex, and that, she said, came with marriage. We both ended up working for Cochton. I was a graphic designer, and she was in IT as artist support. We kept running into each other. You might say we were back-burner pals at first. One-night stands here and there.

I swear I stood over a thousand times. She never allowed me to utter the word *love*. Said it was too dangerous. We got pink-slipped on the same day. Who needs art when you can have fonts? We got drunk to commiserate and we formulated our plan. We went into business together, we lived together, she went to my dad's funeral with me, and through it all she kept saying it wasn't going to last. It wore on me. I sold the condoms and the printer packages. There was always the understanding that if I got caught, we weren't a couple. We would betray each other to save our own skins. Even the name of the bar, Union Station, signifies two separate entities meeting in a shared space. Not a union at all.

"Last year, Maven came to talk to me about her money troubles, and I told her about a fight Bernie and I were having, and the next thing I knew, we were at her place in bed together."

It was humid by the river and my head was pounding. "In bed?"

"We both needed to be worth something to someone, but prostitution is how Bernie saw it, since I told Maven I'd forgive her debts.

"To make things worse, I told Bernie. I guess I hoped it would push the one-off issue. When asked I said Maven had nice breasts and a tighter vagina than I'd expected her to have, and henna tattoos in novel places. Damn stupid mistake. I'm not even a tit man, and Maven and I aren't each other's types. She needs rescuing, and I'm not a rescuer. She needs a simple life, and I don't offer that."

I didn't say anything, and as I'd hoped, he went on talking.

"Bernadette wouldn't forgive me my combination of errors. She wanted me to rot in hell forever alone, but I met you. You insisted on not having a one-off. It drew me in."

A horrible possibility presented itself—what if he still loved Bernadette and I was there to make her eat her words, not because he loved me? "Are my ring and necklace—did you buy them for her?"

"No. I didn't want to get caught asleep at the switch. I met you and bought them in case things went my way."

All sorts of possibilities were jumping in front of me and demanding to be shot down. "Did you call the Washers on us knowing we'd be confronted with a marriage demand?"

"No. She set it up. That was a lucky break for me. I love being married to you. Damn it though. I don't know what I'm going to do about her and Axel."

"Let her be happy, just like we are."

"We're happy, aren't we? Everything happens so efficiently for us, even the baby. I'd like a girl. The world has enough Butzs already."

"She'll be a Butz."

"How about Nellie? That was U.S. Grant's daughter's name."

"Nellie Noelle Butz."

He said, "I like that."

"A Christmas baby. We should've planned better. It happened sooner than I expected."

We walked past a crabapple tree, one of the few flowering plants in all of Cochtonville and pink petals fell onto our shoulders. "A marriage and a baby in the same year," he said.

"Overwhelming," I said.

He said, "Little Honey, you need to be in bed. You're sleeping for two." He went to the curb and stuck out his thumb. A dark car pulled up.

The driver was a middle-aged white guy, average in every way except for his outfit. On his head sat a brown felt hat with a wide brim, like a Mountie or Smokey the Bear might wear. Along with his big hat, he was dressed in a white suit and dark shoes, as if he was Tom Wolfe, the journalist and provocateur from the previous century. We got in. There was the smell of tobacco. He didn't say a thing. Not wanting to give our address to a mute stranger out at a questionable hour, Ulysses told him that if it was on his way, to take us to a busy intersection a few blocks from the inn. The man drove in silence and stopped where he'd been told. We were the only car on the road, for it was nearly 3:00 a.m. When we got out, he said without emotion, "I saw you. Congratulations."

The air was cold and this guy gave me the shivers.

At the inn, I entered the punch code at the door and we tiptoed to our room. We undressed quickly. Waiting until the bar closed to head for home had given us time to talk but had stolen most of my sleep. I had to get up for work in four hours. I left my ugly, new blazer in a heap on the floor.

"That guy. What did he mean by he saw me?"

"He must have seen *This Week at Cochtons.*"

"I can't believe he recognized me," I said.

"It's not like you're just another nerd guy," Ulysses said, climbing into bed with me. "You looked so cute on that show. As pretty as a peony in May. Maybe other guys thought the same thing, or am I a filthy, horny criminal imagining things?"

"You're a criminal and a man of honor," I said, drawing him to me.

"I've waited a long time for fatherhood. All those years with..."

"I wasted time too," I said. "No regrets."

I slept fitfully while Ulysses stayed awake the rest of the night, and when morning came, he called in sick for me. I could hear him talking as I half dreamed. "I might have work. No, not on a Sunday. What's the address again? I'll come if I can catch a ride."

He put down the phone.

"What did Mike say?" I asked, rolling over and hugging the pillow.

"He invited me to a poker game," Ulysses said. "Guess I'll be going."

CHAPTER FOURTEEN

The periodic table is an arrangement of chemical elements in order of increasing atomic number, beginning with the lightest element, hydrogen. Displayed in carefully laid out rows and columns, the periodic table tells a chemist about elemental properties at a glance. There are ninety-two natural elements that speak the language of chemistry.

That Sunday, Jester picked up Ulysses and they went to play poker with Mike and other men from work. I was hopeful the facets of my life might draw together more neatly if Ulysses was friends with the men I worked with. Left behind, Valentine and I were women with our own money. After seeing my announcement, Valentine confessed she, too, was pregnant, about as far along as I was. We walked past the neighborhood shops, looking in windows at baby clothes and discussing our morning sickness. Valentine called it a good thing, a sign the babies were healthy and we were less likely to miscarry or have premature labor. I confessed to her that although pregnant, I craved sex. She told me pregnancy sends blood to the vagina and that some women become more aroused and more orgasmic. She confessed she was tired of prison management and wanted to leave before she had to do anything with the newly reinforced death penalty.

We came to a car lot, closed on Sunday. I was drawn to the idea of buying a car. Having to depend on the bus, or, even worse, strange men with big hats, made me insecure. Once the baby came, I'd want to get home faster and spend more time with it. Plus, I craved the power of owning a car and going where I pleased. As we walked up the driveway to the inn, I saw the lawn was scattered with cigarette butts.

"Look at that," said Valentine. "None of us smoke. It's as though somebody stood here, smoked, and watched us."

We picked them up and went to the trash can behind the inn. I spent most of my outside time on the front porch and was surprised to see what was growing along the back fence—*Valerianus exofficinalis*. This orange flower with a cheesy smell, due to terpenes, had given me my start as a chemist. In high school I'd dabbled in mind-altering substances to earn pocket cash for a laptop. My high school sweetheart and partner in the drug venture, Rex, and I had come up with an extract of *Valerianus exofficinalis* that we called Devil's Bargain because it caused suppression of vital signs followed by a soaring dream in which users often claimed to have met the devil. The resulting powder had packed a two-fisted punch: a dream and an orgasmic near-death experience. I'd slept with the devil, and no man or mind-altering substance had ever measured up until I'd met Ulysses. Rex took off chasing that golden river he'd crossed with the devil's boatman and became a meth cooker.

Around ten p.m. Jester half carried Ulysses into the inn. Ulysses could barely walk.

"Drank too much, I guess," Jester said. "Where do you want him?" Jester and Hans brought him up the stairs to our bedroom and plopped him on the bed.

Jester looked guilty. "He's a great guy. He'll be better in no time."

"Did you do something to him?" I asked. I kissed Ulysses on the forehead. He didn't have a fever.

Jester stared at the ceiling. "He did it to himself. Won fifty bucks though." He held out two twenty-five dollar bills that carried the image of Clarence Cochton.

Hans offered to make coffee. Valentine rushed in and took his vitals.

"He's stable," she said. "Knock on my door if he's still out in the morning."

At sunrise Ulysses mumbled that I should go to work and call in sick for him. I dialed Bernadette on his phone.

"Why the fuck are you calling me?" she said.

"It's Catrina. I don't think Ulysses is going to make it today. He's hungover or sick or something."

"Hungover? He barely drinks. We agreed early on we wouldn't suck down the profits."

"He's not waking up after a day playing poker."

"He hates cards. Take it from me. He's always been weak. I'll have to do it all without him. It won't be that hard. Good luck, sweetie."

I put down the phone. "Are you going to be okay?"

"I'll live. Did I get in a fight? My balls are numb."

"Jester said you drank too much."

"No chance. CochLite was being served. Maybe it's the flu."

Reluctantly I left him. I couldn't use any more sick days since I didn't really have any.

I was in the greenhouse, reaching up, cracking off Mother's leaves with my fingers when someone tickled me under my arms. I screamed in surprise.

"Dingle Butz, go get checked out by HR and make sure you can travel. I want you and Rana to promote No Regrets at the Great Northern Gadget Show."

I clutched the leaves to my chest. "When?"

Mike pointed to me. "You leave tomorrow."

"I can't go. Ulysses is sick."

Mike grinned like a raptor. "Nothing that time away from the sauce can't cure."

"Maybe it was food poisoning," I said. "Did you try to cook?"

Mike touched my arm. "Sassy. Of course I didn't cook."

"I won't go."

"You listen to me. You're pregnant. You need this job. Know what happens to people who can't pay their hospital bills? They go to debtors' prison."

"How many prisons does this place have?"

"An infinite number." He rubbed my arm and looked into my eyes. "Dingle, do as you're told. Is that so difficult? Be a good, prudent girl, like we thought you were when we hired you. 'She won't be trouble,' I told HR. 'She's single. She's nondescript. She'll work hard and keep her nose clean.' How wrong I was to hire a woman. Must I always be chastising you?"

Jester and I were given a rental car and told to drive to what was now another country with a box of No Regrets devices and to promote them to other scientists and health professionals. It was a straight shot and an easy drive. I'd stop home to see my family before we returned. I was a reluctant traveler, but once on the road, I relaxed and let Jester take the wheel.

"Did someone give Ulysses an extra strong drink at that poker party? Because he's got one long hangover."

"They can last up to seventy-two hours."

I gazed at the autos as they zipped by and the new corn in the dachshund-brown, plowed fields. Now and then the scent of concentrated manure lingered, especially by the outlet mall. Despite this, the Granny Smith green of the newly budded trees surrounding the little farmhouses, each with a pond with swans or a patch of lazy cows or a little garden, made me feel cozy in this place.

"It's like a postcard," I said.

"Pretty," Jester said. "So very pretty."

"I could be content forever here," I said.

I watched two little birds chase a hawk. *Can that really happen, the small band together to save their nests?* My eyes grew heavy.

———

The road stretched ahead through the white pines. I was home. A Toyota Cressida passed us on the two-lane road. I was in the car— a big Pontiac—with Granny. It must have been a Saturday. Granny had finally learned how to drive, and we'd gone to the grocery store. It was Granny's birthday. She'd be preparing her birthday dinner. She liked turkey. Gramps preferred a roast, so we'd gotten a roast, large and covered in fat. Fat was the best part when you were a skinny little kid. I asked Granny how old she was. She said sixty. I said I was six. Granny was gentle with wrinkles above her lips from kissing. Granny drove carefully. It was March, the March when Granny turned sixty. The year she'd learned how to drive. Behind us the lights of a police car flashed. Granny pulled to the side of the road near the cemetery in Graafschap, a place carved and shaped by ice and lush with cold loving *Pinus strobus*, the white pine.

The policeman poked his head through the open window. Granny was tiny with neat, gray hair and lipstick. She wore heels and a dress. Her eyes sagged a little, making her gentle. I sat next to her in a booster seat.

"Congratulations, Mrs. Boer. You're my good driver of the day and you've got a cute little sidekick."

"I'm not a good driver, John. I'm a beginner."

"I have two certificates here for ice cream that say you're my driver of the day. You looked great from what I saw."

"You haven't seen me turn, and we both know drivers need to turn."

"I hope to see that someday. I'm sure you'll handle it with grace, as you always do."

"I knew him from school when I was young," Granny said, pulling unto the road. A blush creep up Granny's collar past the fur neck of her coat. In retrospect, I realized she'd done something with him. She'd not settled for Gramps and his criticism of her. She'd not let love pass her by.

Rocky Road was lunch, we decided. We ate the cones in the car. Granny wiped my face with her handkerchief wetted with saliva. "I can drive a little farther."

Granny drove us out to see her brother's Christmas tree farm. How far was it through the pines along the edge of Lake Michigan? Five miles? Ten miles? We'd never been because Granny had never driven.

They were twins, Harmony and Harmon, Granny and Uncle Harm. Harm was surprised by the birthday visit, and to celebrate he'd taken us across the dunes in a four-wheeler with big tires. Uncle Harm called it a dune schooner. They laughed as they dashed across the snow-covered, sandy ground, past the Douglas firs and out onto the sand mountains. It was cold in March with the wind across the lake slapping our faces. Uncle Harm had tucked us in with an old beaver robe. He drove to the spot where the family house had once stood beneath white pines. It was covered with sand now. Trees had been plundered for lumber to rebuild Chicago after the fire of 1871, and without any anchor, the sand had been restless and crept over the house. That happens when roots are gone.

The shadows of winter fell quickly that afternoon. Harm's wife, Martha, sent us off with a bean casserole. Now Granny would need to return the dish. They'd see her again.

We got back to the farm, hours late, and the others were panicked but had soothed themselves with Scotch. Granny was incompetent, stupid, and should never have learned to drive. It wasn't even her car. I told about the policeman and the ice cream. Slumped in his La-Z-Boy, Gramps waved his hand in the air. "Bah. She don't know how to drive."

Granny and I fixed the roast and a cheesecake along with some twice-baked potatoes to go with the bean casserole. By the time folks were done eating, the fog crept in and everyone stayed at the farmhouse that night. I hugged Granny as she tucked me into bed and told me about the foghorns that once warned against crashing on shores you couldn't see.

"Thank you for the ice cream and for being a good driver," I said.

Granny said, "Things are better when you can drive. Just make sure you can drive, honey. Do good in school and take care of yourself. That way, you aren't stuck. Be sure you keep some independence."

Jester reached over and patted my leg. "We made it through The Edge. You've been deep in thought. Is everything swell?"

I sat up. "Yes. I'm buying a car."

"Shouldn't you ask your husband first?"

I pondered Jester's profile. He was distinguished-looking, really. He had a nice jaw. "It'll be a surprise for our birthdays."

"If you act so motivated, you won't get a good deal. You'll jump at the first thing you see."

"Jump at the first thing I see?"

He tightened his hands on the wheel. "Yes. You have no self-discipline. This device we made encourages the worst."

"'The worst?'" I asked. He had his eyes on the road. "What's eating you?" What did nerds really hate? Confusion and disrespect. My life went against his version of what it took for a woman to get respect, thus, it disrespected him and left him confused.

"You don't like seeing me prosper," I said. "That's it, isn't it? It irks you that a female nerd can do the things men do. You think I should suffer because I'm independent. I walked right into your nerd life and upset everything you knew about Nerd Land, didn't I? I can come up with ideas *and* have a baby; I can have sex *and* enjoy it, all without your permission or your genius. I don't bow down to your male version of womanhood."

You could tell we weren't in Cochtonville anymore. A cheery pop tune was playing on the radio. Jester snapped it off. "Yes, I'm jealous of your life. Why are you so happy? What's wrong with me? The way you shed your clothes for a low-life knuckle-dragger shows how impossible women are."

"Hold it right there. My husband is intelligent, and you're the one who holds out for a virgin."

"What are you talking about? You slapped me for even saying it." The car swerved out of our lane momentarily, and he jerked the wheel.

"You were so intent on virginity as some sort of trait. You know what's so sexy about my husband? It's not his looks. He sees me as an equal. He doesn't guilt me for enjoying sex in general, and he's proud of my vocation. Why don't you try that with Jane sometime? She's got a skill set and a profession and her own business, you know. She might even enjoy sex."

He looked ahead at the road and didn't say much.

The two youthful chemists with their handheld device and the appeal of no body fluids captured the attention of buyers. The supply of No Regrets was sold by ten in the morning, and orders were placed all day. We had to admit that moral or not, this invention was a winner.

We drove to my hometown for a family reunion. Granny had given up the house in the country when Gramps died, and the whole family was crammed into a nondescript duplex, white inside and out.

To be in my old town with my mom and Granny was as cozy as a winter evening by the fire. The trinkets of home—delft vases, crocheted afghans—were on display. Dad's collection of his childhood toys filled and toppled from the oak bookcase that sat beside his towering collection of vinyl records. Beneath a furless teddy bear rested my science fair trophies—freshman year, sophomore year, junior year, senior year—all first place. Nothing else would've satisfied any of us. In celebration of our visit, Mom served her signature casserole with sour cream, chicken, cashews, and potato chips. We sat around the table, passing and spooning, discussing my marriage—everyone agreed it was rash—and the possibly reckless pregnancy with the stranger who was my husband. It made me feel like a bad girl, something nerd girls secretly enjoy.

Jester squirmed silently as the outsider. He loyally tried to defend me, saying Ulysses was a respectful and good-looking man and what more could someone want from a partner, after which Dad asked him if he'd ever heard Bonzo Dog Band.

In the course of the conversation, I told them about riding the bus to work, Ulysses's hitchhiking, and about the strange man with the hat.

"He wears a hat because he's bald," said my brother Kevin, a high school senior. He'd been one of those late-life surprises following years of secondary infertility, and this left him entitled. Kevin had none of my ambition. Between his smoking, drinking, and target shooting, he was on his way to developing a nice set of man boobs. Recent studies had linked all of those things to the conversion of testosterone to estrogen. Of course, it wasn't too late for positive change.

Granny said, "I don't use my car now that I don't live in the country. Why don't you take it? Kevin borrows it, but he's going to college in town here and won't need it. He's got to stay on campus and study. I don't like you taking such risks."

"I have friends to see, Granny," Kevin protested. He'd grown. His voice was a baritone, he'd slimmed down a little, and he needed to shave.

"Those friends can give you rides, Kevin. Catrina, take the car. I want you to be able to drive to my funeral, unless the weather is bad. If it is bad, stay safe and don't come. Not that I'm planning on it soon. I like to think ahead."

"The tires need air," said my dad, wearing the same old stained sweatshirt he'd worn every Saturday for two decades. "You'll need the registration. You'll need a license good in Cochtonville."

Granny's car was big and gold—a model not seen on a car lot in over fifteen years. There wasn't time to clean it out or wipe her long-dead cat's white hair from the black upholstery, so I took it as is along with the car blanket and an assortment of facial tissues, cough drops, and the faint scent of her lilac perfume as I drove off in the morning on newly inflated tires. At the last second, Dad tossed my trophies in the backseat, saying he needed more room on the bookcase.

"Thanks, Dad. I'm out of here." I hit the gas and Jester and I left him in my exhaust.

CHAPTER FIFTEEN

Gold, with atomic number 79 and symbol Au, is a heavy, corrosion-resistant, unreactive metal. Unlike lighter elements, gold isn't formed in stars (it takes a nova) and thus is rare on Earth and throughout the universe.

Science passes were golden. I was waved through The Edge, no questions asked. Slabs of concrete maybe fifteen or so feet high hoisted by a crane were being fitted into place. It looked like a gym with no windows or maybe a wall. I knew enough about Cochtonville's lack of investment in infrastructure to be puzzled by it, but I pushed all worry from my mind. I was high with the excitement of ownership of the gold car. Old Gold, I'd named her. No more bus passes, no more worries on that score.

I rushed into Union Station and into Ulysses's strong arms. "I'm so glad you're better," I said.

Behind the counter was a pimply young man with close-set eyes and a lazy smile. The kid leaned forward and nodded sympathetically as he served two women complaining about their bad relationships.

Ernie Ray and Maven were playing pool with the bus driver, Maurice, still in his blue uniform and black tie, an inch of belly hanging over his belt. The television was tuned to the news, and on came City Manager Foil announcing the beginning of construction on a magnificent wall at Cochton's Edge.

"What a stupid idea," Maven said. "Nobody is trying to come here illegally."

"Hell no. It's to keep people in," Ulysses said.

"I saw it," I said. "They've started it already."

Maurice put an arm around Maven.

Ulysses turned off the television and turned on some music.

"Where's Bernadette?" I asked. She was gone.

"Are you hungry?" asked Ulysses. "How about a sandwich?" He scooped loose meat into a bun, poured a glass of water, and brought it to a table. He pulled out the curved-backed chair for me. I sat down. He pushed it in.

"Who's that guy? The new assistant?"

"It is. His name's Zell Bremler. He got accepted to the University of Iowa but didn't make it, and now he's back in town. I thought I might give him a hand."

"Is Bernadette getting the rest she needs?" I bit my fingernail, something I hadn't done since I was a child.

"Little Honey, we have to talk."

"We do. I have a car from my granny." A chill ran under my skin. He was going to say he was leaving me. He'd be mad about the car. It would need a license and who knows how much those were here. I should've tried harder to call and talk it over with him. We'd both been single so long that we hadn't learned to communicate as a couple. "Do you want to see it?"

He drummed his fingers on the table. "In a minute. I got to tell you something important. Eat something first. You must be tired. A car, you say?" He looked at the door and then at the portrait of Grant.

I took a bite of sandwich and a drink of water, foul-tasting, and tried to stay calm.

"Yes. I told Granny about the man in the hat, and she gave it to me in the interest of safety. What is it?" I asked. "What are you dying to tell me?"

He took a deep breath. "When you were gone, something came up. Bernadette and I…"

Here it came. Back with Bernadette. Once again, world, one; smart woman, zero.

"We've had a change in our relationship."

No. I couldn't hear this. The room was spinning.

"You okay, Little Honey?"

"No! What are you saying?"

"I bought the bar. I bought out Bernadette."

I was so relieved. "You bought her half? Why?"

"I couldn't make a dime with Axel prowling around. We had a huge fight about it. I had to get rid of both of them."

"Where did you get the money?"

"My brother gave me the money. He likes to see me entangled in capitalism. I wanted to tell you, but the phones…"

"He gave you money and you took it?"

"I did. As my wife, you own it too."

"I see. Well, we can get back to printing."

"I already made a batch of birds and bees. They were all designed. I just needed Axel gone. They moved out. We can live upstairs. It'll make life so much easier."

"Don't you need her? You were two halves of a whole in this business."

"She's been replaced," Ulysses said.

From behind the bar, Zell said, "Yup."

The door opened and my heart dropped ten stories. It was Axel and Barnabus. So much for Axel not prowling around.

Axel tipped his hat to me and Ulysses. He stood next to the table, his legs wide apart. He wanted me to notice how big he was in the pants.

"How's the family?" he asked Ulysses. All the color was gone from Ulysses's face.

"Healthy and wise," Ulysses said. He put his arm around me and drummed his fingers on my shoulder. "We're doing well. And you?"

"Glad to say we're the same."

"Bernadette should drop by sometime," Ernie Ray said, coming up behind me. "I miss the bounce she added to this place. I guess she's got bigger fish to fry."

"Much bigger, according to rumor," said Barnabus.

I put my hand on Ulysses's leg.

Ernie Ray said, "Speaking of behemoths, I've got a tale for you, an ode to a whale: two million gone, it takes a man to ride that flesh, thar she blows. It could have been a dream, or a fallen star, I rode that whale."

Axel's face grew red at the mention of whales, blowing, and riding flesh.

"Oh, Ernie," Maven said, joining us at the table. "That was kinda bad."

Ernie Ray continued. "Malwear, clothes for criminals, and we'll all be criminals or servants since we're not Cochtons or gunrunning bullies for the state."

"Shut up," Axel said.

Ernie Ray said, "Silent? Hell no. The state has already done enough to me—taken away my hopes. Broken my spirit. My words will remain."

"Hands up, all of you," Axel said. "Ernie Ray, you are being arrested for Word Crime." He and Barnabus grabbed Ernie Ray and handcuffed him behind his back.

"You have no rights," added Barnabus. "Word Criminals have no rights."

"Nobody has rights," Ernie Ray said.

Maven said, "Word Crime? What kind of crime is that?"

Barnabus said, "The worst kind of all."

Axel said, "The dreck of society. The poison of ideas. A canon dangerous."

"He didn't mean no harm," Maven said.

"Yup," said Zell from behind the bar.

Ulysses put his hand on mine as it rested on his leg—a sign we weren't going to cause trouble over this.

"When did this law go into effect?" Ulysses said.

"The first of the month, along with a slew of other laws," Axel said. "It's going to be a busy summer snuffing out delinquency."

"You got no evidence," Ernie Ray said.

"Sure we do. Just heard it. Got it on record. Twice. In this very place."

"I never got a request for any security videos," Ulysses said.

"Request. What's that?" said Barnabus.

"We don't need a warrant. The information was voluntarily given to me by an ex-owner," Axel said. "Now, pal, let's get going."

"What'll happen to him?" Maven twirled her hair around her finger.

"A few days in prison as a warning and a fine." Barnabus put tape over Ernie Ray's mouth. Ernie Ray let out muffled protests and his eyes bugged as he was led away.

Of course, Bernadette couldn't be replaced. Unlike Zell, she was mature and business- and computer-savvy, and unlike Ulysses, she had an entrepreneurial spirit. She'd been the one pushing for new products and writing new programs. Without her, we had production, but no new products, and as for the products we had, printing and selling them by himself made Ulysses nervous. The printer, locked in the bedroom closet, was used for more koozies and fewer condoms.

Bernadette had taken everything, and all we could afford to decorate our apartment was a kitchen table, two chairs, a bed, and a set of towels. Something else was missing. We hadn't had sex since I returned from the conference.

I was eating a tavern sandwich at a table in Union Station when Ernie Ray crawled back in. He watched each bite I took. Finally, I handed him what was left, and he shoved it into his mouth.

"Got no pot to piss in," he said, his mouth full and sauce on his lips. "Muzzled like a rabid dog."

Maven came and put a hand on his shoulder. "Poor Ernie. Keep your chin up. "Zell, come bring him a beer."

"You're not my manager," the young bartender said.

"Here now." Maurice fished a sixteen dollar bill from his pocket and put it on the table in front of Ernie. I'd hardly paid attention to Maurice, who seemed like a decent, safe kind of guy.

Ernie croaked, "Without my words I'm as poor as Job's turkey. Too poor to raise a fuss."

Brown Hat Man walked in, the same disturbing man who'd given us a ride the night of our fight. In the dim light of the bar, his skin was pale and his eyes nearly colorless beneath the hat. He had a big nose with lots of nostril hair. He bumped into Zell as the kid snatched the generous tip for Ernie Ray's sympathy Rainy Day.

Hat Man sat at the table and took out a cigarette. He handed one to Ernie Ray. "Nicotine?"

Nicotine was a plant molecule designed to kill if ever there was one. Ironically, if Ulysses had smoked, it might have been a deal breaker for me, so dangerous is nicotine for the nervous system and cardiovascular health. Gramps had been a smoker and my dad was currently. I blamed nicotine's scourge for their surliness.

"Pleased to meet you," Ernie Ray said, taking the cigarette.

"Don't make it personal," Hat Man said.

"Ernie, no. Don't smoke. It'll wreck your voice," Maven said sweetly.

Zell had been walking back to the bar. "Yo, bitch," he said over his shoulder. "Put it in the suggestion box."

"Show some respect, son." Maurice again put an arm around Maven, almost enveloping her as an amoeba does when it eats.

Ulysses came over to the table. "Don't smoke around my pregnant wife."

Ernie Ray cocked his head toward Ulysses. "Ignore his words. He's walking on broken glass right now."

"I see. We all have two faces," the man said.

"You got it," Ernie Ray said. "Now he's having the family he never expected, and it doesn't sit well with his occupation."

Ulysses grabbed Ernie Ray by the collar. "That's enough news to fill a paper. Take it outside."

"Smart is the new sexy," said Hat Man.

"You too. We're closed." Ulysses went to the door and held it open. "Everybody out. Zell, that includes you. Come back with a better attitude."

As the place cleared, he said to me, "This is no way to make a living."

That night in bed, I reached for him eagerly, but he pretended to be asleep.

CHAPTER SIXTEEN

Anthocyanins are plant pigments that color berries red and purple. They belong to a group of chemicals called flavonoids. Colorful fruits contain a mixture of these molecules. Studies show they can protect the heart, lower blood pressure, prevent ulcers, improve brain function, and prevent inflammation.

Ulysses was making eggs and pancakes as he tried to pretend he'd slept the night before. I'd mentioned many times that I liked his chest hair, but he was shirtless and, to my surprise, hairless. Well, it wasn't up to me to dictate how he chose to groom himself. I sat at the table in the large kitchen, which had a fire escape outside of the window. I was in my silky pajamas, my hair tangled from restless sleep.

"What's up so early besides you?" I asked. Everything was crammed into this area—stove, sink, refrigerator, washer, and dryer. Two pans and one saucepan hung on the walls. The tall window looked out onto an alley below.

"Hope you can keep these eggs down."

He put eggs on a plate. We had two plates—color-changing plastic—experiments by Ulysses and Bernadette during better times. Beneath the eggs, the plate shifted from yellow to red.

"Want catsup?"

"No thanks."

He put the eggs and a pancake in front of me. "Sorry there's no bacon."

"Ugh. Who eats that stuff? Ulysses, that Hat Guy is upsetting, but not enough to keep a person up all night. What's eating you?"

He returned to the refrigerator and pulled out a brown paper bag. "The last of the homegrown strawberries. Cost me a half dozen condoms. They're the little ones that you like."

"More nutrients," I said.

He went to the sink and rinsed them. He kept himself looking nice. He made sure I had fresh produce even though it meant he and the grower had both risked their necks. What more could I want? Besides my suddenly dormant sex life, everything was still perfect.

He put the bowl in front of me. "Little Honey, this country is no place to raise a kid. Ernie Ray was arrested for talking. Talking. *What's going to happen to a condom bootlegger?* I was online all night, except during the outages, looking for a place for us to go. I went and visited my dad's grave. Sat there thinking until the sun came up, wondering what he might do. I'm applying for a job as a brewer's assistant in the US."

"What? You were up all night planning this?" The reality of marriage splashed over me. It was a serious thing, life-altering. I popped a strawberry into my mouth, hoping eating would settle me as it had when I was a child.

"We've got a car. I'm driving to Lakeland next week to interview for a job. I'm taking a sample of Rainy Day with me."

"Assistant? Isn't that beneath you? Suddenly you're a serious brewer? I thought the bar was a cover for your printing business. I know times are tough. We can ride it out." I ate a spoonful of strawberries, packed with anthocyanin pigments.

"It's a stepping stone to a new life as an honest man." He walked to the refrigerator, took out milk, and put it on the counter.

My words tumbled across the strawberries in my mouth. "This is reckless. You just bought the bar. It hasn't even been six weeks."

"A lot has changed."

I put down my spoon. "You just got married. You're expecting a kid. Now is not the time for another major life change."

He held a juice glass to the light, winnowing it for fingerprints. "I want to check it out before The Edge seals, as I'm sure it will."

"Who'll be running the bar?"

Ulysses frowned. "Zell."

"Zell? He's denser than lead. Aren't bartenders supposed to be conversational?"

"The client base is loyal."

"And if you get the position, what will I do? I like my job."

He grabbed a dishtowel from the counter and wiped the glass. "We move together. We're married."

"I don't want to quit my job. I'm in the middle of something interesting."

He poured milk into the glass and handed it to me. "You have a sought-after degree. You can find something else. No need to put cash into Cochton pockets. I didn't say you had to give up science. Your eggs will get cold. We can talk about this later."

I pushed my plate away. "How will it look if I leave a place after a year? Do you even love me, Ulysses, that you would force such a choice on me?"

"I do. We both have a responsibility to the baby, however. This isn't a sane place to be. The noose is tightening, Catrina." He put a graceful hand to his neck and his wedding ring glinted. "I said I wanted the best for the baby. Please eat something." He pushed my plate in front of me.

"Suddenly, I'm less of a concern than a baby? Science is sanity. It's one of the only dependable things. I'm not giving it up. Babies need sane mothers. They need a reliable income. They need clothes and medical care and college someday. All that comes with my stable job." I took a bite of the eggs. My appetite was roaring, perhaps due to the stress of this conversation. "And, Ulysses, what will the people of Cochtonville do without your goods?"

"Add to the fifteen million unplanned people per year on this planet, I suppose. Catrina, kids need security. They deserve to be wanted and cared for. There's no credibility in this place. It's not nurturing. The way things are going, we won't even have public schools." He put a hand on my shoulder.

"You say that word a lot. It's banned."

"What word?"

"Public."

"See what I mean, Catrina?"

I pushed my chair back and leaped into his arms. Oh how I wanted those attachment chemicals to flow. "I need convincing. Come to bed with me." I hated to admit it, but I wasn't going to move for a man who didn't find me attractive anymore.

Ulysses stood like a bale of hay in a field. "I've been under a lot of stress. You've got a baby to worry about. Isn't that enough?" He stroked my hair.

"No. I want a husband too."

He went to the sink and ran water over the egg pan.

"I want to grow in love as we pledged to do." I put my arms around his waist. He was still so handsome, his hair long and sexy, his body strong. "I don't want the truth of us together to slip away. I want to be more than a mother. I need you to accept me as a woman and a wife." Through my silky pajamas, my breasts rubbed across his chest.

"Even though the truth is that we rushed together in haste and tied the knot because of the law?"

And because I wanted to keep that job he suddenly expects me to quit. Because he was rebounding. Because I have daddy issues and a missing component to my life. I released his warm body, crossed the kitchen, and looked out the window. Axel and Barnabus were in the alley near the red dumpster, aiming guns at pigeons on the ledge. I moved away from the window.

"Ulysses, that was harsh. I've been told by the people at work and of course by my dad that I'm a nitwit for rushing into marriage. Won't you be on my side? Can't we wait a few years until we have some money saved? Must we be mired in the lower middle class forever? I want better for our kids. I need the certainty of my job and my data. Can you understand that?"

He embraced me and I put my head on his chest. "I'm so not myself," he said. "I'm sorry. I'm not this kind of man. If I get a job offer, we'll decide together what to do."

I said, "Sex is a strong force. You know what a dry spell does to a person? How ugly and unwanted you start to feel? We're feeling unwanted. Unattached. The chemistry isn't flowing between us."

He touched my hair. "Catrina, I can't. I have no interest in sex. This place is killing me. I have to get out of here. I can feel it as strongly as I feel your heart beating."

I put my hand on his heart. "Baby," I asked, "when did you start shaving your chest?"

He replied, "I didn't."

CHAPTER SEVENTEEN

Androgens are crucial for development and maintenance of the sexual characteristics, bone density, and muscle associated with masculinity. Antiandrogens block androgens from forming or from reacting with the body. They are used to treat prostate cancer and excess hair and acne in women. These chemicals are sometimes given to sexual predators.

The new plants were small against the backdrop of the mature Mother vine crawling up the greenhouse glass. Self-pollinating, Mother displayed brown seedpods, spiraling like those of a locust tree. I wanted to begin analysis of volatiles in young *Muscuna cochtonus*. Volatiles are tricky things for plants. They do all sorts of heavy lifting—they can react to insect damage and call carnivores to consume the pests, or they can wage direct attack by producing toxins and intoxicants. They can, of course, smell wonderful and attract pollinators. It tires the plants to produce them, or so Natharie had told me. These terpenoids, fatty acids, and the vast array of nitrogen and sulfur compounds come at a metabolic cost. Natharie had a new tray of young plants started for me in the greenhouse. A baseline volatile profile was in order before they were hardened by the ways of the world. Plants are far more sensitive than people think.

"Beautiful, isn't she?" said Natharie, stroking Mother like a spaniel. "It wasn't easy germinating such old seeds. Seeds have defense mechanisms to keep them from sprouting at the wrong time. Sometimes they need cold, some like it hot, others want moisture or dryness. I had no idea what this plant desired. I had to score this seed, soak it for a day, then add a touch of growth hormone. She finally sprouted after Mike took me to task for my failure, as if she wanted to prove him wrong. It must have been a response to elevated carbon dioxide from his hot breath chewing me out. I didn't think anything would come out of this crazy Cochton idea to use vintage seeds, but it's been a success. The offspring are fast-growing with no natural pests. This plant is my favorite though. She's the one who started it all."

"Palatable with natural calming properties," I added. "Topped off with a pleasant jasmine scent."

"You make them sound like fine wine. The first batch of feed is being field-tested, or more accurately, confinement tested. Let's hope these beans make the pigs' lives a little cheerier."

A determined clicking echoed in the hallway. A woman with an agenda was tapping out a rhythm with her heels.

"Someone's coming, and it's not one of us," said Natharie.

"What have we here?" Despite the warning footsteps, I jumped at the sound of the harsh voice. It was City Manager Frani Foil with Mike dogging her heels.

Natharie said, "Here we have some fast-growing vines that will be added to animal feed."

"To think how these will fatten the hogs of the world. It brings tears to my eyes." Frani flashed teeth and raised her breasts. "Everyone deserves an affordable pork chop, and Cochtonville deserves the four billion in income from them."

Irrationally, I didn't like the plants spoken about this way, as if they had no purpose except the fattening of hogs, Cochtons, and their spoon-fed politicians. The whole ambushing rollout of No Regrets still bothered me. It had been so disrespectful.

Frani turned her head, releasing an aerosol of perfume. "What inspiring work produced these marvels? Tell me how happy it makes you to snip and sew those genes."

My hair drooped in the humidity of the greenhouse. Natharie said, "No snipping or sewing needed. The seeds, viable and vital, were found in a pocket. We believe they came from Isaac Newton and were passed down to John Locke, then Thomas Jefferson—who rarely changed his pants—and then to one of his children, and from there we're not sure. They're history's secret and nature's miracle."

"If they belong to nature, they belong to anyone," Frani rasped. Her eyes jumped to Mike, who took Frani's arm.

He said, "These are interesting, a token of our diversity of products. If it makes money, Cochton Enterprises will go to the ends of the earth to find it. Come this way, Manager Foil, and view the Cochton's newest corn. We call it Big B—for benefits—DG—for Day-Glo—in the next greenhouse. We've added a fluorophore, cut it right out of pseudomonads and put it in the corn."

"How mind-stretching. How awe-inspiring. Truly *Brave New World*. What will it do?"

"The corn will shimmer and glow like a black-light poster."

"Shockingly clever. It will impress our friends and frighten our enemies."

Their voices trailed off as they left to admire the newest Day-Glo corn. I stood in the greenhouse with Natharie, Mother, and her seedlings. They would serve no noble purpose at the hands of the Cochtons. Natharie watered Mother and then her babies, the silver spray dancing in the sunlight, sprinkling the baby dragons as they arched their green backs. They should belong to everyone, like science, like the Enlightenment revolution. But they didn't. They belonged to Cochton Enterprises, and so did I.

"Look at that," said Natharie. "Mother has expensive taste." A tendril had stretched out and wrapped around the strap of a leather purse decorated with tiny gold pigs.

"How did she do that so fast?" I said. "I didn't even see it happen."

"Hydrogels that rapidly shrink or swell. You should know that."

"Makes sense since you just watered her. The hydrogels are primed. Still, it's unexpected in a bean. She's got faster reflexes than a Venus fly trap. Is that your purse?"

"With pigs on it? Not a chance. It's Frani's."

"Mother's going to get in trouble purloining from a politician."

"Serves that bitch right. 'If they belong to nature, they belong to anyone,'" Natharie said sarcastically. She sprinkled water across the leather of the purse as she drenched Mother's soil. "Drink up, Mother."

"Howdy."

Natharie jumped and water sprayed on our khaki pants and flat shoes. It was Jester. "The bar business must be booming. Jane's been aching for one of those purses, although she prefers the corn pattern."

"It's not mine," I said. "Frani and Mike were here. She must have left it."

"Are you following us?" said Natharie. I couldn't tell if she was teasing or angry with Jester. Being labmates, scientists working together, is an intimate relationship, as complicated as dating, complete with fights and makeups, but usually without the sex.

"Why not? So much beauty in one place."

"Knock it off." She gave him a squirt of water before shutting off the flow.

"Cool your jets. I admit it. I was following Mike."

"Like a dog with your nose up his ass," said Natharie.

"Yeah, kinda."

"Puppy." She patted his red hair.

"Or puppet. I got nothing better. I do what Mike tells me."

"To your credit, you're cute."

Mother's tendril wrapped more tightly around the purse.

"Don't that beat all?" Jester said. "You can see that vine moving. Is it hydrogels?"

"You bet. Mother's got it all," said Natharie. "This plant is my whole world."

The greenhouse door opened with a creak, and Frani strode back from her trip to see the corn, Mike on her arm. With a huff she grabbed the purse, yanking the tendril from the stem. Mother bobbled, straightened, and lashed out a vine that wrapped around Frani's neck.

"Help! Dr. Watson!" she cried, her neck reddening.

Mike lunged at Mother as the vine held tight. Jester and I rushed to help, tugging at the *Muscuna cochtonus*. Mother had the grip of a python! Jester flapped his arms. Mike panted as he tugged at the vine. Frani's face was red and she gasped. Her shoes flew off as she thrashed.

Natharie took clippers from her lab coat pocket and squeezed the blades across the refractory vine. She cut through Mother, who released a gush of fluid, and Frani collapsed onto the gravel floor of the greenhouse.

Frani narrowed her eyes and flashed her teeth. "That plant is a menace. Dispose of the thing or I'll have you all shot."

"You tripped into it and tangled yourself," said Natharie, pointing the clippers at her. Mother sprung back behind her, recovering from her cut tendril.

"No," said Mike, helping Frani to her feet. "Get rid of this plant at once or you're fired." He brushed dust from Frani's suit. Frani slid on her heels and they left arm in arm.

"Golly wow. Was that illogical or some freak accident?" Jester said.

"Maybe Frani fell and got snarled. Her heels were kind of high and she wasn't watching where she was going," I said, trying to stay calm and consider multiple possibilities. I clasped my hands because they were shaking. Who ever heard of a chemist with shaky hands?

"Staring into Mike's eyes," Jester said. He wiped his brow. "Close call. Has this happened before?"

"No," Natharie said, her ring flashing in the greenhouse sunlight as she waved her hands frantically. "No. No. Never."

"The worst thing to do in the face of a lab accident is to panic," Jester said. "One time I had an azide explosion and—"

"I'm panicking. We've got to save her. She's a gorgeous plant, not some killer." Natharie stroked Mother's leaves. "I'll trim her and transplant her. Maybe she's root-bound. She's out of her habitat. She needs further study."

"Mike said to destroy her," Jester said. "We've got to do as he says."

"How about keeping leaf, stem, and root samples and tossing out the plant?" I said, keeping my distance. I didn't want to draw a hasty conclusion, but I didn't want to get strangled either.

"No," said Natharie. "Mike said to get rid of her, not destroy her. He only did it to impress that Foil woman. Otherwise, he would have said to kill all the plants, and they're too valuable to Cochton Enterprises. Jester, I love Mother. She needs another chance. My car's in the shop. Help me sneak her somewhere where I won't be accused of gardening. I'll make you dinner."

"I'll be a hero. Right-o. But promise not to tell Mike," Jester said. "We'll plant her somewhere. In my backyard behind the garage."

"No. That would be too obvious. There aren't plants in yards in Cochtonville. Even I know that," I said.

"Yeah. Dad would think her a weed and bust out the herbicide. He's got some dementia but he still likes to kill stuff. I've got an idea. But we can't tell a soul about it or what we just saw."

Jester parked the hearse, and the three of us got out near a fresh grave. I felt as if I'd been punched in the gut when I saw it—a heart-shaped tombstone with a cement angel leaning her cheek on the name on the right-hand side: Jill Rana. Jester bowed his head in respect. "This is the place."

"Your mom? Jester, I'm so sorry," Natharie said as he put

Mother's heavy pot on the grass beside the grave's new dirt. I studied the dates on the stone.

"The week of Catrina's wedding reception," he confirmed. "I didn't want to bring everyone down, so I didn't say anything. It was her heart. It broke. Nobody would believe what she carried in it. Right after your wedding, Juan killed himself. It came out in a letter he sent her."

"Dad's a wicked man. He abused her. He hit all of us. Some of the boys got it worse than others. Some older boys did it to the younger ones. We were only orderly on the surface. Yet there was, you know...not only hitting but touching. Admirals for the Brotherhood of the Mounted, they called it."

I got the chills. "Incest? You looked so beautiful together."

He sat on his mom's grave and put his face in his hands. "Let's say that besides Dad, Jehosophat is a monster. He left home when I was small, so I was spared. Things settled down, but I saw the fallout. Dad stopped hitting, stopped bringing us into the embalming room to point out what we'd be like if we told anyone, but he still yelled."

We sat next to him and put our arms around him. The atmosphere here in Cochtonville was villainous with smells.

"Things like this happen everywhere, I'm sad to say," said Natharie. "It's no judgment on you."

"Mom told me that her father had been the same way. She'd married Dad in a hurry to get away from home. It wasn't the refuge she'd hoped for. That's why I fear for Catrina and her speedy marriage."

He picked up a cigarette butt that had been tossed on the grave. "It's his. He smokes this brand." He threw the butt.

"Who are you talking about?" said Natharie.

"Jeho. My brother. He doesn't come around much. He was back for the funeral. I haven't seen him since. How can Mom be dead and he and Dad be alive? My hope all along was that after Dad was gone, she'd find peace at last, but he outlived her."

The wind ruffled my hair. "Did you notice," I said, "that this is the only place in Cochtonville where flowers grow?"

"No," he said. "There's another place. I'll show you."

After planting Mother on Jill's grave, we got in the hearse and started home. A short ways down the road, Jester turned onto a gravel road.

He said, "I need to show you something. I've been meaning to do this since we met, Catrina."

The hearse bumped across the uneven road past corn so huge it could have been alien invaders.

"This must be the Big Yields Corn," said Natharie.

"It is. It's ours," Jester said, hunching over the wheel as we traveled through the tunnel of corn. "Of course, we don't own any of our science," he said. "I mean, it all belongs to Cochton Enterprises. Have you ever thought of that?"

"Not anymore. Mother is ours now," Natharie said.

Jester slammed on the brakes as we met another car at an intersection obscured by corn.

"Gets dangerous out here," he said.

"It's like we're in a maze," I said. "You can't even see where you're going."

"I know where I'm going," he said.

We stopped at a field of grass shot through with white, yellow, and purple flowers.

We got out of the hearse and stood in it with the grass blowing around us.

"Well," he said at last.

"Well what?" I said.

"How do you like the remnant prairie? It's cool, isn't it? Crammed with species. It turns over with the season like nothing else you've seen." He took my hand and we walked into it. He was right. It was a cottage garden of spiky leaves and petite blossoms. All sizes of bees traveled over it taking inventory. Scattered through it were beer cans and condoms.

"I'm not sure how this little haven escaped. It might be future cemetery plots. Once prairie like this covered eighty percent of this area. Now a tenth of a percent. Sad, isn't it?"

"Yet we're helping destroy it by promoting only a few kinds of crops and your pigs." said Natharie.

"I know. I have such conflicted feelings. I work for them and they are ding-donged nice to me, but my family once owned three hundred acres of this land. The Cochtons bought it and a hundred farms. Farming is dangerous work and the offer was good. The next year they bought more farms. Gobble gobble, and I don't mean turkeys."

"Now they own it all. Every bite we take fills their pockets and we're at their mercy," said Natharie.

Jester picked a purple flower and tucked it in her hair.

"Thanks, Jester, for saving Mother," she said.

"Thanks, ladies, for being my friends. I couldn't ever tell another man about..." He wiped his eyes.

As we drove from there, a plume of gravel powder flowed from the hearse like dust from a comet's tail.

CHAPTER EIGHTEEN

Estrogen is a sex hormone and steroid associated with female sexual characteristics such as breast tissue and the menstrual cycle. It's responsible for growing the uterine lining. Estrogen levels increase during pregnancy. It plays a role in bone formation and cardiovascular function. Estrogen lubricates vaginal tissues. Estrogen in water can harm male fish, reducing their fertility.

That night when Ulysses came to bed we lay face-to-face, half in slumber. I took his head in my hands.

"If you get that job, I'll go with you. I'll do whatever you want," I said. Mother had a lesson for me. The prairie had a lesson. The world could shift in a moment. All I had was my struggling love for Ulysses and this baby. I had to make this work even though I didn't know if it would, if I could. I still had that empty spot, but I was inching closer to filling it with substance. I almost had it.

Ulysses kissed me. He kissed my neck. He kissed my tender breasts. He went down on me until my back arched like a cat and I imagined that the baby fluttered. When I went to return the favor, he was a broken water balloon.

"Is it me?" I asked. On the street, a siren squawked. A traffic stop in the dead of night.

"Forget it," he said. Really, nothing had been right since Bernadette left.

"Can I do anything?"

His breath was hot on my face. "I'm not feeling it. I'm just not feeling it. Maybe I've been standing too long. Or God, I'm meant to be a one-off guy and not a husband." He rolled over and we lay there, together and alone.

The next Sunday, he left with the big gold car, a quart of Rainy Day, and hopes for a future without Washers.

Come Monday morning I stood at the bus stop, the wind tangling my hair, the city moving in front of me like a lazy river. The bus pulled up with a hiss of hydraulic brakes, and the door opened with a screech. Maurice Diamond broke into a chubby-cheeked smile that quickly became an eye roll and a glance behind him. Ernie Ray in a V-neck, white T-shirt, and jeans was slumped on a seat with his hand over his face while Hat Man in his white suit sat next to him as alert as a German Shepherd. Hat Man touched the brim of his brown hat and wolf-whistled. Oh why had I ever been on that television show? I'd attracted a creep.

"Catrina," Ernie Ray said, sitting up. "Where's Ulysses?"

I fixed my eyes on the back of the bus, pretending not to hear or see them. I was delighted to spot Valentine a few rows back.

"Hey," she said as I scooted next to her. "How're you doing? What brings you here?"

"Ulysses took the car for business."

"Back to the back of the bus," Valentine said.

"There are some shady characters from the bar sitting up front," I said.

"Aren't we used to shady characters by now?"

"I should be. How's work?"

"Your device sure made my life easier. Lots of blood tests at the prison, and now no blood—genius. The baby icon is cute. I look at it every day and I can't believe it. Aren't we lucky?" She was mentioning a side of No Regrets I regretted. Pregnant women were monitored at work to make sure they were still pregnant.

"They say we can't have it all," I said. I was considering how I'd balance my life.

"Who are *they* anyway and what do *they* know? Just a bunch of cautious naysayers."

We compared abdomens, hers stretching her scrubs and mine the Cochton polo. Our sickness had passed and we were in the second trimester. Our bellies were still little bumps, not demanding any maternity clothes, yet we couldn't wait to buy them. For all the trials and stress of being working women, having our own money and our own babies under our hearts was like being able to fly. We knew we'd be dropped like bombs, our bodies stretched, our sweet lives disrupted soon, with those bundles of so-called joy, but right now we held the whole world in our souls.

We talked about the flutterings we felt, how we hadn't bought a thing for our babies yet. Here it was illegal to know anything about your baby's sex or health before it was born. The fear was that people would sneak to another country to get abortions if they got disappointing information. Valentine whispered of a nurse who did secret ultrasounds off-hours.

"If you want to get one, we could go together. Text me that you want to go shopping. It would be fun to know."

We worried about being late for work. Traffic was bad. Blocking the bus was a pickup with a hay bale in the cargo area. It was going slowly. The struggle of the truck brought my own struggle to mind.

"I hate to ask for free medical advice, but I'm desperate. Ulysses can't—or won't—have sex with me these days. Is it me or is it him?"

Valentine thought for a moment. "How old is he?"

"Thirty-five."

"Unless he has some sort of condition, he should have plenty of testosterone at this point. It drops only one percent a year. Was he active until this pregnancy?"

"Yes. It was what brought us together. That and loneliness."
Was that even right? Had I been lonely? I'd been a competent and confident

chemist when I met Ulysses. In control yet incomplete. Being in control of lab data isn't the same as being alive. I hadn't desired anything beyond lab results as I had even given up being accepted and loved. Some can say they don't need erotic love, but for most of us it just isn't true. Love is a catalyst. It makes things proceed more easily. In this regard I was like most everybody else. He'd given me that, and it had been withdrawn. How I wanted his touch again.

Valentine frowned. "Hmm. He needs to get it checked out."

An older woman sitting behind us leaned forward. "My guess is another woman."

"You emasculated him," said her friend.

This possibility and their intrusion shocked me into silence. It was plausible. Shaving his chest. No interest in me. Now a mysterious trip. I was losing my husband. If my thesis committee had rejected me, I could have considered bias or the old-man stubbornness those groups are known to harbor. I would've squared my shoulders and gotten to work. This was my husband, the man who knew me most intimately, who had pledged to love and cherish me. No matter how smart I was, it couldn't protect my heart from hurt. Nothing could replace the buoyancy of being wanted, loved unconditionally. Every scientist knows that science is progressive. The next generation stands on your shoulders and you are replaced. But a wife, no. No one enters that state with the goal of being downgraded; you enter it with all hope. It wasn't just my pride at stake. My confidence was shattered.

The bus paused at a stoplight. Ernie Ray leaped to his feet, Hat Man at his side. He croaked in his bullfrog voice, "Ladies and gentlemen, this is a poetry ambush." People began to chatter.

"Silence," said Hat Man. "This man will speak poetry until we get donations."

Maurice put his hands up. A knitting woman paused briefly, her hands tense on the needles. She was considering stabbing the man; it flickered across her face before she put them in her purse and raised her hands.

Ernie Ray said a few lines. "No news is good news. No soul like an old soul, who dares speak of *plutocracy*."

The patrons gasped. He'd obviously said a word not to be mentioned. Hat Man removed the hat, showing a huge, bald head, pale as a ghost.

Ernie continued. "*Monoculture* of thought. *Public*, are you so afraid? What should we do to improve our lives? Plenty of corn. Hidden hogs. A poverty of art."

People covered their ears with their hands.

Across the aisle, a man in a Cochton Big Yields cap, a symbol of nationalism, stood up and shouted, "There will never be enough corn!"

"Had enough?" said Hat Man. "Make a donation and we'll go away."

He walked through the bus as people tossed coins and bills into the hat. They stood before me. I opened my billfold, looking for the smallest amount of money I could find. Fifty cents.

"Thank you for your donations. Only the brave have words, and it's been a pleasure speaking for you," Ernie Ray said after the cash had been collected. "Now if you'll excuse me, we've got to scram. Let us off or we'll speak again."

Maurice stopped the bus and the robbers jumped down and dashed across the cracked sidewalks of Cochtonville.

"Ugh," I said to Valentine. "I'm going to be late."

Sure enough, we'd gone just three blocks when the bus stopped again and Axel and Barnabus got on.

"Oh no," I said. "That smaller Washer married Ulysses's ex. We've got bad blood between us."

"I know him," said Valentine. "Good-looking but arrogant. Didn't he crash your wedding reception?"

"Yeah, and danced like a dream."

Barnabus's hair was askew. He was missing a button. Axel was detailed like a luxury car. His hair and nails were trimmed, his nose was straight and so were his teeth. The Washers went through the bus, asking riders what happened.

"They were beggars," said one woman.

"They threatened us with poetry," said a man.

"They said bad words," explained another.

Barnabus took notes. Axel gave me a look of recognition and strode over.

"Mrs. Butz, I didn't expect to see you here. I'm sure you can confirm the identity of the suspects, being as your husband deals with lowlifes on a daily basis."

I didn't correct him by pointing out that my name was Dr. Butz. "One was Ernie Ray, and the other I've seen before but don't know his name."

"Any guesses as to the motive?"

"Ernie Ray used to be paid for his poetry, but now it's illegal. I imagine he needed money."

"I see. You got that, Barn?"

Barnabus was smiling at Valentine and fluttering his long eyelashes. "Nice to see you, doctor," he said to her. "Need a ride to work? We're going that way."

"What a sweetheart! I'd treasure a ride in your van. Will we leave soon? I'm running behind." She winked at me. Valentine was better than I at playing helpless. She was getting the Washers out of my face and getting a ride at the same time.

"Sure. Could you take a look at a carbuncle that popped up on my side while we're at it?"

"I'd be happy to. Does it hurt?"

Of course, I was late for work. I had to report to Mike to get scanned with No Regrets. He was less angry than I expected.

"Word Outlaws. That beats all," was the sum of what he said.

I met Jester in the hall.

"You okeydokey?" he asked.

"Yes, I rode the bus and there was a holdup. Some men demanded cash for withholding poetry."

"What happened to your car?"

"Ulysses has it. He's gone," I didn't want to explain too much. I didn't want Cochton Enterprises to know Ulysses was looking for a job.

"Is he coming back?" Jester asked.

"I think so."

His eyes scanned me, looking for flaws, for any unhappiness that would show I'd made a mistake by marrying Ulysses, proof that professional women have to make a choice: love or career.

"Golly gee whiz," he said.

The reality was that I was a person who flew best on the wings of security. If an experiment fails, you learn; you try again. What had I learned from this besides what I already knew? I was attracted to men but they hurt me. All I'd needed was one on my side, just one, but obviously even that was beyond me. I, the celebrated chemist, was tumbling to earth at the suggestion that Ulysses had another woman. Even worse, I'd lost my sense of wonder and awe. I had no curiosity about the mystery of life. Without that, I wasn't a scientist anymore. I was just a technical person who knew the moves and talk of science without having it in my soul.

"Nothing is worth anything," I said.

"That low, huh? How's the research?"

"I have a fecal study coming up." My voice was as dead as a flat ball.

Jester ran his hands through his hair. "Oh shit."

Union Station was silent that afternoon. I sat at the bar where Zell was eating pretzels with one hand and serving beer to a big-bellied man with another. The couch was empty. Maven was in a booth brushing purple polish on the nails of the woman who'd been kissing on the couch during my first visit to Union Station. Each of them had a half-consumed glass of Riesling at her elbow, the rims red with lipstick. More bottles of polish sat between them.

"Do you want some sparkle on top?" asked Maven.

"No." The woman sighed.

"A little flower?"

"No."

Maven capped the bottle of polish. "That's good. I'd rather be done with this."

The woman's kissing partner was playing pool with Maurice.

"Hey, you took an extra turn," said Maurice to her partner.

"No, I didn't."

Kissing Woman stretched and yawned, her arm hitting her wineglass. The Riesling spilled onto the floor. I ran to the bar and grabbed a towel.

"Look at that mess," I said to Zell, hoping he'd get the hint.

"Look at all *this*," he said, opening the cash register, busting with bills. "Everybody's drunk and depressed."

"Slow it down. They're spilling things." I went and wiped the floor. Kissing Woman stepped over me on her way to the bar to get another drink.

Axel came in and stood in the doorway. No one looked up. No one greeted him, as they usually did as a form of warning to the others. He spoke to Zell briefly. Zell pointed to me on my hands and knees wiping the floor. Axel came my way.

"Morgues have more going on than this place." He put money in the jukebox. A slow song about an angel visiting earth sobbed to life.

He came up to me, his shiny boots in my face. "Dance with me."

"I'm not a good dancer." I made a final swipe at the sweet, fruity wine.

"I didn't ask if you wanted to."

"Dancing is art."

"Only a display of dancing meant for an audience. Otherwise, it's exercise."

"I've got a mess on my hands."

"More than you think." He grabbed my arm and pulled me to my feet. I tossed the wet towel next to Maven as Axel drew me toward him. He held me close to his muscular body and we swayed together.

"Where's the ball and chain?" he asked. He had deep brown eyes, like the lush soil of Cochtonville, with whites like porcelain.

"What are you talking about?"

He moved me away from the tables to the area cleared as a dance floor. No one joined us here.

"The husband. The old man," he said, shifting as his accessories floated with him.

I didn't want Axel to know anything about my personal business. The one joy I got from this intrusion was the awareness that he hadn't an erection. Finally my emasculating powers had some use.

I wouldn't let him carry me along with this dance or this conversation. "He's not a ball and chain; he's my inspiration."

"Where is he?"

"He's ill."

Ernie Ray came in the door with Wilma. They tried not to stare at me dancing with Axel as they headed straight for the bathrooms.

Axel pulled me closer. He smelled spicy—orange and menthol. "How about if I go up and check on him and if he's not sick in bed, you get arrested for treason against the city-state?"

"All right, then, if you must know. He's off on business." I was glued to him by his tight embrace and my fear of arrest.

His step quickened. "Funny thing, Bernadette is away visiting her sister. I don't believe in coincidence."

I was punched in the gut. "You're not suggesting they're together, are you?"

"Of course I am. I'm the law. I look for vice." The music stopped. He went to the jukebox and put in more money. Zell was serving up pitchers of beer.

All eyes were on me. I was left at the altar. I was holding a Kick Me sign. The residents of Cochtonville gulped their alcohol and watched me with mouths hanging open like carp.

Axel swept me up and snuggled me as if we liked each other.

"When did he leave, that husband of yours on who so much of Cochtonville depends?"

"I don't know what you're talking about."

"Don't play innocent. When did he leave?"

"Yesterday," I said as Zell pushed more pitchers across the bar.

"He's banging my wife, I'll bet you. Don't tell me you don't care."

My mind went blank as if he'd taken a match to my brain and incinerated it. I'd been expecting this but didn't want to hear it from the Washer. I didn't know who the enemy was, only how unlovable I was.

"What are we going to do?" I asked as Axel kept me in his arms.

"There's no *we* in this. I'm going to have a cup of coffee, drive there tonight, and if your husband's with my wife, I'm going to hurt him. Even if he's not, I'm going to punish him for making me think it might be happening."

My scalp prickled. I didn't want that, no matter how distraught I was. Axel read my face. "Don't think of calling him. I blocked both of their phones."

"You can do that?"

"We can do anything. The only safety is clean living. I'm enjoying our dance, aren't you?"

"I have to go to the bathroom."

"No, you don't."

"I'll pee on your boots."

"They're waterproof."

"Are you telling a pregnant woman she can't empty her bladder? Holding it could hurt the baby." He loosened his grip enough that I was able to wrench myself away and run to the bathroom. My stomach was in a knot.

The pink-walled bathroom held just two stalls. Wilma came out of one of them. She wore a miniskirt and white boots. Even a sixty-year-old woman put me to shame.

"Is that Washer gone? I need more cartridges. There's a run on Classic Just Be You. I need to print the old stuff. All I have is Dipstick."

I went and leaned over the toilet, seeing a dark rim of organic matter in the bowl.

Wilma stood behind me and held my hair as I vomited. "You gonna be all right? What was he saying?"

I gagged out the words. "Ulysses is with Bernadette." Then I puked in the dirty toilet again.

I grabbed toilet paper from the almost empty roll and dabbed my mouth, hoping I had vomited out the shame that came with being left. It wasn't just sex I was missing. It was the connectedness, the bond we'd felt when we'd first met. The confidence. The acceptance. Neither one of us had confidence now. Any touch reminded us of what wouldn't be done.

"Don't believe it. That Washer's messing with your head."

"It's got to be true. I'm not lovable. Just smart. I should stick to making money for the Cochtons. But even that's gone. I don't have a thought in my head."

"The Washer is doing it. He wants you to talk, to rat out Ulysses in anger." She took a brush from her purse and straightened my part.

I wiped my eyes on the back of my hand. "The Washer doesn't need my confessions. Bernadette could tell him everything."

"Her new image of purity keeps her quiet."

"Or she still loves and sleeps with Ulysses. I can't win for losing."

"I doubt she sleeps with him. *No* man in Cochtonville can get an erection. Am I right?"

I was floored. I hadn't considered this. "I haven't tried them all, but no. No, he can't. Yes, you're right."

Maven came into the bathroom. "You need to go put on some

happy music. People are going overboard with the giggle juice and the tomcats are getting fisty with each other. The Washer Wagon's gonna come."

Wilma said, "You getting any, Maven?"

Every bit of Maven wiggled as she shook her head. "No. Squat. High and dry. Maurice is lit, like he don't want to be with me. Do I look fat in this dress?"

Wilma put an arm around her. "We're all singing the blues."

"Where there's trouble there's Cochton Enterprises," she pouted.

"Exactly," Wilma said.

They both looked at me as if I'd dropped the class guinea pig.

"You're not poisoning us, are you?" Wilma said.

This was it. The final cut. Even other women were turning on me.

"I'm suffering as much as anyone," I said defensively. Yet deep inside, the ashes of my curiosity flickered. I had to figure this out. And I could. It had to be a chemical disruption.

The distinct crash of tables being tossed over came from the bar.

"Bar fight. Make war, not love," Maven said.

I peeked from the bathroom. Axel was gone and Maurice had Kissing Man in a stranglehold while four guys in seed corn caps shoved each other. A fifth was struggling under an overturned table. A river of beer ran across the floor as two more men rolled across it, locked in struggle, their wet shirts rolling up to show their white-whale beer bellies. The women sat picking at their split ends and staring at their phones, unimpressed with the pugnaciousness.

I went to the jukebox and selected "Shiny, Happy People." Its cheery inanity had no effect. The whales rolled on and seed corn caps flew as another table overturned.

At this moment, Ernie Ray came out of the bathroom.

"The outlaw rides!" said a whale-bellied man, sitting up on the floor.

Maurice loosened his grip on the hapless kissing man. "Speech, speech!" he shouted.

Kissing Man righted a table. "What's the word, bird?"

Wilma ran to Ernie Ray and put her hand on his chest. "Nobody can fuck worth a shit, and it's making us owly. Only words can stop this hot mess."

"No," I said, holding my hands out like a traffic cop. "Nothing illegal. We just got rid of the Washer."

"Catrina, words are all we have right now," Wilma said.

"We're not alone," Kissing Man said. "He speaks the inexpressible."

I had no leverage with anybody.

"What's eating Cochtonville?" croaked Ernie in his bullfrog voice. "Let me tell you.

"Who has seen the Cochtons?
Neither you nor I,
But when we all bow down our heads
You know they're here like spy
Boner fatigue
Washers
Itinerant corn
Demands our obsequiousness
If you don't kneel to it
You're cast aside
Like the elderly in an efficient colony of ants
There's no more play
No more love
Work, citizens, work for the Empire
Produce nothing beautiful
You won't see the Cochtons
They're better than you
The corn is everywhere like sin."

"Oh Ernie," Maven said. "Nice going, sugar."

"Eight to the bar," said Maurice, hugging Maven.

"On fleek, bae," Wilma said.

The patrons clapped for Ernie Ray, poetry outlaw. The heavy door flew open and Hat Man walked in. He took off his hat.

"Your donations are as cherished as liberty." He held out his hat in front of Maven and Maurice.

"Who are you? Some grifter?" asked Maven, tugging her hair nervously.

Hat Man bent slightly at the waist. "I'm the poet's business manager."

Ernie Ray said, "This is no swindle. A man can't live on art alone."

I had to get them out of here. I went to the bar and punched the cash register. It opened with a ding. How much did Ulysses pay Ernie Ray for performance? I fished out a thirty dollar bill and gave it to him.

"No soliciting. Go. I've had enough of Washers up close for one night." I held open the door. "Everybody out. We're closed."

The customers sipped their beer. Wilma grabbed Ernie Ray and pulled him onto the couch.

"Take over for me," I told Zell.

"Yo. Right-o," he said.

I went upstairs to the apartment and flopped onto the bed. I grabbed my phone from the nightstand and tried to call Ulysses. Maybe Wilma was wrong and he could have sex with Bernadette. No answer. Maybe Axel had already gotten to him. God, I didn't even know where he was exactly.

I wasn't going to sleep. I got up and went out into the hall. I had to get to Ulysses. Where was I planning to go? How would I get there? I had no car and no directions.

I turned and went back to the apartment as the sound of boots on wood came up the stairs. I locked the door behind me.

A key turned in the lock.

"Hello?" I said, my voice shaking. Someone turned the knob.

"Catrina?" It was Ulysses.

"Oh God," I said, rushing to embrace him. "You're okay!"

"I didn't mean to surprise you. My phone isn't working. How are you and Nellie?" He put his hand on my abdomen.

"Fine. Just mad and shaken up. It's been a terrible day. Ernie Ray defied the law and recited poetry both on the bus and here in the bar. So glad to see you're not hurt."

"Why would I be?"

"Axel came by and accused you of sleeping with Bernadette. He said he was going to find you and hurt you."

"You didn't believe him, did you?"

"I did at first."

"I'm a failure as a husband if you can't trust me."

"I thought you didn't find me attractive anymore. I was a failure as a woman."

"To match my failure as a man."

The situation had us both so shaken we could barely love ourselves, much less another person.

"You're not alone," I said, reaching for him. "No man in this whole place can get an erection."

"How do you know that?"

"I have it on good authority. Wilma and Maven say it's true." I sounded silly and unscientific with my hearsay, but it made sense. I had to start somewhere.

"No wonder condoms aren't selling."

"It's got to be fact. When did it all begin?"

"For me, after the poker game." He sighed as if he were an old man.

"Obviously not every man in Cochtonville was at that poker game," I said.

A flash of lighting peeked through the thin curtains. Thunder rumbled and rattled the windows. Precious rain, fresh water, hit the glass. I smoothed away the worry lines on his forehead. He was caving in to fatigue.

"Welcome home," I said, changing the subject. "Let's get you to bed."

He pulled me into his arms and kissed me. "We've got to keep meeting like this. It brings the rain."

"How did your interview go? I've been thinking about it. You're right. I'm ready to get out of here."

Ulysses ran his hand through my hair. "It could have gone better. Even our rainwater in Cochtonville has a scent of pig to it. We're used to it, but once you're gone from it and you come back, you can smell it again. I don't think Rainy Day impressed them like I wanted it to. They said they'd call."

My heart fell eleven stories. My hope for a clean getaway, a fresh start for the two of us, was gone. Ulysses took off his clothes and climbed into bed with me.

"It was damn hard to get across the border and back. I had to fill out paperwork about why I was traveling. I said I was going to try to sell beer. I got a thirty-hour pass." He yawned. "God, I'm tired. Sixteen hours of driving, four of interview, and an hour delay for interrogation each passage through The Edge. I couldn't stop to sleep before driving home. I'm not going to do that again and call attention to myself."

"It'll be okay. It will. I love you." I held him as I'd hold a child.

CHAPTER NINETEEN

Amino acids are twenty protein building blocks. The name comes from Amon, the Egyptian sun god, sometimes portrayed with a ram's head.

In my lab the next day, I asked Natharie, "Have you noticed that the men of Cochtonville are having troubles?"

"No. I've vowed to stay away from them because I hope to be successful." She was holding an open laptop.

"They can be hazardous to your health," I agreed.

"It's true. History has examples of the dangers of erotic attraction across all cultures. I don't give two shits about men, or sex for that matter." I must have looked surprised. I'd never heard her use such language. "I'm gratefully asexual and aromantic," she said matter-of-factly.

"I'd call you Isaac Newton since he hated romance, but you're nicer than he was." I respected her candor and self-awareness.

"I have to be. I'm female, yet as joyfully unattached as Newton ever was. Despite the issue with Mother, Cochton's has a huge test plot of the beans, and after they are in a product and launched, I'll move on to a new species. Maybe with this company, maybe somewhere else. I don't need a man holding me down with a hand in my purse or my pants. What's the trouble with them this time? War? Rape? Oppression? What are they forcing on us now?"

I was almost embarrassed to say it. "Something's going on with the men and they can't get aroused."

"Aroused?" She wrinkled her nose.

"No erections. Soft as a stick of butter at a summer picnic."

She narrowed her eyes. "Have you tried them all?"

"No, but I'm gathering information from others."

"It sounds pathetic. They are so fixated on such bother. Don't look too far for a cause. When there's trouble in Cochtonville, Cochton Enterprises is responsible. I'm sure."

"I am too."

"How are your bean studies coming? That's why I'm here. And because I value your friendship."

There was a knock at the door. Natharie opened it with one hand while balancing her laptop with the other.

Rhonda struggled in with a cage that smelled like sawdust and sick-sweetness. She placed it carefully on the slate lab countertop, a few feet away from the pH meters. I didn't welcome such dirtiness near my equipment. I needed to avoid cross-contamination.

"Mike sends his best along with these rats for the animal study," said Rhonda.

Of course it would be Mike sending something I didn't want. I peeked in the cage. Three rats gripped the bars with their pink paws and wiggled their whiskers at us. One was the typical white Sprague-Dawley rat, another a hooded rat—black head with white body—and the third a black rat with white paws.

I said, "Why are they here? I didn't ask for rats. I thought I'd just be getting the droppings." Wow. Not only had I not gotten any sort of raise or bonus for No Regrets, now I had to collect rat shit for analysis myself, even though Cochton Enterprises had a veterinary group that could and should have done it for me. I was working my ass off for Cochtonville while bearing a child in accordance with Cochtonville's wants, and nobody really gave a crap about what I had to say. Axel could stalk my husband and I couldn't stop him. The Cochtons were invisibly raking in money from Cochton Enterprises, not working themselves, never even showing their faces. Ernie Ray was a clandestine hero for going up against them. What did it take to succeed here anyway? Not hard work or loyalty or even clever ideas got me respect at Union Station or in the workplace. Yeah, Jester was right. Dad was right. I was dumb, naïve, toothless, and a sucker all rolled into one. If I'd been a kid, I might have cried.

"Mike said you would harvest the droppings," said Rhonda, brushing sawdust from her silk blouse. "Why do you need them?"

Natharie piped up. "For an amino acid absorption study to finalize the processing and storage of our beans. Red beans, for example, are more nutritious after they've been dried and rehydrated. Catrina's found the amino acid content of these beans. Amino acids make up proteins, you know. We'll feed the rats a known amount of beans and test the feces for excretion of amino acids. Less excretion means more use of the protein to build the bodies of the rats."

"Feces?" said Rhonda. "Like in poop?"

"Yeah," I said.

Natharie said to Rhonda, "The beans grow in extreme temperatures, smother weeds, and pests haven't a taste for them yet. They're the perfect crop. We may work for the evil empire, but we're doing good things."

"I hope so," I said. The new plants showed no sign of developing the hydrogel that gave Mother her dangerous reflexes. Of course, there was still time.

"Have you found a secret ingredient yet, Catrina? I don't want to rush you, but I'm being pressured for a report."

I was a far better chemist than I was a lover. Of course I'd found a special molecule in the beans. I'd found several.

"Ingredient? There's a psychoactive compound," I said absently. I still had the erection problem on my mind.

She laughed again. "That sounds like we'll have hippie hogs."

"How about an agent to act against snake venom?" I said,

distracted. Yes, that was in the beans too, but how would that apply to hogs in confinement buildings?

"Could sell them to tropical regions, then," said Natharie. "I'd love to see these out in the world helping more than just the Cochton family. These beans need to spread over the entire planet. I know this. They just must."

"If it's profitable, the Cochtons won't share it with the world," said Rhonda. "They'll screw the world over and have them begging for it."

"Males, I see," I said, peeking at the rats. They didn't have erections, either, not that I knew what a rat erection looked like. The women of Cochtonville were right. It had to be Cochton Enterprises. There was a molecule responsible for the fatigue of all the men in Cochtonville. Something Mike tried on Ulysses that leaked out and affected everyone. I could take samples or be efficient and go to the source. Or more accurately, to someone close to him.

"According to Mike, I clean them," said Rhonda. "I've named them Cappy, Stetson, and Shady." She filled the water bottle from the lab sink. "Shady is the black one." She slipped it into the rat's cage.

I said, "I'm sure Mike did something suspicious with a chemical and my husband. Rhonda, did you take any memos about human studies?"

"No memos. I get coffee, give backrubs, fetch rats...stuff like that."

"Jester knows. Think he'll tell me about it straight up?"

"He won't betray Mike," said Natharie, waving her diamond ring. "Getting the sober truth out of him will be like walking on broken Pyrex."

"I could get the unsober truth though."

I walked down the hall to Jester's lab. He closed the sash and took off his chemically resistant purple gloves.

"Catrina. Long time no see. How's Ulysses? What can I do for you?" he asked cheerfully. Natharie was right—the direct approach wouldn't yield results in his own territory. He could never admit to anything here at work. I looked at my reflection in the fume hood and fluffed my hair. With enough pressure, or even better, Rainy Day, Jester could become a stool pigeon and tell me what took place at the card game.

"He's fine. Things are great. I'd love for you to come to the bar with me tonight. Say hi to Ulysses. Grab a bite to eat. I have a friend who needs a pool partner."

"Golly, it would be swell to, but I'm kinda sorta taken."

"Are you married?"

"Not yet, but gol darn I will be. I'm still nervous about asking. I need a push to get over my barrier."

"I can't give you that, but I'll buy dinner. Don't be a stranger. Meet me at Union Station tonight at seven."

Two tavern sandwiches, a hotdog, a mini pizza, and a glass of Rainy Day later, Jester was playing pool with Maven. This was an age-old plan: some alcohol, a pretty woman, and flattery would get a confession out of Jester, for few honest men can carry a secret alone.

Maven shook her hair at Jester, the glimmer of henna leaping from each silky strand. "Are you any good?"

"I've never played." If it hadn't been for his baggy Cochton Big Yields T-shirt and innocent, polished face, Jester could have been the whole package: strong, smart, and even good-looking. Fortunately, Maurice was in on our scheme. The entire bar was, and we were all on edge. The fat, white men I called whales hovered close to him in a pod. If Jester didn't confess to something, I'd have to begin at the beginning, looking for a needle in a haystack of chemicals. If he told us he'd done something, we'd be halfway to solving the problem. The situation was like in the 1960s when birds were disappearing and Rachel Carson discovered it was because DDT took calcium from their eggshells. Only now it was mammals that would be disappearing.

Maven licked her lips. "For beginners, we need to pick a cue with a tip that's not too hard."

Jester looked at the tin ceiling. "That sure is a lucky thing."

"Why don't you hold it?" Maven put the cue in Jester's hand. "And cast me an eyeball, sugar."

He gave her a shy smile. "I'd rather have you hold it."

"Later, daddy. Let's practice your shots. Slow and straight. Easy now. I'll help you with your strokes." She put her arms around him. "I like to take things slow."

"Me too, but my foot is on the gas pedal right now. Just don't call me 'daddy.'"

"Oh, deluxe. How about you pop the clutch?"

This went too far. Jester moved away from her and slapped his forehead. "No! I've got a girl. I'm just here for the food."

"It's cool, baby. I was just being friendly. I got a beau myself. What do you do at Cochton?"

"I synthesize things."

"Oh, do tell! Catrina, will you scram? You're cramping his style and being a gooseberry."

"Yeah. Scram," Jester said. He went to the bar and I sat in a booth with Wilma.

"Hey, Ulysses, long time no see," he said. "Did you know there's acetaldehyde in beer?"

"Not if it's properly sanitized and brewed," Ulysses said. "Do you have anything else you want to explain to me?"

"I need a couple of beers," Jester said, already bold.

Ulysses filled a pitcher and handed it and two glasses to him. "Can you manage that?"

"Sure." Jester slopped beer as he walked back to Maven and put the pitcher on the pool table. She poured a glassful right on the felt, tempting fate.

"Cheers!" she said, handing him the glass. "Can you handle your liquor?"

"Ethanol is such a wimpy molecule. Of course," he said, draining his glass. "Ethanol has a health hazard of two. I'll have you know I've worked with acetaldehyde before. It's a three, like nicotine," Jester said as he poured himself another. "The hazard numbers go up to four."

"Uh-huh. That's cool," Maven said. "Let's talk about you. You got a girl, but she's not here. I like that in a man. Does any of whatever you do in your lab have to do with sex?"

"Well, yeah, it's agriculture after all. Where'd we be without it?"

"Agriculture or sex?"

"Both, but I meant, uh...." He drank deeply from his glass.

She leaned forward, her cleavage winking at him. "You can say the word, my sizzling steak."

"S-s-sex."

"Don't it feel good? Tell me all about what you do with sex. Impress me, man."

"We came up with a chemical hog-castration molecule." The pod of whales edged closer as one, as if breaching the water simultaneously.

"Unreal. People need that? You slay me." Maven forced a laugh and a smile.

Jester didn't catch her insincerity. "Spot on. There's a problem with the new Cochton hogs. Yes, they have big litters of fifteen to twenty, but the males aren't right."

"Not right? Like in the dick?"

"Kinda. You see, the majority of the males born to these hogs can mate, yet their testicles aren't all the way descended, and so they can't be mechanically..." He took another loud gulp of beer. "This is the best damn beer I've ever tasted."

"Mechanically what, big guy? You can tell me. I've been around the block a few times."

"Castrated."

"No way. Why ever would you do that to the poor things? Can you imagine people not having any sex drive? You wouldn't have any poetry, or art, or love. Poor piggies."

"There's a whole good reason for what we did. When males have, um, testicles, they fight, and the meat can have a bad taste called boar taint thanks to the active, um, testicles."

"If I ate you, you'd have a bad taste? Is that what you're saying?"

"Well, kinda. Only, I'm sure I'd taste good if you ate me."

"Later, gator." She winked. "Let's have more beer and you can tell me about castration."

She poured him another beer. She was speaking his language and he was eating from her hand.

Jester took a drink of Rainy Day. "This stuff's good."

Maven poured herself a beer, put her finger in the foam, and then put her finger in her mouth. She looked Jester from head to toe and smiled.

"I was saying," he said. "What was I saying?"

Maven whispered in his ear.

"Right-o. The male hogs can mate, and because they have testicles, ones you can't cut off, their meat has boar taint. Not everyone can taste it, but there are elevated levels of androstenone, skatole, and indole in the meat. It's a crying shame when you have to discount the meat. The Cochtons needed something done. We developed a chemical." A whale broke from the pod, grabbed the pitcher from the pool table, and refilled his glass.

Maven twirled her hair. "Tell me more about the testicles."

"The chemical we came up with causes the testicles to go dormant. It's an antiandrogen. No male chemicals produced. Isn't that genius? Just call me the Cock of Cochton Enterprises."

My anger mounted like thunderheads. I knew where this was going. Wilma put a hand on mine.

Maven said, "You do this?"

"Sure do. It's an injection. Calms them down and makes the meat taste great. It's called Boardoze. Sounds kind of like the wine, don't you think?" He grinned stupidly.

"Oh yes. I adore wine. Give me a taste." She pulled him onto her lap and gave him a wide-mouthed kiss.

He shook his head. "Wowy, that packed a punch."

Maven looked at me and at the gathering whales. "I hope that's the only punch you get tonight."

"Yeah, right. I guess I need to be going before I get in trouble with the old lady."

Maven looked momentarily panicked. We were on the verge of a confession. "Oh, don't go just yet. I promise I'll be a good girl. You're such a swell guy. You tempt me. Have another beer, handsome. Then we should talk about it some more. The chemical, I mean. It intrigues me."

"Let's talk about him. That guy bugs me." Jester pointed the pool cue at Ulysses.

"Ulysses? You're an Einstein. Poor Catrina's got some problems."

"Hey golly. It's not my fault. I bet he's a gold digger. Nerd girls always go for the men with flaws." Jester's voice grew louder and he was slurring.

"I'm not a nerd girl. I'd go for a man like you for sure. But gee whiz, Ulysses wasn't flawed in the dick when they met. Now the poor girl thinks he's steppin' out with his ex."

"Nooo waaay is he doing that."

"It's bad. She's like Alexander without Jade. Like Phil Collins without Peter Gabriel."

"I don't follow," Jester said.

"Oh, baby, you know. She's like the moon without the stars, just kind of hanging there in the dark like a wallflower," Maven said.

"Oh yeah, got it. What are you talking about?"

"She's no good at her job now. That's what she says. Her squeeze is gone."

"Golly. Yikes. We need her ideas."

"I know just how she feels. My tomcat won't touch me. Do you think I'm fat?"

"No. Your boobs are big, that's all, and boobs are made of fat."

"My guy's got someone new. I'm all alone just like Catrina, without a thought in my head. Jester, baby, do you like my perfume?" She held out her wrist and he sniffed it, lingering over it.

"Handsome," she said, "you can tell me anything. Is there something you can't hold inside any longer?"

"Her husband isn't cheating," Jester said with conviction.

"Says you. I don't believe it. Have you seen his ex? He's gone back to her."

"Impossible. He's fixed."

"As in 'fixed his wagon'?"

"Kinda." He leaned over and played with her hair.

"Kinda how you're so smart. I know you know it all. Tell me, baby."

"Women need to make a choice, be a man or be a commodity. That's what Mike says anyway."

"Baby, that's crazy talk. Who's this Mike? Can you talk a little louder? I can't hear very well."

Jester raised his voice. "Mike, he's our boss. He reasoned that unless we intervened, there'd be no end of the babies Catrina'd have, and we didn't want to lose a good chemist. They're rare, you know, chemists who gets results all the time like Catrina."

"Oh, such a problem," said Maven, giving him her full attention.

"Nooo shit, Sherlock. We solved that problem. We gave hubby an injection of Boardoze at a poker game."

Wilma said, "Wow. Crap."

I leaped to my feet.

The white-bellied whales moved in toward Jester, surrounding him. I shoved my way past them and grabbed him by the shirt.

"Catrina!" shouted panicked Jester. "Golly. I forgot about you being here. What'd you hear?"

"Enough to want to hurt you." I drew back my hand to slap him.

A whale stepped up. "Let me do the honors. This shit. We all got it in the blood, don't we?"

"N-n-no. Why would we care if *you* had sex or not? It's injected."

"The hog piss gets drained out to a lagoon," a whale said.

"Those things ain't secure. It's in the water," another whale said. "It ain't just Ulysses. It's all of us."

"I got it too. It's in my dick. When can I expect this wearing off?" said the seed-corn-cap guy, his man boobs jiggling. Boardoze had hit him hard.

"Yeah," said Couch Kissing Man, advancing on Jester. "When?"

"Golly gee. We're not sure. The hogs become hams before we can discern the long-term effects. We figure within five years."

"Five years," I said shrilly. I looked around for Ulysses but didn't see him. I hoped he was in the cellar checking the latest batch of Rainy Day and hadn't heard all of this. The whales moved in.

Jester raised the pool cue to defend himself. Maven jumped and pulled me away for my own safety. I wanted nothing more than to see Jester suffer.

"That little stick ain't gonna save you." A whale yanked the cue from Jester and cracked the tip off.

"Now it goes up your ass."

"No, please. I was trying to help. We all rise with Cochton Enterprises."

"We ain't rising. That's the trouble."

A whale lunged at Jester but he dodged, only to fall over a chair. I put my foot on his collarbone before he could get up. I thought blood might squirt from my eyes. He'd betrayed the sacred bond of being labmates together. "How much? How much did you give him? I need a concentration—a dosage." I pressed my foot into him for emphasis. Jester would have been the lackey and gotten the injection ready. Mike never touched anything but employees in his labs.

"Yow! Calm down. I can't remember. Uh, quarter of what we'd give a hog. Didn't want an overdose."

"What is it? What's the formula?"

"It's the first sample I ever gave you. You labeled it 427.1."

Kissing Man sat on Jester's chest and slapped him in the face. Just then, Axel and Barnabus came through the door.

"Bar fight," said Barnabus cheerfully. He reached for a club hanging from his belt. "Who do I crack open first?"

"Him," I said, pointing to Jester. "He's drunk. Get him out of here! He's caused all the trouble."

"Come on, pal," said Barnabus. "Disturbing the peace." He and Couch Kissing Man yanked Jester to his feet.

"Drunk as a skunk," Barnabus reported to Axel.

Axel strode up to him. "Never seen this one before. Who are you? Give me your ID."

"No," begged Jester. "I'm getting married. I need my job."

"A bachelor party, eh?" Axel said. "You picked the wrong dump for it. Barn, check out his story, and if he's not engaged, make sure he is before the night is over."

"Congratulations," I called as Jester was taken to the Washer van. "Enjoy your honeymoon."

Axel looked over to the bar for Ulysses. He was still absent. The only one behind the bar was Zell, with his crossed eyes and mouth hanging open. Axel came close to me. I trembled. This was all too much – the revelation and now the Washer in my face. Once again he pulled me to him to demonstrate his power and my helplessness.

"You get a citation for overserving," he said. I must have looked scared enough to please him because he let me go. "A warning. Just a warning. Tell that bum husband of yours to man up and stand by your side. There's nothing worse than abandoning your wife and kid."

"Y-you got that right," I said. Axel looked pleased with himself as he left.

I found Ulysses behind the bar slumped on the floor with his hands over his ears. I sat next to him.

"Did you hear it?"

"Yeah. Damn shouter."

"It's not you and me at all," I said, as embarrassingly human tears leaked from my eyes.

"*This* was their way of dealing with your home-workplace balance? Damn, my bitterness units are off the charts right now. How long will this stuff last?"

"I...I don't know. I'll take a urine sample once you stop drinking the water and adding more to your system. From that I can estimate the half-life. It will take eight half-lives."

"Eight half-lives," he said. He embraced me and held me close. "Eight. What a nightmare. I imagined the worst—that I didn't love you, even though you'd done nothing to cause me to feel that way. I thought I was unable to accept commitment."

"I thought so as well."

"We're so used to being beaten-down rejects, not fitting in, that we accepted it. I know I did." He put his face in his hands. "I was such a sucker for Bernadette. Always at her feet and groveling. It wore me down. Made me a fool."

"I'm a fool too. I don't know what I need to do to be accepted at work. I do everything they want and more, and still they don't trust me to make my own personal decisions. Now they've harmed you."

"You should leave me. It's your time in life to have kids, and you're going to miss it if you wait this out."

"We have our one kid. That will be enough." My heart dropped with disappointment, but in reality, it would be a perfect compromise. It was the sex I would miss.

His mouth twitched like a bug that had been sprayed.

"Do you want that?" he asked. "You don't have to keep proving and sacrificing yourself to me. That's what the powerful do to us—beat us down so we're so insecure we have to keep on proving." He wiped a tear from my cheek.

I loved him. I admired the way he went about bettering society, putting himself out there for others without bragging about it.

"I'm not proving anything. I'm doing what my heart desires."

"You desire a condom outlaw? Certainly I'm not what you dreamed of as a little girl."

In a way, he was. I wanted to be a scientist, and he fanned the flickering flames of my questioning scientist self. The woman who stood against bullshitty authority. Rachel Carson, Darwin, Galileo —they'd all spoken of a reality that the powerful didn't want to hear, and they had the strength of observation backing them up. As fringy as he was, Ernie Ray had a point with his defiant words. He allowed people to see behind the curtain of manufactured truth. Wilma's insistence that women deserved to have and could find their own pleasure had taught me to seek my own truth about my body and its needs. It was all about balancing personal freedom and public responsibility—and about being a genuine scientist— not just a lab worker but a seeker. I'd found my tribe.

"I dreamed of a balanced life as a girl, and one where I had freedom. In other words, I dreamed of science and I dreamed of you."

He took my left hand. "You stole my heart, Catrina Pandora Van Dingle Butz, although you're a fool for sticking with me."

I covered him with kisses and pulled him toward me as we sat on the cool floor behind the bar, the patrons scattered by the Washers. "I'm a fool for not realizing it was Boardoze! I love you too. In fact, I'm convinced we're made for each other."

He put his head in my lap, and I stroked his hair. "I wish we could have makeup sex. How long until this stuff wears off?"

"I aim to find out."

I wasn't sure what we were going to do, but I'd come up with something. It was all just chemistry, after all. But right then, I cried.

CHAPTER TWENTY

Testosterone is a steroid and an androgen that promotes male characteristics such as facial hair, penis enlargement, and voice deepening. It binds to and moves into DNA, where it activates genes for muscle mass. It's found in small amounts in women.

There was no reason to panic. I'd make things right, do a work-around as always. In the morning, I went to the grocery store. In the coffee section, I found some packets of carbon, little balls meant to take away aqueous impurities and improve coffee flavor. I bought every pack on the shelf along with a glass pitcher with a red lid from the housewares section. I'd add the carbon balls to the water in the pitcher to draw out the Boardoze. We'd drink boiled rainwater too, as much as could be collected. I may have lost a lot of my self-esteem, but I still had my smarts.

In the checkout line, a woman asked for my autograph. "I just found out I was expecting!" she exclaimed. She thrust a paper bag from the bulk items section and a pen from the same place at me. "It was so easy to find out, and you're the reason. I hope my baby goes into science." I was stunned by her recognition of me and signed the paper bag *Congratulations from Catrina Butz, developer of no Regrets.* I made sure to use a lower case *n*, for I had regrets about my premier product.

She said, "I'll be careful. Look, I've got a bag of kale. I'm growing brain cells after all." Guilt ran over me like honey and my envy piqued. How had she managed to have sex these days?

"My husband was out of the country for three months on business, and as soon as he walked through the door, he threw me on the floor, and well, it happened," she bragged. "I got tested right here in the store. I can't wait to get home and tell him."

The woman beamed, and I had my first shaky data point. One guy, three months. It would probably take longer than that after an injection, but at least one person had recovered from Boardoze exposure.

As I was leaving, I was stopped by Barnabus and Axel at the door.

"I enjoy that look of terror on your face," Axel said, "but it's a routine grocery store stop. Nothing special."

As I clutched my plastic grocery bag, Barnabus scanned me with No Regrets. "Free to pass," he said, looking disappointed. "Still clean."

"And if not?" I asked.

"You'd get quarantined with the rest of the deviants," Axel said. "The Cochtons built a new home—the Asylum for the Impure. Private prisons are a growth industry, you know. Lots of jobs to be had in corrections."

Yup. That was the way things were here in Cochtonville. You had to keep on proving yourself until you dropped dead or got arrested. Even if you started out with No Regrets, they'd find you.

The sun beat down on my forehead as I walked to my car. I was in acceptance hell working for a boss who both appreciated and betrayed me in a place that constantly tested me and made me regret my accomplishments. I couldn't make a move, for with any step things might get worse.

It was a hot Friday in July, and Union Station was packed. There was a run on Rainy Day. Ulysses was swamped, and I considered canceling my after-work date with Valentine to help him.

"Where's Zell?" I asked

"Good question. He'll be here shortly. No need to stay," he said. "Go change. I know you're looking forward to tonight."

He had no idea what we were up to. I changed into a simple sleeveless dress and went to pick up Valentine. We were telling everyone we were going to Cochtonville Night in Celebration of Agriculture. In truth, we were going to get illegal ultrasounds at the prison.

"How's Trent these days?" I asked Valentine. I needed to tell her about Boardoze and get her valuable opinion.

"Traveling a lot."

"Good thing, because there's a chemical in the water that castrates men," I said, dropping the bomb.

"No! Did Cochton Enterprises make it?"

"Of course. They didn't intentionally pollute. They were sloppy."

"Will it eventually decompose?"

I put a hand on my belly. "It should decompose, and carbon filtration removes most of it. Just get those balls meant to be put in your coffeepot. Might it hurt the baby? What's your perspective as a doctor?"

"Perhaps. Hormones are tricky things."

"I suspected. This ultrasound will give me some peace of mind."

"This is serious. Are you going to tell anybody?"

"Once I get enough data. The company is in love with this product. They won't give it up easily, and I don't want to be fired right now. What good would that do in the long run?"

The correctional facility consisted of a poured-concrete building with three adjoining wings: one for the insane, one for the deviant, and one for common criminals and outlaws. It was a colorless place surrounded by enough floodlights to illuminate a stadium and a chain-link fence topped with barbed wire. Inside the gates, crab apples burst with unripe fruit. Birds would be happy here. It was clever of Mother Nature to break in with beauty.

I stopped at the gate.

"The guards know this goes on; everybody here does. It gives them pocket change. I don't want you traced in case there is suspicion," said Valentine. "So I'll sign you in as my sister. I don't have a sister." She got out of the car and wrote in a ledger. As she got back into Old Gold, the guard opened the gate and waved us in.

In the building, full of marble and with a winding main staircase, we walked quickly to the centrally located medical facility.

"By day, cranial ultrasounds. By moonlight, fetal ultrasounds," said Valentine. We entered the empty clinic.

"Here it is," said Valentine, folding her arms across her abdomen. "Nervous? I am."

"No," I said. "It is what it is, right? There aren't any side effects, are there?"

"No. It's not that. I get skittish at revelations."

"I'll go first," I said. I couldn't see how knowing something could make anything worse. However, after I removed my dress, stretched out on the table, bared my abdomen to the gel and the probe, and the image came on the screen, I thought otherwise. There in shadow and light was the earth-changing being inside me, kicking at my bladder. I wasn't an expert, but seeing this future human told me there was no little Nellie. I burst into unscientific tears.

"It's amazing, isn't it?" the technician said. The hundred dollars in cash I'd paid her—swiped from the back of Grant's portrait— was safely in her purse.

"Ah, sure," I sobbed, waiting for her to tell me the news, what I knew I was seeing. Not that it was bad. It was simply overwhelming.

"Perfectly formed," she said. "Is this your first?"

"Yes. Yes."

"Congratulations. He's beautiful. See it here? The legs, the umbilical cord, the penis."

"The penis?" This was why I'd cried. I focused on the light and shade, an image resembling animated plaster. "Are you sure?" He'd be a good man like his father, wouldn't he? Not a Jester or a Mike or an Axel. There were so many bad ones.

"Is it...okay? Is he okay?" I let my mind wrap around the word *he*.

"Yes. I've seen a lot of sonograms. You've got a keeper. A nice straight spine. See his face? I bet his daddy's handsome."

I tried to focus on the face—he had my big eyes and his dad's straight nose along with that pensive brow we both had. He was trying to cover his ears. I couldn't, however, get past the fact he was a boy. Ulysses wanted a girl. I couldn't even have the baby he expected.

"Yes," I sniffed. "He most certainly is handsome."

She handed me a tissue. "It can be emotional," she said. "Tell him you'll meet him in December. Do you have a name picked out?"

"No," I sobbed. "He's okay. You said he was healthy, didn't you?"

She touched my arm and gave me an abdominal wipe. "All is well. Your placenta is in a good spot. These ultrasounds are so useful. They put your mind at ease, don't they?"

I walked to the lobby and sank into a hard chair. Valentine was reading, her brown curls falling around her face. She looked at me with soft eyes. "Did it go well?"

"Yes. It's a boy and we wanted a girl, that's all. Your turn,"

She came out with a dreamy, dopey smile.

"A girl?" I asked. She nodded. "Congratulations." I turned up the corners of my mouth.

On our return, we passed through the section of the city known as Old Town. The brightly trimmed brick buildings blended together as I sat at the stoplight, that is until the car behind me honked.

"It's green," said Valentine softly. I pushed down the accelerator and Old Gold jumped into the intersection, but not fast enough. Another car honked. In the mirror I could see the man in the car behind me mouthing ugly words—"Lady driver."

"This country isn't very loving," I said.

Valentine said, "A bunch of jerks. Now I really have got to get out of here." She put her hand on her belly. "This is no place for a girl."

"It's hard to believe women's rights so quickly slipped away. And here's a crazy thing. A friend of mine got in trouble with the law and got out of it by saying he'd get married, as if it's a punishment. He's been nothing but a team player at work but was still in terror of being fired."

"This place makes no sense. People are more than willing to see the Cochtons as better than they are and deserving of rule, even if they rule unfairly, cruelly."

"I'm pretty much stuck here. I have a husband and a job. I like the science *I'm* doing. I'll have to shoulder the disrespect as women have done for eons."

"Well, I don't plan to. I get no maternity leave. The mother-infant bond sets the stage for the baby's future mental health. Everything from how the baby handles stress and takes and gives love depends on it. Motherhood and bonding is such a tricky thing, a combination of relaxation and vigilance."

"Oxytocin and cortisol," I said.

"Exactly. You need to hold your baby and not be stressed. You and the baby must develop mutual rewards. Societal factors can interfere. Stress can throw a wrench in it. You could become temporally disorganized from long hours at work followed by infant care. Depression is likely and will create risk to you and the baby."

"We'll be strong. We'll rise above," I said, although she had me scared. I saw clearly how women became oppressed. It was less traumatic to go along with the status quo, and stress was very bad for maternity. No wonder so many suffragettes and birth control pioneers were older women, and no surprise that an aspiring empire like Cochtonville would want to keep women pregnant! We were less trouble that way. They'd blown it with Boardoze, hadn't they? It was almost funny.

Valentine looked out the window at people walking to Cochtonville Night. "You know what mouse studies have shown? That once we give birth, the oxytocin receptors in our brains will plump up and we'll be in tune to our infant's cries. What before motherhood we might have dismissed as noise will be a call to action!"

"That's all interesting, but I have to work. I need financial security and I need a doctor for the delivery, unless you'll do it, but you're going to be busy with your own. What are we going to do?"

"A hospital has been recruiting me—it's in Illinois. Maternity leave. Sane hours. Even the option of part-time work. I'm the only doctor at the prison. It's exhausting. Cochtonville sucks!"

The car behind me honked again, and a second chimed in. I still wasn't going fast enough for them even though a car in front of me was pulling out of a parking space. What was so wrong with caution?

We were at a stop. The ugly, impatient honking resumed. The cars behind me were mansplaining how to drive.

We proceeded through the intersection until the car in front of us stopped suddenly as another backed out of a parking space. I stomped on the brake and Old Gold screeched to a halt. Our purses flew forward and our seat belts tightened.

"Are you doing okay?" Valentine asked.

"Apparently not," I said.

"Me neither."

She leaned down and grabbed a plastic card that had flown forward from somewhere during my abrupt stop.

"Driver's license," she read. "Is this your brother's ID?"

"Kevin?"

"It says Roger."

"Roger? No. I don't know him."

"It says here he's thirty years old." She held it up.

"It's fake! That barely looks like him. He must've used it at bars. What a deadbeat." I laughed. "Well, he's lost it now. Put it in the glove compartment, please, and I'll tell on him as soon as I get the chance."

It was a beautiful summer evening and humanity was savoring it. The scent of the hog lots was a distant undertone that, if you had imagination, might be mistaken for jasmine. It was Cochtonville Night, devoted to the wonders of modern agriculture and the success of Cochton Enterprises. Parents pushed strollers across the sidewalk and Valentine and I eyed the babies. Next summer, this would be us. I longed to be normal. I watched the crowd of normal people. Upon close inspection, many of the couples were arguing.

Ahead on the street, a black pickup was stopped in a tangle of traffic. Walkers were filming and taking selfies. Ernie Ray and Hat Man—his hat filled with money—dashed out of Upmarket, the pretentious restaurant where Valentine and I had planned to eat, and jumped into the black truck. For a moment, the truck was stuck in traffic. I got a look at the driver—young and dumb. Most certainly Zell. It broke away, veered right, and sped over the curb and into City Park, almost hitting the Civil War cannon commemorating all wars. Diagonally it went across the grass, past a display of tall cornstalks and combines, and through bushes, over a bed of petunias, nearly hitting a child on a bike and woman walking her dog. It plowed through a pen of display hogs and the powerful animals bolted past the surprised citizens. Frisbee players and ice cream vendors sprinted away in all directions, like water from a sprinkler, as the truck ran across the corner opposite and down Main Street toward the highway.

"Are those the poetry bandits?" Valentine asked.

"Yes. Wow, what buffoons," I said. "Lucky they didn't hit anybody."

Ernie Ray and his gang were gone, and the squirrels in the park leaped across the grass.

Valentine said, "Sure takes away my appetite. Would it be all right with you if I just went home?"

I dropped Valentine off. The bar was still hopping, although there was more drinking than dancing. Boardoze was doing its work. There were no couples. No chemical attraction except for that of loner to alcohol. Ulysses was trying to keep it going all by himself, and sweat bloomed beneath the arms of his black T-shirt. I went behind the bar to help him out. At least the beer business was picking up now that we were without any new models of toys and not selling condoms.

"Ernie Ray strikes again," I said.

"Did he panhandle you?"

"No, he hit Upmarket, or so it appeared. We weren't in it at the time, but we had a narrow miss."

Ulysses passed a beer to a customer. "Great stuff!" the man said. "Got that added kick to it."

Another man put a bill on the table. "Got to ask for a raise. Rainy Day 2.0, please."

People came to the bar in rapid succession. The whoosh of the hospital helicopter cut through the noise of the bar.

"You'd better go get some rest," Ulysses said to me.

"Not when we're so busy. Let me help serve. It's too early for sleeping."

"He'll show up here later. It's half the reason for our surge in popularity."

"They headed out of town." I put on an apron.

"I imagine Zell was part of the robbery since he never showed."

"He drove the getaway car, I think. And badly too. He tore up the park."

"Ernie Ray never had a lick of sense," Ulysses said.

"How'd you meet him anyway?" I asked, taking a handful of popcorn from the bowl on the bar and shoving it in my mouth.

"Believe it or not, he's Bernadette's cousin. That's how he knows so much about her."

I took another fistful of popcorn. Missing dinner wasn't going over well with me or Baby Boy Butz.

"Wow," I said. "And Axel arrested him."

"Yeah, Axel's an asshole. I almost feel bad for Bernadette."

"Rainy Day 2.0," said a man in a seed corn cap.

"Sorry, bud, all out. Just served the last of it," Ulysses said. "How about a CochLite? I can add Sprinkle and mix it in."

"I guess," said the man.

"I promise you'll like it. Sprinkle is the magic ingredient in 2.0." Ulysses poured him CochLite and powdered it with something that resembled parsley.

"What is that?" I asked.

"A new secret ingredient," Ulysses said. "It's the other reason for our newfound success. I need you to take a look at it and give me advice. The old secret ingredient was neroli oil, but since it's not produced in Cochtonville, it was getting hard to come by. This is something local. I need your opinion on it. Maybe tomorrow."

We'd worked for another hour or more when the bar doors banged open and Ernie Ray and Hat Man stumbled into the bar to cheers from the crowd.

They laughed together while patrons held out napkins for autographs.

"Ulysses," Ernie Ray said in a voice swelled by excitement, "a beer here!"

"You smell like you robbed a liquor store. I won't serve you more alcohol." Ulysses poured Ernie a glass of water and handed it to him.

Hat Man signed a napkin held out by a man in tight pants, flat in front.

Ulysses said, "Where's Zell?"

Hat Man said, "You fired him."

"Nice try. I did no such thing." Ulysses sounded like an experienced teacher or professor.

"He got what he deserved."

Ulysses said, "Pal, gaslights haven't been used for over two hundred years, so don't pull an illusion on me. Did you do something to him?"

"Of course not. You insult me," said Hat Man without emotion.

Ulysses turned on the television and Cochtonville's twenty-four hour news.

"Turn it off," Hat Man said. He wiped the dirty knees of his pants with a napkin.

Newscasters stood at the curb of a tree-lined street while ambulance lights flashed. They reported that a man and a woman, deep in disagreement, stepped in front of the getaway car and were struck down. The unlucky couple, City Manager Frani Foil and Dr. Mike Watson of Cochton Enterprises, were in gravely critical condition. A search was on for the black pickup truck.

"Opinion has turned against the Poetry Outlaws. They are wanted," the newscaster said with dramatic seriousness.

"Who cares what they say?" Ernie Ray said, picking up his cigarette. "The public is worse than any autocrat." He laughed. His voice wheezed.

"Don't speak so ill of autocrats," said Hat Man "They know the difference between bloodshed and pasquinade."

"Most definitely," Ernie Ray said. "Ulysses, do you have an ashtray? My nerves are getting the better of me."

"No," Ulysses said flatly. "I don't carry them."

"Nervous Ernie," Hat Man said. "I'll be seeing you," and he walked out the door. The newscaster interrupted the weather report to give an update. Dr. Mike Watson of Cochton Enterprises was dead.

CHAPTER TWENTY-ONE

Creep or cold flow in material terms is the tendency of solids to crawl away from stress over a long period of time. Creep occurs in plastics, uncured concrete, and materials that get hot.

After Mike's funeral, our minds brimming with death and loss, Ulysses and I went to the graveyard. We weren't there to lay Mike to rest. That had been done before the service. I would finally see the grave of his father. We swung by the little cottage and picked up Blossom.

We hadn't seen Blossom as much as I'd expected to over the summer. She had teacher conventions to go to and courses to take. She was kinetically busy. We'd been surprised when she called and asked to be taken to the cemetery. She carried a bouquet of pink and white phlox from her garden, and the petals shed in the car as we drove to the graveyard. She was dressed in that teacher way, practical in scalloped knit shorts and a green top, also scalloped. Her gray hair curled across her shoulders, and she wore big sunglasses and sneakers.

I'd never even seen the grave of my father-in-law, only that of Jester's mother. Being here made me uneasy and guilty. I worried about leaving Mother and her tangling vines unsupervised. The ground was wet from last night's thunderstorm. We drove through the gate and turned left, past the Cochton Mausoleum and the little stand of pine trees, beyond the gnarled oak. My discomfort grew. Both graves were in the same section of Peaceful Knoll Cemetery.

Sprawling from my shapeless sundress, my bare legs stuck to the leather seats of Old Gold. We pulled to the side of the little path, so close to Jill's grave that I could see Mother and an alarming tangle of seedpods. We should have destroyed that plant. She was self-pollinating and reproducing with the speed of an insect!

Blossom laid the flowers on the grave of Hiram Butz, killed ten years ago, not long after, as I privately noted, Ulysses had first met Bernadette.

"He was a kind husband," said Blossom. "I've missed him."

"He would've loved being a grandpa—he adored kids," Ulysses said. He put a hand on my shoulder. "Dad, this is my wife, Catrina. We're expecting."

My face burned in the heat. The summer air was heavy with particulates and humidity. Blossom got on her knees, her legs white, and put a hand on the grass before the headstone.

"Hi, it's been ten years. I've missed you. This whole place has gone to shit."

Ulysses took my hand. "Ma, please excuse us. Catrina and I need to talk and walk for a bit." Following his lead, I walked with him to the resting place of Jill Rana near a grove of pine trees. Ulysses stopped right in front of her grave and Mother sprouting from it with a tangle of leaves and pods. He touched the plant tenderly.

"You know about plants. What is this thing?"

"*Muscuna*," I said. There was a cigarette butt on the grave. A breeze ruffled stray hairs around my bare ankles. I was already having difficulty shaving.

Ulysses stroked one of Mother's trembling pods. "I was here earlier in the summer visiting Dad, and its blooms smelled so enticing, I picked them and put them in Rainy Day. Beer is better with volatiles, you know. I also put them in that additive I call Sprinkle. Thank God, because sales of Rainy Day and Sprinkle have gotten us through the summer. I haven't printed anything. I haven't the interest or the heart, and it's too dangerous now with Axel prowling around. The flowers give Rainy Day a nice bouquet. It's 'estery.' You know what I mean?"

"Yes, that's chemistry talk for sweet-smelling," I said, glad to be sharing a language with him.

A vine wrapped around his finger, perhaps in response to touch. I panicked.

"I wouldn't handle the thing. It could have toxins. Plants can kill, you know. In fact, step away." I was unreasonably worried about what had happened to Frani, an isolated incident. This plant made me nervous.

"It's got these seedpods now. Do you think I'd get caught if I picked a couple?" asked Ulysses.

"It might be called gardening. I wouldn't go near. They'll be bursting soon anyway and the seeds popping all over. You won't have to touch the plant to harvest them." The twisting tendrils of Mother loomed larger and healthier than last week.

"Do you think you can grow the seeds?"

"I'm sure I can. We don't have a garden, though, and never will, so let's be going."

"Maybe someday a house, a garden, a brewery," he said

He tugged off a few pods and stuffed them in the pocket of his jeans. It was true that I'd snipped parts from Mother and her babies with no repercussions so far, but his handling of the pods scared me. She could strike at any time and I didn't know what triggered her.

"I'll leave the rest for nature," he said. "I can imagine a whole field of these, fighting against the smell of the pigs."

"Fighting back for sure," I said. "Now let's get out of here."

"You doing okay in this heat?" he asked. "I don't know why Ma chose today of all days to visit."

"I need to tell you about this plant. It's one I'm studying. A weird thing happened. Something unbelievable, so I haven't mentioned it."

A figure came out of the grove of pine trees. It was Hat Man in his hat, stained white suit, and black shoes.

"Here's the happy couple," he said. "Tell me how happy you are."

"We're not that happy," I said, instinctively disagreeing with him. "And I'm not giving an interview."

"Happier than Jill, I imagine. She's the patron saint of family troubles." He clasped his hands to his chest. "Poor Jill. Her life was brutish, her husband, a lout. He passed it on too."

"What do you want?" Ulysses said sharply.

Hat Man removed his hat, showing his hairless head sweating in the heat. "I'm here to pay my respects to my dear mother."

Mother! He was Jester's brother. He had a strong chin like Jester's. He had to be Jehosophat—Jester's abusive brother.

"Additionally, it would be interesting to see you hanged."

"Pleasant thought," Ulysses said.

"Let's go," I said to Ulysses.

"I'd cherish seeing your wife cry. I have repugnance for efficacious women. Were you raised a hippie, that you let your wife be free-range?"

"How I was raised is none of your concern."

"Raised to be a cuckold," said Hat Man, coming closer. "She needs her retribution and so do you, sheath master. It's a crime against men what you've been doing. In the name of the Brotherhood of the Mounted, I take you both into custody."

His hand dipped into his pocket. Before he could withdraw whatever it was he reached for, Ulysses kicked him squarely in the stomach. Hat Man doubled over. He fell onto Mother as the wind came up, and a vine from Mother wrapped around his neck and dragged him down.

Ulysses grabbed my arm. "Run."

CHAPTER TWENTY-TWO

Coumarin is a food flavoring agent and gives a pleasant scent to mulled wine and pipe tobacco. It was first discovered in the tonka bean in 1822. It occurs naturally in cassia cinnamon, vanilla grass, and grapefruit juice. It's a complex molecule containing oxygen and is an antioxidant. Coumarin is considered a mild toxin that could cause liver damage. It's an antibacterial and antiviral agent. For plants, coumarin defends against these things. Some forms are antifungal. It dilates blood vessels. It can keep apples from browning and could be used as a food preservative. It's also used in perfumes and aftershaves to give scents of newly mown hay, vanilla, and licorice.

I retrieved the results of the water testing and studied the data surreptitiously. It was good data, and by that I mean unequivocal. There it was in every sample—Boardoze—in the tap water, in the river, and in the urine of my poor husband. A whopping 20–30 parts per million. The boars had to have been swimming in it because the men of Cochtonville were.

Jester, wearing a plain, black suit, slunk into my lab.

"What's buzzin', cousin?" he asked, his gaze on the ceiling.

I put my water-testing data facedown on the lab bench. "I've finished an interesting study with the bean volatiles. They contain jasmine, and other indoles, and chemicals found in colas—

monoterpenes, and sesquiterpenes, isoeguenol as in cloves and sweet coumarin." This wasn't the data I'd been looking at, but it wasn't a lie either. No wonder people were chugging Rainy Day 2.0. It made them happy despite Boardoze. It made them brave. It tasted great, and enough of it would make them resistant to snakebites.

"Good golly Miss Molly. Makes me want to eat that hog food," he said.

"Plenty of indole-based compounds in there that probably have psychological effects. Some are close to psilocybin's structure. We could have some high hogs out there. I'll get you a report."

His breath was on my neck.

"You have something to tell me, don't you?" I asked.

"I've been meaning to mention this. I'm married." His tone was businesslike, almost dead.

"Congratulations." My ears were ringing. I put my hands over them to stop the din that came with having Jester near me. The Boardoze debacle left me with *hang*, a brewer's term for bitterness that won't go away.

"To Jane. To keep out of jail, but I wanted to anyway. She's gorgeous. She moved her hair salon to the mortuary. It's now called Sleeping Beauty Salon. She wanted me to tell you, if you ever need anything, she's there for you. Her dad knows Ulysses. Don't that beat all?"

"I'll drop by when you're not there," I said, annoyed at his lack of remorse for what he'd done to Ulysses.

"I know you're sore with me, and I want you to understand that Boardoze hurts me too, Catrina. Some wedding night I had. First, I had to pretend to be too drunk and then too busy with work."

"It's not as if you were injected with it. You did it to yourself."

"How much is in the water?"

I tapped my fingers on the slate lab table. "Let's just say your best seller has neutered every man in Cochtonville."

"We can modify the formula. We're already working on it."

"Are you going to officially tell people?"

"No need to cause widespread panic and anger." He was already sounding like what they called a leader in Cochtonville.

"Jester, when science doesn't help people, we need to stop. It's not whole without helping people, giving them what they need for better lives, making the planet healthy. Science is for humanity, not selfishness." I suppressed the twitch at the side of my mouth. I'd found my half of the whole, my missing ingredient. It was my connection with humanity. This was why I wanted to have a baby. It was why I'd fallen for Ulysses and his noble business of helping people control their fertility. I was searching for a connection.

"Neither one of us can afford to buck Cochton Enterprises. We were born middle class."

"I imagine we were hired for that as much as we were for our intellect."

"We were. We're scientists but we're serfs. The sooner we accept it, the better things will be for us. There are crazy laws in Cochtonville, but a person can find happiness and contentment here."

"And a flower can grow in a crack in the sidewalk. But why should it have to? Well, Cochtonville's done itself in. Nobody will want to move here once this gets out. With no libraries and no art and no sex, what there is of the next generation won't know beauty, passion, or curiosity. There won't be any new ideas. There won't be any new science. Science needs all of those things for fertilization."

Jester put his hand on my desk and leaned toward me. "You know what I need? I need security and safety. I don't need someone moralizing to me, gol darn it. I've had enough hurt to last a while."

"Why the hell are you here, Jester?"

"I have what will seem like bad news," he said in a hushed voice. What an odd way to put it. Why couldn't the man ever say what he meant?

"Spit it out. It isn't as if bad news is something unique these days." I glared at him. He had a faint citrus odor of limonene.

"Don't be sore about this." I immediately generated alarm chemicals. "We both found great success under Mike's leadership."

"Uh-huh," I said. Had he no concept of what that Boardoze had done to my life?

He went on. "I got a promotion. I'm stepping into his shoes. I'm your boss."

My anger chemical—wasn't it catecholamine?—spiked and so did my blood pressure. I could feel that great river of life pounding in my head. I worried it would harm the baby, and I took some deep breaths before I said anything.

"*You* are *my* boss? Who decided this? Even you must see the unfairness of it."

"I've been productive. Boardoze is a best seller. You'll be busy in a few months and won't want the pressures." He put his hand on my shaking shoulder.

I bowed my head, pretending to stare at the paper I'd been reading. My hair fell around my face, covering what must have been my horrified expression.

"No one even asked me. The decision was made for me," I said.

He bent over and brushed my hair from my face with a clumsy sweep. "We make decisions for those we love, Catrina. It's human nature."

I turned my head away. "I'm not your child. We're the same age with the same credentials. Don't touch me right now. Not my hair or any part of me."

He pulled his hand away and put it in his pocket. "I hope you can accept this and see the wisdom of it. By golly, I'll be the best boss you've ever had."

"I was expecting someone with more seniority." I gave him my meanest look.

His hand flew over his eyes. "Please, neither one of us needs a jolt of cortisol right now. This isn't good for either of us."

"Okay. I guess it isn't your fault."

He peeked through his fingers. "You're a peach for understanding." He held out his hand for me to shake, and I ignored it. "Could you get me a report on the rat growth? Make it look good."

"How can I do that with no control group?" My stress was jumping again.

"You're a swell clever girl. I'm sure you can manage." He cleared his throat. "Along those lines, Catrina, another thing. I'm supposed to tell you that we don't have a maternity policy here at Cochton Enterprises. The day you get released from the hospital is the day you report to work."

"I figured as much."

"I can pull some strings."

"Thanks ahead of time. Get out of my lab now. Please. I need to concentrate." I handed him the data on Boardoze. He studied it, his wholesome face crumbling as the numbers and scans sank in.

"Good golly. Look at the levels. Heavens to Betsy. Holy crap. Catrina, I'm sorry. I didn't mean harm. I was going for big yields and that success that's supposed to be in my head."

"Well, I know one place where success is *not*."

"It was boneheaded. I owe you and Ulysses." He handed the data back to me. He went to the door and stood silently in the doorway. He peeked into the hallway.

"Gee willikers. What's this?"

Steps rang through the hall. The sharp smell of aftershave arrived three seconds before Axel did. We were surprised to see someone from the outside here in the building and in my lab. Most nonscientists enter a lab timidly, but Axel strode in and posted like a marble statue.

"Who are you?" Jester said.

"What are *you* doing *here*?" I said. Marriage had been good for Axel. He was jaunty and fit. His black shoes gleamed in the harsh, bright light of the lab.

"I'm looking for Jester Rana," he said.

"I'm Jester Rana." Jester stepped forward.

"What now?" I said. "How did you get in?"

"The Patrol gets in, Catrina. You can't escape the Patrol. We see clearly. I need this fellow." He pointed to Jester.

"What do you want?" Jester said, shifting uneasily.

"Bad news. A dead guy." Axel took out his tablet to show Jester a picture of the body. "Found on your mother's grave. Nary a mark on him, except for striations around the neck. Can you explain?"

Jester clenched his fists as he looked at and then away from the image on the tablet. He said, "That's her son. My brother." He met my gaze. My spine crawled. Hat Man had been Jester's brother, and now he was dead. Killed by Mother. "The mark is from birth. Check his medical records. He came into this world with a noose around his neck—the umbilical cord."

Axel let out a long *hmmmm* and stared at Jester for any sign of a resemblance. "Her son. Your brother. Same big head. You've got a forest of hair. Makes a world of difference."

Jester ran his hand through his gorgeous, red locks. "My wife is a beautician. Sleeping Beauty Salon."

"I'll have to try it. Her son, you say? Older, I imagine. Or had a rough life."

"Both."

"That gives credence to why he was there. Who is he?"

"His full name was Jehosophat Rana."

"Spell that."

"J-e-h-o-s-o-p-h-a-t."

"And?"

"R-a-n-a."

"There were shoeprints. Show me your shoes. What size are you, son?"

"Eleven and a half."

"Not yours. These are smaller prints from loafers."

Ulysses! I steadied myself on the lab bench.

"Did he have any medical conditions?" asked Axel.

"He died of a broken heart, I imagine. He and our mother were close. Too close." Jester clenched his jaw.

"We'll have the coroner take a look, if we have a coroner these days. I imagine he could have been dehydrated. Awful hot out there," Axel said. "Bad luck, man." He touched Jester on the shoulder tenderly.

"I'm sorry, Jester," I said. What had I expected after walking away as I had?

"It's nothing," Jester said coldly.

"You don't seem too shook up about it. Better work on that, although I'm not sad he's dead. Lead poor Ernie Ray down the path of destruction." Axel spread his legs apart, as if his balls needed air. Jester and I each wiped away a crocodile tear.

"No need to get maudlin. My condolences. You'll need to claim the body."

"I don't want it. I want no part of him."

"If you pay for transport, the City will toss it to the pigs. Otherwise, he's yours."

"I'll pay," Jester said, getting out his wallet. "I've got the bread. I just got a promotion. I don't want to see him again. Do you take credit cards?"

"Sure do," said Axel, pulling a device from his belt.

When the transaction was complete and Axel left the chemistry floor, Jester slumped against my lab bench.

"I lied," he said. "My brother wasn't born with the umbilical cord around his neck. It was Mother. We were negligent in planting her there. She killed him."

"Will we be implicated?" I was guilty of leaving a man to die.

"She did the right thing. He was crazier than a hoot owl. It's for the best. It was my hope when we put Mother there. He'll be eaten by pigs and no one will be the wiser. But how can a plant do this?"

"I don't believe it's intentional. She's a vine and she wants something to climb. She's grabbing for tall things that cast a shadow on her. She thinks they're trees. It's why I've always been safe around her."

He pulled a folded paper from his pocket. "It all makes sense. But you're wrong. It's intentional. I have one more thing to share with you, now more than ever. I need your opinion. I found this in Natharie's lab coat."

"You were sneaking through the lab coat pockets?"

"That's what bosses do. Get a load of this."

He showed me a copy of an archived newspaper page that bore the tale of Old Pa Corduroy, nicknamed for his pants, a bean sharecropper who burned his crop and disappeared after a series of mysterious strangling deaths on his farm. First the father-in-law who demanded a dowry, next the pastor who pestered him about his drinking, and finally the landowner himself. The trouble was, Old Pa Corduroy had only one arm due to an accident with a mule and a plow, so he wasn't convicted of strangling them.

"Is this real?" I said.

"These things can't be the crop of the future," he said. "They're killers. Not just Mother. All of them have the potential."

I said, "They're already in the first batch of feed and another crop has been planted. The plants are dehiscent. They have popping seeds. They're loose."

"These incidents aren't accidents. The victims were all oppressors. These are the seeds of rebellion! We need to stop the experiment right now. These beans have to be contained or there will be chaos. We can't risk it," he said. "Can you find a new crop?"

"I'll have to, won't I?" I said.

"You snoop. Going through my pockets." Natharie strode into my office and snatched the newspaper article from Jester.

"Were you going to tell me this? Mother killed my darn evil brother."

"She killed. That explains it," said Natharie.

"I thank her for it."

Natharie said, "I went to water her, and all that was left was a black stem and a pile of goo. The strain was too much for her. She gave her life. She's gone."

CHAPTER TWENTY-THREE

Theobromine, produced by cocoa plants, is one of the over four hundred compounds found in chocolate. It's similar to caffeine in structure. It primarily stimulates smooth muscles as opposed to the nervous system. It's toxic to dogs but much less so to humans.

When I got home, the bar patrons were glued to the television set above the portrait of Grant. The newscaster, who resembled Frani—a look people here apparently found appealing—was in a cornfield, the ever-present prairie wind blowing her hair from west to east. With a breathless lisp, she reported that a decomposing body had been found, an unidentified young man in his late teens or early twenties. Most disturbing, an unused condom had been found near the body. The camera zoomed in to the condom on the ground, surrounded by crime scene tape, and I saw that it bore the image of Ulysses S. Grant. My Ulysses was white and trembling. His illegal goods were now associated with murder, and the general couldn't have been more incriminating.

"Oh crap," I whispered.

"Who could it be?" asked Maven. She was looking especially fetching in a pink spaghetti-strap dress, her skin sun-kissed to nearly a burnt sienna. Her mouth was tense and her mascara smeared.

"Bad news for sure," Maurice said.

On cue, Axel came into Union Station, walking to the bar in quick steps.

He said in a clipped tone, "Butz, I need you out in the car."

Ulysses took off his apron. We traded fearful glances. Axel escorted him to the Washer van and they got in. The lights flashed as the two sat in the front seats. From what I could tell, they were studying images. Ulysses was as glum as I'd ever seen him, almost transforming into Edgar Allen Poe before my dizzy eyes.

"This can't be good," said Maurice, peering out the window.

"What's it about?" Maven asked. "Tell me it's not that dumb kid in trouble."

My heart dropped at the thought, but where else was he? Axel and Ulysses came back in.

Ulysses wiped his forehead. "It's Zell, everybody. He's dead, I'm sorry to say. I saw the photos."

A whisper of condolences swept across the room.

"Who did it?" asked Couch Kissing Man.

"The bus driver," said a man in a seed corn cap.

"Ernie Ray," said another.

"Now, Butz, show me the condoms," said Axel in a scratchy voice.

Maven spoke up. "His wife is pregnant. That should prove he don't use condoms."

Axel snorted. "There was one on the body of his employee and my wife might say different."

Ulysses clenched a fist. "We were strictly business partners."

Axel grabbed his elbow and escorted him behind the bar. "Don't worry, Butz, I compare favorably. Nothing like a past with a reprobate to make a woman treasure the present. Let's take a look around behind the counter, why don't we?"

Axel opened the ice machine and scooped through it. He slid over to the cocktail shakers and shook them. He picked through the swizzle sticks, coasters, koozies, napkins, bottle openers, and decks of cards. He popped open the cash register. I took my place beside

Ulysses and looped my arm through his. Ripples of tension poured off him. Axel ate a few olives, then pulled open the cash drawer where we stashed anything over the petty cash in the register.

"Nice haul," he said. "Bernadette was wondering how you were managing."

"How is she?" Ulysses said under his breath, as if he was ashamed to ask.

"Beautiful, devoted, and appreciative of supply-side economics," Axel said. "Open this drawer here."

Ulysses unlocked the condom drawer. Everyone in the room stopped breathing. The drawer slid open with a groan. Light from the Tiffany fixtures glinted in. The tray inside was empty.

"Take it out," Axel said gruffly. Ulysses hesitated. "Get it out and hand it over, Butz," he ordered.

Ulysses removed the blue plastic tray and handed it to Axel. Underneath the drawer was a copy of the magazine *Naked and Wet Women*.

Axel whistled and the patrons gasped.

"How'd that get there?" Ulysses said haltingly.

"That might be enough to put you away," Axel said triumphantly, taking the magazine. "You guys think if you go paper the Patrol won't find out. I'd say intent is evident."

"It's mine," I blurted out.

"What?" asked Ulysses.

"It's mine. Give it to me." I yanked it from Axel's hands and desperately flipped through it, past big breasts in the shower and at the pool until I came to a woman on a beach.

"There," I said. I pointed to the beach grass in the background and hoped Axel and the Patrol knew nothing about beach grass.

"See that? It's *Ammophila mammas*." Wow, I'd made up a particularly stupid scientific name.

"Hmm," Axel said. "What's that supposed to mean?"

"It's clearly something the Cochtons will be interested in, and as their natural products chemist, I need to find this location and collect a sample. It could be the next forage crop—not to replace corn, but grown on marginal lands. That sand looks marginal, don't you think? And that grass looks marvelous." I held up the magazine.

"I've seen better," Axel said.

"Me too," said Maurice, raising his glass of Rainy Day 2.0. "If it's the woman you're referring to."

"Yes," said Axel, squinting. "I am."

"Gentlemen, there you have it," I said. "The finest part of this magazine is clearly the grass."

Axel grabbed the magazine. "I need it as evidence."

I snatched it back and hugged it to my chest. "I need it for scientific research. You'll have to issue a warrant to my boss. This is Cochton Enterprises property."

"We'll see about that," Axel said "Meanwhile, you can check that know-it-all attitude."

He ran his hand through the drawer. "Ah-ha." He held up a pumpkin seed. "I suppose you'll say this is yours too."

I grabbed it. "Of course. I have a permit to carry seeds. Would you like to see it?"

"No. Damn, you're tiresome. Always an answer."

His phone blipped and he pulled it out of his pocket and checked it, reading the text a couple of times before returning it to his pocket.

"Butz," he said, "you're off the hook. For the moment. Ernie Ray is wanted for the murder of Zell Bremler. He's missed his curfew and the state can't locate him. Innocent people don't run from the law. Plus, he has size ten-and-a half feet, just like the prints found next to the corpse. Until the murderer's been caught, this city-state won't be safe. I'll be monitoring this place looking for him and keeping tabs on all the single people and other troublemakers."

He grabbed the magazine from me. "The Patrol doesn't need a warrant. And Butz, don't go anywhere."

Axel settled onto the couch. "I'll stick around and keep an eye on things."

Maurice put an arm around Maven. "Baby, things are crazy tonight. I've been wanting to say this for a while, and I finally got up my nerve—let's get married. You make the world less nuts."

Maven flipped her hair. "I love you, baby. I'm real gone. But are you sure? Considering the way things are, do I have much to offer you?"

Maurice said, "If you'll have me 'as is,' I'd be honored. More than honored. I'd be blessed."

"I understand, baby. Yes. I do. I don't need a cock to be loved."

The patrons clapped as our newest couple, so much in love that even Boardoze couldn't get in the way, kissed.

"That's the spirit," Axel said. "Nothing like marriage to kill any thoughts of deviance. It's a guaranteed way to be respectable. The Butzes being the exception to the rule. He brought her down."

"Free toast on the house," Ulysses said. "Catrina, come with me to get the champagne."

We went to the cellar beneath the bar. It was lined in white plastic to keep the crumbling walls at bay. It was here where cases of wine, mostly white Zinfandel, were stored at a constant temperature and where the Rainy Day was brewed, which gave the space a sleepy haze of carbon dioxide.

Illuminated by the one dim dangling bulb, Ulysses grabbed two bottles of champagne. He still carried the dour aura of Poe.

"Are you doing okay?" I asked.

"Except for my life flashing before my eyes, yes. I kind of forgot about that magazine. I was trying to get myself aroused at one point, but Boardoze works far too well. Not only did the magazine not get a rise out of me, I forgot all about it. Good catch with the grass story."

"I aim to please," I said. "I'm going to get a permit to study the grass. I'm taking you with me. We'll cross The Edge and not return."

"Little Honey, that was brilliant. And the seed. Glad you've got the permit."

"What is it with no seeds and no birth control? They don't seem to go together."

"It's all about a centralized means of production. The city controls the seeds so we can't get too independent. That way, the babies we make will conform and be valuable commodities for the empire."

"You're the brilliant one. You're helping people maintain control over their lives."

"Axel is right. I brought you down with my selfish desire to make you mine. Keep in mind that if someday he hauls me away, no heroics. Get your ass out of here and save yourself. Promise me you won't get involved. Claim you and I are separated and you know nothing about condoms or vibrators."

I shivered in the damp cellar. "What are you talking about? You don't have them these days, do you?"

"No. No interest at all in condoms. Nobody's even asking for them. But that general will ambush me. I'm sure of it."

"There's no proof. We'll be long gone by then. You'll recover from Boardoze too. It has a half-life of thirty-one days from what I can discern from the urine study, so within a year..."

"Come on upstairs, now. People are waiting."

CHAPTER TWENTY-FOUR

P-coumaric acid is an antioxidant common in plants. It's prevalent in corn at a concretion of 4 percent by weight. It could have anticancer properties.

It wasn't hard to convince Jester of my need to study the grass, to get one more discovery launched before the birth of my child. It would make us both look good, and as far as he was concerned it would pave the way for a replacement for the *Muscuna cochtonus* beans. Natharie would have no trouble growing grass. The HR woman eagerly stamped the border-pass papers, her eyes glazing over as I mentioned p-coumaric acid and its antibacterial properties. Certainly, as a forage crop it could cut the use of antibiotics. Maybe this is why dogs eat grass.

"You want an assistant to do your dirty work and heavy lifting?"

"How about a good-looking male?" By this I meant Ulysses, posing as my assistant.

"I've added that to the paperwork," she said, handing me the form.

As he walked through the door of Union Station, Ernie Ray looked like the farm cat Screwby who used to run off all summer and slink back to Granny's each winter in need of food and a trip to the vet. Ernie Ray was skinny, shaking, and missing an incisor.

Ulysses instinctively poured him a glass of milk and pushed it across the wood bar along with a bag of peanuts. "Ernie. How you been?"

"You're looking good, Ernie Ray," I said, meaning that he was alive.

"Are you blind? He looks like hell," Bernadette said, waving her hand in front of her nose.

"Damn, they got the wrong man and I'm sick as a dog," he said, pulling his skeleton to the bar. The stench of sweat and an ass half-wiped rose from him.

"Tell me all about it, cousin," said Axel, placing a hand on his shoulder. "We'll get the right man, believe me." He took his tablet from his belt and turned it on.

"Where ya been, Ernie? What happened?" Bernadette said.

Ernie Ray took a shuddering breath. "I let Zell drive the getaway truck. He was useless as an outlaw. He only wanted costume jewelry and shiny trinkets. He was a klepto too, pocketing stuff from the gang before we split the profits. He had crap from the bar, Ulysses: swizzle sticks, pool chalk, and urinal cakes."

Ulysses nodded. He'd known this already.

Ernie Ray continued. "We held up the restaurant, and damn if Zell didn't get us away in record time. Jehosophat told Zell to hit that couple crossing the street because it's always funny to mess with people. Zell was stupid. I didn't stop him though. It was that batshit city manager with some guy that looked like a suit. The kind of dude who puts rocks in your socks and boulders on your shoulders. I tell you this, there's something wrong with the empire's take on what it is to be a man on top and what we say strong is. So there we were, thinking we were big men, outlaws. Truth is, we all had that boner fatigue that's been going around. You gotta be noticing it, Ulysses. No man needs a condom."

Nobody said anything, not wanting to admit to boner fatigue or condoms.

"And at the crosswalk he played hero, stepping in front of the girl. Why would he do that when all lust is ashes-cold in Cochtonville? He's dead now, they say."

"Ernie," Bernadette said, "you're barely making sense."

"Just have something to eat before you say anything else. Want more milk, Ernie?" Ulysses said. "You look awfully skinny."

"Skinny, hell, yeah, and my mind's blown too. I've been hiding from Jeho. He's a killer."

"You mentioned Zell hit the man," I said as Ulysses gave Ernie more milk.

Axel sounded sympathetic. "Tell us more, Ernie."

"We ran the guy over. No stopping that, and Jeho told us to hide out in the cemetery. We stopped by a grave. Believe it or not, the place smelled divine, and it gave us a heady feeling. We were hungry and Zell emptied his pockets. He had some coffee creamer from the bar, some of that cheese you put on microwave pizzas, and a pint of pilfered vodka, Ulysses. He had one of your condoms too. He was playing with it, flipping it with his fingers. Jeho took note of it."

My blood ran hot at further mention of a condom, and Ulysses stood as still as a rat before a snake.

Ernie Ray went on, unaware of his incrimination. "We started talking about what we'd always wanted to do. I mentioned I'd always wanted to take Maven away from Cochtonville, and Zell said he'd always wanted a dog. Jeho needled him, asking why he had a condom and wanted a dog. Was he going to fuck the dog? Zell said he never took the condom, that Jeho'd put the condom in his pocket to make him look bad. He got mad and hit Jeho in the chest. It knocked him back. Zell packed a wallop."

Axel leaned in. "By Jeho do you mean Jehosophat Rana?"

"I think that was his name. The dude with the hat."

"This condom. Was it the General Grant condom found near the body?"

"It sure was a General Grant condom. Jehosophat mentioned it and said that no outlaw would be caught dead with one. Men don't bridle their pride, he said, and not with a Yankee general."

"What happened, Ernie? Why is Zell dead?" asked Bernadette.

"I've got no idea. Jeho told Zell if they played family style together that he'd get Zell a dog. He had a gun. Said they could play target practice. Took him to a cornfield and came back without him. I was drunk by that time. We came to Union Station, and I don't remember the rest. You'll have to find that man with the hat."

"He's dead," Axel said. He reached out to grab teetering Ernie Ray. "I'll escort you to the State Home for Rehabilitation in exchange for your confession. You might give us further insights on that condom."

Ernie Ray rose to his feet and stood swaying. "No. I won't go. Inside me a poet lives on and art must be free.

"I've had enough of hero's tales.

They're nothing more than howls.

Knowledge is not death

Unless you're chained to corporate bowls.

Fill ears with wax and consumption tax

Until your belly growls."

"Ernie," said Maven, "what's going on? Are you all right?"

"Yeah, man, you're not Edna St. Vincent Millay," said Maurice. "Don't even try to rhyme."

Ernie Ray went on, oblivious to this interruption.

"Have you been with that man

Who lead you afoul?

Who is your master?

The dove or the owl?

You can't hide the sin with shovel or trowel."

He clutched his chest. "Heartburn." We weren't sure if this was part of the poem or not.

Ernie Ray went on, bent over and nearly breathless.

"Time to throw in the towel.

Love is all there is.

Forgive me, Zell. I'm dust."

He tumbled to the floor.

Bernadette rushed to his crumpled body, rolled him over, and began mouth-to-mouth while Maven did chest compressions. I tried to call an ambulance, succeeding after five or six tries. It arrived too late. Ernie Ray was gone.

We closed the bar and went to our apartment, into the kitchen. Ulysses opened the window. The night was cool.

"Are we going to run?" I asked, looking out on the alley.

"I need some air." Ulysses took my face in his hands and said, as he had before, "You never intended to get caught up in all of this. Don't throw your life away. Poor Ernie."

"What's the punishment for condom distribution?" I said, tears falling like glitter in a snow globe.

He said, "It depends on what facility they have an opening in. If it's the insane asylum, I'll be insane. If it's the treatment center for deviants, I'll be a deviant. If it's the prison, I'll be a criminal."

"You're none of those things. We need to fight."

"Please, just get on with your life. I'm useless as a man. You've given me the best year a guy could have. I wouldn't trade it for anything." He kissed my cheeks, wet with tears.

"I'll be coming for you. I'm not leaving you to rot."

We held each other as steps came up the stairs. "Let them take me, Little Honey. Don't jeopardize yourself. I can't bear the thought."

I stared into his eyes. "I'm not going to lose you."

He set his brow. "I'll get our marriage annulled to keep you out of it. We should have known a renegade isn't meant to settle down."

I was sinking in mud, struggling. "Don't do it. A wife can't testify against her husband. You said so yourself."

"You won't have to testify. I'll confess."

A key turned in the lock. The door creaked. We could hear someone taking long strides through the living room. It was Barnabus and a new cop, a tall guy.

"Washers," the new guy called out, his voice crackling with energy.

Barnabus lifted his big gun. "Ulysses S. Butz, you've been selected! You're under arrest for morality crime and being an accessory to the death of Dr. Mike Watson." Ulysses touched my hair.

"Don't do anything rash," I begged.

He held out his wrists to Barnabus as I clung to him. "I go willingly. Put away the weapon."

"You're a smart man, Butz," said Barnabus. The tall man pushed me aside and handcuffed my husband, who stood stooped like a broken man—his hair hanging raggedly around his lean cheeks.

"Where are you taking him?" I asked.

"Yet to be determined," said Barnabus. "Scan him, Manny."

"He's clean." The tall Washer read No Regrets.

The Washer tapped his tablet. "He's clean, so he isn't a deviant. Don't worry, missus. He'll be too ugly to be someone's sweetheart. We'll let him off easy if he gives a list of customers."

"I'd rather be dead."

"That's another option. Time to go, Butz."

Ulysses said, "Catrina, you've got your whole life ahead of you. Go study grass."

Barnabus said, "You married a smart woman, she's not going to listen to you. You should've known that. How about you sign the annulment app right now? I get a bonus if you do—Commissioner Whitehead wants to please his wife—and this little woman won't be touched by the law."

"Hand it over," Ulysses said, wiggling his fingers in the handcuffs. He didn't even pause.

"No!" I cried. "Don't let her get her way with you one more time."

"Catrina, I'm sorry. We've got to do this. It's not about her. Nothing about us was."

"Please, no," I said, my panic rising as I saw the determination on his face. "Don't do this, I beg you! Don't let them take you!" I was sick, hot and cold, my heart crumbling like a sandcastle.

The tall cop held the tablet in front of him and guided Ulysses's finger to the right place. Without looking at me, Ulysses poked the tablet, slicing me from him as sharply as beach grass slices bare legs.

"Now give me your rings," said Barnabus. He smiled as he pocketed them.

"Ulysses, don't go. Please don't take him," I pleaded. "He didn't do anything."

"He contributed to the injuries of city manager Foil and the death of her friend by stimulating the poetry outlaws with a condom."

I stood at the top of the stairs as Ulysses was led away. He didn't turn around.

I rushed to the window and watched the Washer van slip into the night. Misled moths sparkled beneath the streetlight. My heart was in my throat. Ulysses was right. The rational thing to do would be to move on. It would be almost as easy as my quickie wedding ceremony. One child, a job, and Whisper Whizard as my lover would be manageable. It would be easy and sensible. I'd still be the achiever my parents and Cochton Enterprises wanted me to be. I'd move into the upper middle class. I'd keep the baby safe this way. I could make it work as chemists do. I'd be a success. Yes, I'd die alone, but there was no shame in that. Dora Jordan, Marilyn Monroe, and Prince all left this life solo. Of course, they were entertainers, not scientists, but it didn't matter. I was a human first and scientist second. I swallowed.

CHAPTER TWENTY-FIVE

Carbon filtration: originally done with charred bones, this method of purification relies on highly porous carbon that has been exposed to oxygen. The material will adsorb many organic chemicals. They adhere to the surface of the carbon through chemical interaction and are removed from water.

I was whipped. I was dead inside. The dark paneling of the apartment was more oppressive than all the corn in Cochtonville. I ran down the stairs and out to the sidewalk. Venus rose bright in the western sky, defying the city lights. I knew those alchemical tales about her power were silly. She was just a planet. I wasn't religious. I didn't believe in signs. Yet I was learning to know myself. I wasn't aromantic. I had the need to love romantically. The light of Venus bore down between my eyes. Science wasn't my be-all and end-all, but it had given me a set of skills for dealing with the natural world. What no one can take is my expertise. My smarts would save me, my husband, and our baby. With help from science, love would win against Cochtonville.

Hans, holding a plate of chocolate chip cookies, opened the door to the inn a crack. "So sorry, Catrina. I'd ask if there's anything we can do, but I fear the answer is that we can't do anything. We're in a bad way. Jan had a brush with the law, you see. He grew a butternut squash behind the house. The Washers showed up and took him to the Gardener Rehabilitation Center for a week. He's been released; claimed it was buried by squirrels. We can't afford more trouble."

"Let her in, you damn coward." Wilma tossed open the door and I rushed past Hans into the familiar charm of the Brownstone Inn. The spicy smells and the plate of cookies calmed me. My plan was going to work. It was.

"I need to talk to Valentine and ask her if she's seen Ulysses in prison. I'm going to break him out. I need to know where they're keeping him. I can do this if I have enough insider information."

"Oh no," said Hans. "They'll shoot you. You have another life to think about."

Wilma snatched a cookie. "It's her life too." She took a messy bite and a crumb fell to the carpet.

"I won't live without him and neither will the baby."

"My dear, no. You're in shock. How about a cookie?" Hans shoved the plate at me.

"You know what you need?" Wilma said. "A pardon. Would that Frani bitch give Ulysses one?"

"She's in the hospital and will surely be guarded," said Hans, stooping to retrieve the crumb.

"A pardon. Of course. I need someone to get into the hospital and have Frani Foil pardon Ulysses. She's all for marriage, and she'll want to keep mine together."

"I have a friend who delivers flowers. I can call her," offered Hans.

"If she's who I'm thinking of, she's bought some products," Wilma said. "She'll be one of my many happy customers."

"They won't let her into the room. She's not a doctor. Is Valentine in?" Followed closely by Wilma, I ran up the stairs without pausing and burst through her door eager to make my entreaty.

I was surprised to find Trent there. Valentine was bent over a suitcase, her toothbrush in hand. I hurriedly explained my plan.

"Ulysses was arrested?" Valentine was stunned. "You need me to go to the hospital and ask Frani Foil to pardon Ulysses?" she said, blinking nervously. "I could if we went right away." Trent stood wide-eyed, most certainly weighing if his wife should risk this for me. I didn't want her to.

"It's okay. I can come up with something else. There's this flower person Hans knows. You're leaving, aren't you?"

"We wanted to go as soon as possible. Trent got me a guest pass to travel with him on business. I have tomorrow off. By the time they realize I'm not going to show up, we'll be across The Edge. Nobody on the outside is going to extradite us to this place. They hate it as much as we do."

"Do they know you at the hospital?"

"Not really. We try to keep the prisoners contained in the facility, so I don't get out much."

"I could have Wilma print your ID with my picture on it," I said.

"That'll work. All it takes is a white coat and a badge. The hospital, like the prison, is for profit and cuts corners on everything, including security."

Wilma said, "I can make an ID. It needs to resemble Valentine in case someone knows her. Catrina, got any hair dye?"

Trent studied me. "If you changed your hair, you could pass."

"A little contouring and you'll look just like her. Back shortly," Wilma said, rushing off.

"He's right. You can be me. Wear my white coat." Valentine went to her closet. "And here's a dress. Doctors dress up, you know." She was talking fast, relieved to be able to help and not feel as though she was overtly abandoning me as she fled to provide a better life for her baby. "Take anything, really. Take my room here. You can come and go exactly as me. We need to travel light. If asked, I'm saying I'm traveling with Trent on business for just a few days. When you get the pardon, go to the prison and visit Ulysses dressed as me. People there have a tendency to look away when things aren't right, so as long as you have a resemblance, nobody will admit to being the wiser. Clear Ulysses for release and all that. I haven't informed them I'm leaving. Wear gloves and prescribe antibiotics if you get asked to look at patients. Many of these guys haven't had the resources to care for themselves. If they've got a hot rash it's probably MRSA. Prescribe StaphEX." She explained it all in a rush. I prayed I'd remember everything.

We went downstairs to arrange with Jan and Hans for me to take her room. I'd give the bar to Maven and Wilma. On the stairs, Valentine stopped me.

"Watch out for Warden Carmine. He's flirty, and I flirt back to keep my job. He's got a gold tooth and a beer belly. He'll call you Pixie and you need to call him Pumpkin. He's got a bit of *fetor oris* from chewing on cheesy chips and drinking on the job. Fortunately, he has bad eyes and is too vain to wear glasses."

"This is the most harebrained scheme I've ever heard," said Hans. I on the other hand, believed in it. If we could work together to get a confession from Jester, we could work together to pull this off too.

The neon sign still stood in the front yard. The lettering of *Rana Mortuary* had been turned off, and a window sign read, "Sleeping Beauty Salon." I had an appointment with Jane.

"I need your help," I told her as we stood in her salon, the former embalming room. I showed her Valentine's ID. "I want to look just like this."

She bade me to recline in her chair. I hung my head over the stainless-steel sink. As she washed my hair, she praised it while hatching her plan to change it dramatically. Her banter relaxed me, made me feel normal, like any other woman in on whatever all woman talk about. She rinsed my hair and added shampoo that smelled like cherry-almond—in other words, like benzaldehyde.

"I join others in praying that your plan to free Ulysses succeeds," she said.

"What are you talking about? I...I just want a new look," I said, fake smiling up at the ceiling as my stomach knotted.

"Thousands of us hope otherwise."

"Thousands?"

"Yes, he's widely recognized and loved. Didn't you know? How could he do what he did and not be? He's an underground celebrity. My father is a fan."

"I knew he was known, but I had no idea."

"I'm proud to help you in any way I can." She hesitated. "Jester tells me you're a woman of experience. I have a question. Are all men alike in bed?"

I was flummoxed by the question and by Jester's disclosure. "Why...why do you ask?"

"I'm curious."

Oh crap. How do I answer this honestly?

"I'd say that different men can treat a woman differently. However, these days, they are all the same in bed. At least here in Cochtonville."

She massaged my scalp. "How so?"

"There's a chemical in the water that makes them all unable to perform sexually. It explains some things, I imagine."

"It certainly does. I thought it was a joke—that phrase 'there's something in the water.'"

"It was in hogs, and now it's in our men." I reached up to feel my hair.

"It doesn't affect the hair products. I gave a perm this morning and it turned out fine. In the water...it really is astonishing," she said, rinsing off the suds. "How connected we all are. Guess I'll sit tight. It's not easy. Will it be gone soon, that chemical?"

"Talk to Jester about it. It's up to Cochton Enterprises. Oh, and those carbon coffee filters remove it. Put a couple in a pitcher of water and pop it in the refrigerator."

A perm and a dye job later, thanks to chemistry and Jane's skillful hands, I had gorgeous curls, the color of the mahogany chairs at the Brownstone. She also transformed me with makeup contours and pink-petal fingernails. I had a new identity. I was Dr. Valentine Bliss.

CHAPTER TWENTY-SIX

Isopropanol is a solvent closely related to ethanol. It evaporates easily and leaves nothing behind. It's used as an industrial solvent and cleaner and as a skin disinfectant. When concentrated, it may produce respiratory irritation and headaches. It was first made in 1920 by Standard Oil. When mixed with water, it's known as rubbing alcohol.

I straightened my ID badge and inquired at the front desk of Clarence Cochton Community Hospital about City Manager Foil.

The receptionist squinted at my badge. "Is this about a patient of yours at the prison?"

"Yes, it is. I need to ask for a pardon. He's innocent."

She waved her hand in the air. "They all are—or so they say. Hand over the badge."

I unclipped my ID and she ran it over a scanner before handing it back to my shaking hand.

"Third floor. Go easy on the coffee next time, doctor."

Thank you, Wilma! I waited until the elevator emptied before getting on. I didn't want to be stuck alone with someone who might ask questions and figure out I wasn't a doctor. The rise of the elevator dropped my stomach into my uterus. The doors opened, and across the hall, decorated blandly in maroon and beige, was another set of elevators. The uncertainty of where to go and the peril of my mission had my head spinning. I turned to the left and saw the nurses' station.

"Can I help you, doctor?"

I cleared my throat, relieved the young nurse assumed I was a physician. "I'm here to see City Manager Foil."

"Are you a consultant?" she asked, staring up from a long counter.

"No. I'm with the state. How is she doing? Better, I hope."

"Open-book pelvic fracture and hypovolemic shock," the nurse said.

Having no idea what that meant, I nodded and said, "Hmm," thankful that my experience in the working world had taught me some skills in pretending to know what I didn't.

The nurse went on. "Bladder rupture. Lost an ovary. Don't take too much time. I need to change her dressings soon. Poor thing. Complains about shortness of breath. She's getting supplemental oxygen. There's an order in to radiology, but we're high census."

I nodded and followed her to the room.

The nurse put her hand on the latch. "You're not going to be upsetting her, are you? She needs to relax. I'm hoping her shortness of breath is just nerves."

"She's had an ordeal," I said. "I won't take long."

The nurse opened the door and then returned to her station, leaving me alone with the city manager. I took two steps into the room and restraightened my badge.

Frani was in bed, her head on the thin pillow. The sight of the vital signs monitor, the tubes and wires, put me at ease. Here was a place where measurements were taken seriously. I took a deep breath. The city manager turned her head toward me, coughed, and croaked, "Who are you?"

"I'm Dr. Bliss from the prison. I'm sorry for your loss."

She didn't respond.

"I came to ask a favor."

Her eyes were hollow, her skin the pale color of a pelican's wing or a plastic bag.

"I'm so happy you're recovering nicely," I said, trying to break the ice.

She didn't move. She coughed again. This was going worse than I'd ever imagined it could.

"Forgive me. I'm here to ask a favor," I repeated

She coughed, put her hand on her chest and grimaced.

"I'd like to entreat you for a pardon. Ulysses Butz had nothing to do with your injuries and is unfairly implicated. He's a family man, not someone who provided the poetry outlaws with condoms," I said, trying to keep desperation out of my voice.

Frani began to pant.

The nurse came in with a cart of supplies and asked, "Are you through, doctor?"

"Not quite," I said. On the monitor, blood oxygen dipped to 89 percent. Frani coughed and a trickle of blood came from her mouth as she sank farther on her pillow.

I took five steps back at the sight of blood.

"Manager Foil," the nurse cried, rushing to her side. "Frani, are you okay? Are you okay, Frani?" The nurse took her pulse. "Thready," she said, reaching to Frani's neck.

"No!" I said, unsure of the proper reaction. Frani was unresponsive.

"No peripheral pulse and a weak central pulse."

"That's bad," I said.

She glanced at the monitor. Frani's blood oxygen was dropping; her heart rate was soaring.

The nurse shouted, "Help in 327."

I yelled out the door. "Help! Help!"

Two more nurses rushed in, and the three worked in coordination like figure skaters, gliding around Frani, unhooking the monitor cables and tubes and attaching a smaller, portable tank of oxygen through a tube in her nose. They were pros with tubes and tanks. Frani was the color of limestone. The nurses whisked the bed past me, brushing my hip.

I steadied myself on the doorjamb. I'd failed. I made my way blindly to the exit. Hans had been right. This was a stupid plan.

Tripping through the dark parking garage, I had no guideposts. I was foolish to think this scheme would work, stupid to think I could rescue Ulysses so simply. At last I found Old Gold. I got in and turned on the headlights. The darkness sucked them away until there was nothing ahead of me at all.

CHAPTER TWENTY-SEVEN

Venom is produced by over 100,000 animals on earth. Venomous substances contain a wide variety of chemicals. Most are peptides or proteins, often proteins or enzymes that interrupt heart rhythm.

I sat trembling, my hands in my lap, goose bumps popping on my arms, my mind as blank as the wall in Valentine's examining room. I had no nurse to help me deal with the patients and no notion of how to find Ulysses here in the prison. I was on Plan B and not sure what it was. All I knew was that I had to see Ulysses.

Barnabus, bags under his eyes, brought in my first patient. He was exhausted, too tired to recognize me.

"Doc, got one for you."

"Tell me your symptoms," I said to the muscular prisoner with two missing teeth on the left side.

"My butt hurts," he said. "It itches."

"Hemorrhoids," I said. This doctor stuff wasn't difficult.

"No, my cheeks hurt," he insisted. "I can't sit down."

"Do they feel hot?" I asked, worrying about MRSA.

Barnabus shrugged and yawned.

"Well, get up on the examining table and drop your pants."

I was shivering inside. I didn't want to look at a butt rash.

There were reasons I didn't go into medicine—blood, guts, rashes, vomit.

The man did as he was told, smiling and sitting on the examining paper without complaining.

"Lie on your stomach," I ordered.

"I've been doing squats," he said, rolling over. "Aren't you going to tell me my ass is cute?"

"No," I said. "I don't see anything to make it itch either. Where exactly does it hurt?"

"Down here." He pointed to the lower right quadrant. I bent over cautiously. The man flexed his buttocks and released a loud, stinky package of gas. My hands flew to my nose as he laughed rudely.

"Finally got you, Doc."

I tried not to look rattled as he sat up, dangling in front of me.

"You're getting slow," he said.

Barnabus laughed and said, "Off your game today, Doc. Me too. I was up all night watching baseball. The Cochtonville Kernels are kicking butt."

"I'm not myself at all," I replied, wondering how I would ever get through this day with its steady stream of patients and problems I wasn't equipped to solve.

The next prisoner was clearly suffering.

"I'm pissing blood," he said, slumping on the examining room chair.

My mind raced. Infection. Bacteria. You needed to know what kind before giving antibiotics, didn't you? That required some kind of culture. This place had to have a lab, didn't it? Maybe it was kidney stones.

"How long has this been going on?"

"A few days. I can't sleep. Up all night with it." I skimmed his chart. He'd had this before. I selected the same drug he'd taken previously.

"We'll need to give you another round. Follow up in a week."

I put in an order for an ultrasound. I was out of my league on this one. First, do no harm, wasn't that it? It was a suitable motto for every profession. This man needed a real doctor. I hoped he'd have one soon.

Warden Carmine, with his gold tooth and tight shirt, hustled in a prisoner. My heart leaped like a sunrise when I saw the patient —Ulysses.

"Who have we here?" I said, trying to hide my enthusiasm.

"This guy needs to be declared fit to execute."

"Execute!" I put my hand to my forehead to calm my panicked neurons. Of course, nothing worked. Me losing it wasn't going to help Ulysses. "When?"

"It was decided an hour ago."

"How long? How long does he have?" I had to do something but of course I needed time to think.

"A week. He won't agree to his plea bargain, so he's going to get offed in style."

"Style? But...but death is such a waste." I was tipsy in Valentine's heels. The room was rushing me.

"It won't be a waste. More like a warning. That new Vice Patrol commissioner insisted this guy be able to choose his means of execution, and the criminal picked death by asp."

"Asp?" I was alert. Every possibility was upon me.

Ulysses piped up. "They gave me a choice. I picked that one. Will my ex-wife be notified? She had nothing to do with this mess. I want her to move on."

"She'll see it on television after the fact, like everybody else," the Warden said.

Ulysses slumped. He'd picked asp on purpose so I would save him. We were still meant to be together. Boardoze, Bernadette, bumping off—none of it would keep us apart. He understood me. He knew I'd come to rescue him.

I snatched a stethoscope from my desk. "A noble man to sacrifice for his wife," I said. "He looks fit enough. He looks very fine. Do you want me to examine him?"

"A dope, but yes. Examine him for dramatic effect. It doesn't have to be much."

I motioned to the examining table, and Ulysses sat. I put a stethoscope on his chest. His heart was pounding as he read my nametag.

"Dr. Valentine Bliss. What a beautiful name," he said suspiciously.

"What's in a name?" I said, pulling the comet necklace from inside my blouse.

His eyes widened as he recognized me and stammered, "But I prefer blondes."

"Damn right you do," I replied.

His words rushed out like a waterfall. "Such a lovely woman is out of place in this joint. What are you doing here, Doctor?"

Warden Carmine cleared his throat impatiently.

I said, "Saving lives, as doctors do. Of course, some scallywags are awfully tough to save."

"If you see my ex-wife, give her my love."

"We'll see about that. Mr. Butz, you may have visitors come to bid you goodbye. I suggest you open your arms to all. Don't turn anyone away. *Kiss* them goodbye," I said, adding quietly, "and don't forget to swallow."

He shook his head. "Sounds like a night in Vegas. I'll do that, Doc, if you insist."

"Hurry it up. I haven't got all day," said Warden Carmine.

I asked the warden, "This asp—who's going to handle it? How's this execution to be carried out, Pumpkin?"

"We're working out the details. The Cochtons were delighted with the choice of this prisoner and method of death and wanted to take it to a new level. It'll be broadcast. We're calling in a snake handler. Gonna get a scientist from outside Cochtonville. He'll pose as one of those old-time religion guys. The mayor saw it as a way to get people flooding to Cochton-approved churches and scare them at the same time." He put a hand on my shoulder. "You see, Pixie, appealing to people on simply economic terms is only partially effective. You gotta have hell to scare the others into behaving themselves."

He looked into my eyes. I looked away, fearful he'd catch on. "Well, something's got to do it. You're so wise."

"He'll get paid handsomely, I hear. More per hour than I get."

"This place can be so unfair, darling. You are handsome and deserve a handsome reward. Certainly, you're worth more than a snake man pretending to be someone he's not. How much involvement will I have?" I ran my hand down his black tie. Cheap material.

"You'll declare him dead, of course, Pixie. You all right? Seem kind of nervous and nasally."

"I *am* nervous; I admit it. It's a dumb way to die and a painful one."

"It's not up to you, Tinker Bell. You look a little puffy today, like you're losing your looks. It's awful when that happens to women." He stared at my ID badge.

"I beg to differ," Ulysses said. "She's beautiful. A woman is more than her looks."

"Stop trying to butter her up, Silver Tongue," the warden said. "You're a goner and nothing's gonna stop that." He poked me in the ribs. "When you gonna tell your husband I'm the father?" I was horrified until I realized he was teasing.

I tried to sound playful. "Right after you tell your wife. Now, let's discuss this patient. Unless you let me administer an antiemetic, he'll vomit all over. We can't have things so messy. We don't get paid enough for that, and it will make for bad television, don't you think, Squash Blossom?" I fluffed my curls at Warden Carmine.

"Guess we could allow it, if you ask nicely and smile for me," he said. "Did I ever tell you how much I love your hair?"

"Many times, my benevolent pumpkin. And I love, um, your..." I looked down at his spit-polished shoes. "Your feet. Nice shoes. So sexy, that black leather. Makes me think of whips. And we all know what big feet mean." He grinned as I went on. "And those eyes of yours, so clear and strong. Nothing gets past you. Now to the matter at hand. I'd like to meet with the loved ones and prepare them for the gruesome event they'll witness."

"It can be arranged."

"We must keep the lights low. The medication works best in dim light." *And so will my false identity.*

"Whatever you say."

"You're so reasonable, Pumpkin. Not like this criminal. The man is a damn fool. Death by asp. Absurd. It makes things so difficult for those of us trying to do our jobs as efficiently as possible."

"Creative though. It'll draw viewers, clicks, likes," the warden said, his tooth glimmering. "Gotta hand it to the guy. He knows how to go down with style."

"That he does," I said, brushing my hand across Ulysses's thigh.

CHAPTER TWENTY-EIGHT

Terpenes are nice-smelling essential oils produced by plants, marine sponges, and some insects. Conifers and cannabis are noted for their terpenes. Such chemicals are hard to make in the lab and difficult to purify from plants. Vitamin A is a terpene, and turpentine is made from terpenes.

I had a week, *a week*, to save Ulysses. I had a mental template around which ideas assembled. I needed to keep my confidence, not have it beaten down, and not be so cocky as to be reckless.

Jester owed me. We shared the bond of chemistry. His wife would be on my side. I returned to his house, sat in his aqua-blue kitchen, and told him and Jane the plan. I'd have visitors kiss Ulysses goodbye and slip him a bean each held in their mouths. He'd swallow the beans and, with enough kisses, spread out over the right amount of time, he'd become resistant to the bite of the snake.

My excited words danced out of my mouth. "The peroxidases in the saliva work to produce the antivenom. It was my thesis project, isolation and detection of antivenom from the unique tropical jack bean *Canavalia aspernot*. Most antivenoms are made from horse plasma. My adviser collected *Canavalia aspernot* and other beans in Costa Rica. The idea was to isolate unique terpenes —essential oils—used as muscle relaxants. Agricultural workers there told him about their local cure for snakebites using beans, and he smuggled them out of the country to our lab. We found they work well against the bite of *B. asper* in particular, the asp! The execution death is to be by asp! How fortunate that one of Mother's secret ingredients turned out to be the very same antidote—aspernot."

"It makes sense if the species are closely related," Jester said slowly.

"Yes. No surprise. Now I've got to get Ulysses these beans."

Jester sat frozen, saying at last, "There are variables. The antidote is probably water-soluble, so it will dissolve in the mouth of the kisser. It's a kooky plan."

"Timing is everything."

Jester stared at the ceiling. "But if the asp bite doesn't kill him, they'll just shoot him."

"I've already thought of that. I'll have to inject him with a sedative and declare him dead. I'll make one from *Valerianus exofficinalis*. I've got a history with it. He's already susceptible thanks to the Boardoze." I felt my face getting hot as I remembered the high school escapades with Devil's Bargain. I told HR I had the flu and couldn't come in. Can you get me a syringe from work? I'll need a rat too, to test the dosage. It's been a while since I made this stuff."

He bit his lip. "Against my better judgment, I can. This is dangerous. You're not a doctor or a synthetic chemist."

"Here's where you come in. You'll pose as a mortician and haul him away in your hearse. It will be important to be prompt on this, and you're prompt."

"I am, but I'm not a mortician. I can't just pretend to be one and take away a body."

"You've got all the gear for it and the doctor arranges for the mortician. I've already looked into it."

"Where's the body supposed to go?"

"Bring it here. We'll put him in my car, and I'll head for

Cochton's Edge. This place runs on a shoestring. Is anyone going to care?"

Jane touched his hand gently. "Jesse, it's so romantic. We've got to try to help. I'll volunteer to deliver a bean!"

He stared at the floor and wrinkled his brow. "It's illogical. I got the annulment notice. He's not your husband anymore. He might never be able to have sex again, and, golly, that's the whole center of your relationship. I need you here. I need you for your mind. What about your patent? The money won't transfer to another country. Let the man go and start fresh. If bread's the problem, I can arrange a raise. I'll give you maternity leave. Let's not take foolish risks."

"Foolish risks? Don't say that." I wanted to cry. I needed someone to believe in my plan.

Jane took his chin and lifted it until he met her eyes. "Jesse, don't make me wonder if I've married the devil. Catrina, your plan will work."

I picked all of the cheese-scented *Valerianus exofficinalis* I could. I took them to Valentine's room and soaked them in isopropanol overnight. The next morning, I poured off the liquid and evaporated it in the microwave. I redissolved the powder in vodka and poured it into a screw-top vial with a lid that had a septum for needle insertion. Here, for better or worse, was the sedative I'd pass off as a drug to prevent vomiting. A man is not a rat. I needed to extrapolate the dosage as best I could. My hands were shaking as I put Shady the rat to sleep and laid him in the bathtub. In the morning he was awake, sitting up, sniffing. Jane was right. I was right. This plan would work.

At the prison, I shook hands with the loved ones there to view the execution—Blossom, Jan, Hans, Jane, Maven, Maurice, Wilma. They each had two magic beans filled with antidote, distributed by Jane.

"You'll want to kiss him goodbye," I said. "Let's work in intervals of thirty seconds to give him time to swallow." I went to the execution chamber—just a modified break room with windows looking into the hall—to wait for Ulysses and got a most unwelcome sight as Axel wheeled him in on a gurney. Axel. Of course it would be the interfering asshole. Suddenly, I wasn't sure of anything.

"Got a live one here, doctor. Just not for long," he said. Our eyes met for half a second—long enough for him to recognize me. He whispered, "Don't be so terrified. It's not your execution."

To make things worse, Bernadette, all in black, was now among the viewers.

"What do I have to do to get you off my back?" I said quietly.

"Get him out of my life one way or another."

One by one the designated kissers came in and bid farewell as tears flowed and Ulysses tried not to gag on the beans delivered on the lips of his dear ones.

As I leaned over Ulysses stretched out supine on the gurney, my tears fell on his face. The comet necklace glistened at my throat in the harsh lighting. If this didn't work, I wouldn't live without him. I couldn't go on.

He swallowed his last bean and coughed. His eyes focused on the necklace.

"You know why I'm here," I said, my wavering voice nearly betraying me.

"Doc, do what you've got to do."

I said quietly, "For now, you need to sleep as the dead do. Trust me."

The tattoo eye of Ulysses S. Grant stared at me. I slipped the needle into his iris.

"Good night, sweet general. Close your eyes and dream of

peace." I injected Ulysses with my sedative. It would make him look dead, or dead enough. He passed out immediately.

I listened to his heart with a stethoscope. Pumps are fragile. I knew this from working with lab equipment. The first thing to go was always a pump and its seals. His was steady and slow. Perspiration ran down my back like a river. The snap of the door opening made me jump.

The snake handler wore a tan seersucker suit and carried a briefcase.

The scientist-turned-fake-pastor took the bright green snake from his briefcase. He held it up in a fat fist. "This is Emerald. Want to ask her anything before she kills a man?"

Emerald was wide as a fire hose. It was hard to imagine, but things had just gotten worse. Much worse. How had I expected to take on the Boss Hog that was Cochtonville?

"Excuse me." The words squeezed from my throat. "That's not an asp."

I put my palm on Ulysses's chest. His heart beat steadily. He wasn't fathoming my fear at this unknown snake species. I had no idea now if my antivenom would work or if I'd given enough. This was an enormous snake. I leaned on Ulysses as the world swirled around me.

"Asp. Who uses those anymore? Not reliable, rather weak venom, and anyway the term is vague," said this fake.

"It's a damn snake," said Warden Carmine. "Deadly as any of them, isn't that right, Reverend Terapin?"

"Sure is," said the "pastor." "One of our newest ones. Parishioners like flash these days. It's hard to keep people interested in this era of nonstop entertainment."

My mind was tripping over itself. What kind of venom would this aberration have?

"She's new. A bit hard to handle," said Pastor Terapin.

To make the situation even more dire, a new snake freshly captured would likely have more venom. Snakes handled in churches don't live long and lose their poison due to the stress of being touched by people.

Looking down at Ulysses, I shook with chills.

The warden said, "He's out like a bulb. Hurry and get this over with."

"The mortician's not here yet."

"As long as he's here before he's stiff, it don't matter."

The room was as hot as the forges of Vulcan. The snake shook its tail in anger.

"He's not even suffering," the preacher said, wagging his head toward Ulysses. "Shouldn't he be begging for the Lord's mercy?"

"He's sedated. It's either this or he pukes all over," the warden said. "It's the doctor's call and we're short on custodial staff."

I studied the clock. In ten minutes Ulysses would go into his death trance.

The faux preacher waved the twisting snake. "Since when do men take orders from female doctors? Or females of any sort? Women's suffrage is a sin." He was enjoying his false persona too much. No scientist would believe such a ruse.

"Since women earn less than men," the warden said. "This is a private prison and we cut costs where we can." Warden Carmine put his hand on his holster. "Now get on with the killing of this menace."

"I take my time with these things," the reverend said. Blossom sobbed, her arm draped across Bernadette's shoulders.

The pseudo reverend started his spiel. "Behold, I give unto you power to tread on serpents and scorpions, and over all the power of the enemy: the enemy is carnal knowledge and lust. This man has aided in the destruction of society."

"This is ridiculous. This man did nothing wrong," Bernadette said from the gallery. To have her speak up now was shocking. It was a little late for her to develop a conscience and I didn't need her help at this point. The snake's tongue whipped like a beach flag.

The preacher cleared his throat. "The law says to let your

women keep silence in the churches: for it is not permitted unto them to speak." This man had prepped for his role.

"Fuck that," Maven said. "This joint ain't a church."

"Double fuck that," Bernadette said, licking her lips. "I speak when and where I wish."

She and Maven leaned forward, their breasts pouring from their blouses. The warden, the preacher, and Barnabus ogled, caught by their own objectification. The snake rattled its tail. Around this time, Shady poked his nose from my purse. How had he gotten in there? The snake snapped her head in the direction of the rat.

"Hide my eyes from sinful women," the minister said, overcompensating.

"Here now, my wife isn't sinful," Axel said. "It's not a sin to be gorgeous and brainy. Defamation. Buddy, I'm going to detain you for Word Crime." Axel was trying to stall the execution, not understanding I was on a tight timeline if I was going to pull this off.

"No need to be a moron, Whitehead," the warden said. "We need to kill this man and not take all day doing it."

"Warden, you work for me, not vice versa."

My scream broke the stalemate as Shady jumped out of my purse and down to the smooth floor. Ulysses opened his eyes, and they dimmed as his pupils dilated. His mouth fell open. I wanted to vomit. I'd seen Rex like this, but I hadn't loved Rex. I'd viewed his body hanging between life and death with curiosity and detachment. This was something else. My cool indifference evaporated like morning fog. I shielded my eyes with my hand.

Shady scampered across the concrete and through the preacher's legs. The snake lashed at the rat, missed, struck again, and sank its fangs into the preacher's thigh. He yelped, his eyes filled with surprise. He dropped the snake and doubled over. I pressed my foot on the snake's neck to halt it as Shady slipped under the door. Emerald thrashed, pinned at the neck. Axel stomped on her. Her body writhed and flexed and was still.

Warden Carmine grabbed me. "Do something!"

"I did. The prisoner is dead."

"The prisoner is dead?" Warden Carmine said with relief. "Yee Gawd, he looks terrible. He weren't bit though," he said in wonder.

I glanced at Jane and she gave me a thumbs-up. Where was Jester?

"Yes. Yes. I killed him with the injection," I said hurriedly. "That wasn't the right snake and I take no chances. Get the mortician in here right away."

"Hope you know more about killing men than you do snakes." The scientist, red in the face, clutched his thigh where spots of blood bloomed through the suit.

"Get him a chair," I ordered Axel. There were no chairs in the execution chamber and Axel ran off as the warden steadied the sham Reverend Terapin.

Unbelievably, the keg deliveryman strode though the door left ajar by Axel. It made no sense that he was here. There weren't kegs in a prison facility. He wore a badge: Rana Mortuary. I stared at my hands. Had I spilled Devil's Bargain on myself and was now having visions? Surely the devil wouldn't come as a man who delivered beer.

"Here to pick up the empty," he said. "This one done?" He grabbed the gurney on which Ulysses lay as still as a corpse.

"Goddamn, he's dead. Get him out of here," said Warden Carmine. "Even dead he's making a muck of things."

Terapin vomited.

The deliveryman flipped a form in my face. "Sign the death certificate, please." I was blind with fear and confusion. He offered me a pen, and I signed the form as he smiled at me as if I was buying a keg.

"Where are you taking him?" Nothing was going as planned and no one was trustworthy.

"Rana Mortuary. I come with the blessing of Jane Rana. She says to tell you that your hair looks fabulous. We'll be taking this criminal to where he can do no harm."

Axel had returned with the chair, and the "pastor" was slumped in it. Warden Carmine stood over him with his head bowed.

The deliveryman seized the end of the gurney. "We're doing this by the book. Hold the door for me, please, and come verify the transfer of the corpse."

I followed the deliveryman through the halls of the prison. The floors were wobbly. I put my hand on the wall to steady myself as the man in tan swept the gurney through the corridors. We picked up speed, dashing through the halls past closed doors. Footsteps followed distantly. I didn't turn around, fearing I'd look guilty. In the parking circle at the rear of the facility, we picked up Ulysses and put his limp body in the beer delivery truck. A rush of prickly fear swept me along with the thought that I might have killed him. We shut the door.

"Thanks, Dad." I jumped out of my skin. It was Jane!

"Jester couldn't get access to the prison. We hadn't filed paperwork for the hearse. Who knew? This place is so unpredictable. So I called Dad. His truck has a permit, and he came. I knew he was a fan of Union Station. Is he safe? Ulysses, I mean."

"As peaceful as the Cedar River and nearly as full of chemicals. We've got to get out of here. I need to get him across the border before he wakes up. Did anyone call an ambulance for that pastor? I don't have my phone."

"Wilma did. Let's go."

At Jester's house, Jester gave his father-in-law a high five. "Thanks. You're a lifesaver. Jack signed the death certificate," Jester said, handing it to me. "He doesn't know his ass from a hole in the ground, but he can still sign his name. I checked the box for transport over the state line. Let's get Ulysses out and zip him up so you can be on your way."

Ulysses was stiff and unresponsive. I listened to his steady heart with the stethoscope.

"Looks dead," Jester said.

"He'll be okay," I said, although Jester was right. Ulysses was frozen and ghastly.

Jester slipped a body bag over Ulysses and hoisted him into the back of Old Gold. I put the body-transportation papers and death certificate on the seat. I slipped off the doctor's coat and stethoscope. I was now Dr. Catrina Butz, transporting the body of her ex-husband and leaving the country to study beach grass. I felt sick. This lie seemed preposterous and the danger insurmountable.

Jester embraced me. "I need to apologize. Jane told me what a hero Ulysses is. He's all yours, Catrina, and you are his. Travel safely. Let me know if you need a reference."

With a wave and a glance in the rear-view mirror, a pine tree air freshener hanging from it, I was off to The Edge. With luck, I'd never see this place again.

CHAPTER TWENTY-NINE

Shooting stars can be caused by the icy debris of a comet or, more rarely, parts of an asteroid or planet that flew between the moon and Mars and fell to Earth in the form of meteorites. Most meteorites are primarily made of iron, often alloyed with nickel, and may contain calcite, gypsum, olivine, and pyroxene. They differ from earth rocks in that they are denser, more irregularly shaped, and often are magnetic. Those that make it to Earth are called falls.

I drove through shimmery fields on the strip of straight road to Cochton's Edge. The corn fields were dreamy and powerful. There was so much corn, hypnotic as it danced in the light and reached for me. A hog truck came up behind me and pulled up by my left side, almost drifting into my lane as it clattered past. Pig snouts poked from the oval vents on the trailer. I kept my sweaty hands on the wheel while the semi zoomed on.

In the back of Old Gold, the body bag stirred. My heart jumped. Ulysses was waking up. I needed to claim to be transporting a body. The body couldn't be moving! I almost collided with a truck at a corn-obscured intersection. My hands started shaking. I reached for my purse and, with one hand on the wheel, dumped out the contents. As I feared, the syringe and

Devil's Bargain weren't there. I'd left them in the execution chamber as I hurried to leave. Ulysses groaned. I accelerated. Ulysses cried out, a product of seeing the devil. He'd be awake soon with a horrible story to tell. I had fifteen minutes to get through the border. I wasn't going to make it.

A road sign read "Tuckaway Prairie." I pulled over on the dirt road that lead to the remnant. Jester was right about prairies. The palette had turned over to green and yellow and the grasses were reaching for the clear sky. I shut off the car, and the roar of the air conditioning gave way to the insistent chirp of crickets. The humidity packed a punch. I rushed to the backseat of the car and unzipped the bag. Ulysses's eyes were wide and as wild as his hair. I smoothed it.

"How are you?" I asked, the rush of relief at seeing him alive bringing the tears again.

He shook his head and yawned. His eyes weren't focusing.

I tapped his cheek. "Ulysses. Are you with me?"

He coughed and shivered in his cocoon. He struggled against the white fabric. I opened the bag to give him some fresh air. The humidity was pressing, crushing, like an invisible hand. He clawed free from the gauze and sat up. "Catrina? You're here?"

I touched the necklace. "It's me."

He put a hand on my belly. "She's still with us?"

"We made a tough baby."

"Where are we?"

"In the country, dodging the law."

"Not in hell? You didn't kill me off?"

"No. How sensible would that be? A fool for love is hard to find in my profession."

He put both hands to his temple and shook his head. "Glad to hear you're still rational. I don't remember a thing. Why am I in a bag?"

"It's a body bag. I had to make you look dead so I could smuggle you out of the prison. Can you stand up and shake this thing off to give yourself some air?"

I steadied him as he extracted himself from the bag. He swung his legs over the seat and took a coltish step from the car. He was standing barefoot in a prison uniform in the rippling prairie.

He put his hands over his face. "I'm grateful. It was what I was hoping for, but damn, what a mess."

I swept him into my arms and put my head on his chest. "It's me who's grateful. You're alive. We're going to make it through."

"Are we still in Cochtonville?"

"At the edge."

He smiled, the crow's-feet sprouting to show he was truly happy. "What's the plan, smarty-pants? I know you have one. I'm certainly a wanted man."

"Ulysses Butz is a dead man. I have the death certificate in the glove box. You'll need to get back in the body bag before we go on."

His smile vanished. "No. Oldest trick in the book. They'll inspect it. I won't be dead. To the slammer I'll go, and so will you. Shit. Maybe I can hide in a hog truck and meet you on the other side."

"No, too dangerous. I'm not letting you out of my sight."

We clutched each other. We'd come this far only to face an impasse.

He said, "The fence can't be everywhere. We can find a spot where I could cross. You can drive through with your paperwork and distract them."

"No," I said. "Yes. The paperwork. You're right. The paperwork. You've given me an idea."

I rushed to Old Gold and fished through the glove compartment for the grass study paperwork. My eyes scanned it. Yes, the forms said I could have an assistant. I groped for Kevin's fake ID. It didn't look much like Ulysses, but maybe we could pull it off. He'd be my assistant—a visiting scholar.

"I have paperwork that says I'm traveling with my assistant. You could show my brother's fake ID if we get asked for one. You've got to change your clothes. I've got some for you in my suitcase. Ditch that uniform. Leave it in the dirt. Hurry, before I lose my nerve."

Ulysses pulled off his shirt and sniffed under his arm. "Yuck. I'm as skunky as light-struck beer."

"It's probably the antidote I gave you. I made it from plants that smell like cheese."

He slipped off his prison pants. He had a huge erection showing through the baggy, white boxers. I was stunned at the sight of it.

"Wow. What've you been doing in that prison? Not drinking the water, apparently."

"It's just angel lust from almost dying," he said, looking between his legs.

"I don't think so. You didn't almost die. The snake bit the handler."

"It did?"

"Yes, poor man. Axel killed the snake."

"He was there? I only remember the sexy doctor."

"He was in the gallery. Bernadette too. She cried." I opened my suitcase and held out a pair of jeans.

"So did Judas. Speaking of, I saw her when I was under. She told me she was letting me go to be with you. I thought it meant we were both dead." He put his fist to his mouth to keep from crying. This was no time for tears.

"The dead don't wear shoes. Here they are. I packed them. Get dressed."

He slipped into the jeans. They were formfitting, especially in the front.

"These are twenty years old," he said. "Vintage."

"I hadn't time for laundry. Here's a shirt from the bottom of your closet."

He held up the gray T-shirt. I hadn't noticed that it read, "I'm with stupid."

"This is Bernadette's." He slipped it over his head. "How do I look?"

"Everything's too tight. You look lewd. You'll have to settle down some before we meet other people. You owe me some of your legendary makeup sex. Once we cross the border."

Black ink poked out from beneath the tiny T-shirt.

"And cover your tattoo. It's too incriminating."

He ran a hand over his deltoid. "How will I do that?"

I dug a pen from the glove compartment.

"With this lab marker." I handed it to him.

"What do you have in mind? I know you've got something."

"I don't. You're the artist. Do what you can."

"Upside down?"

"Yes."

"With this?" He flipped it skillfully in his long fingers.

"Old school. No technology."

"Now I feel really naked."

"Hold that feeling," I said.

He scribbled across the tattoo, giving Grant a longer beard and changing his name to Gus Adams.

He handed me the pen. "Are you sure you don't want to kiss me goodbye and end it all here and now?"

"You know me better than that."

He pulled me toward him and touched the comet necklace. "I'm the luckiest man alive. Are we still married?"

"Not anymore."

"Let's do it again, if you'll share a life with me."

"Yes, let's. We understand each other well enough to make it work this time."

He said, "I've got a hell of a deviance. If we wait for safety, we might wait forever."

"Let's not wait. We've never been good at it."

We kissed and our tears fell like the rain. He put his thigh between my legs as men do when they are testing you, prepping you. I moved across him like waves on a rock, and he was as solid as I was laminar, smoothly flowing. I was flying, I was lost in his arms, on a treasure hunt, I was bursting. We were breathing in sympathy. A force ran through me that I didn't know I had.

———

We were stopped at Cochton's Edge. I showed the papers. The lazy-eyed guard glanced at them. "Studying beach grass," he read.

I said, "Cochton Enterprises needs this grass."

"Your last name is Butz?"

"He was my ex. He's dead. Would you like to see the death certificate?"

"No. I'm not interested in the dead. This shaggy guy here is another scientist? Get a haircut."

"He's my assistant. See that part on the forms?"

He went to the passenger side of the car. "ID, please."

Ulysses flashed Kevin's ID and froze his face in an imitation of a Botox brow.

The guard grabbed the ID and entered information into his tablet.

"You don't match any records of people who've entered Cochtonville for science. How can you be here?"

"He's been working with me. Came in June. Here on a summer pass. I guess I've forgotten to bring that. Absentminded me."

"Scientists are absentminded, and our records are shit. I'll fix the records." He snorted. "Oh boy, says here you have an outstanding prior."

"Oh, does it?" Ulysses said. His eye twitched.

"Yup. Firearms violation."

Ulysses clenched his teeth and growled in imitation of a seed-corn-cap-wearing bar patron. "A man can't be a man."

"That may be true. Get out and put your hands on the car."

Ulysses did as instructed. The guard patted him down.

"Clean. I should've known you wouldn't have a weapon in those tight pants. Too bad. I could use a new gun."

The guard peeked in the window.

"Ma'am. He has a weapons violation. He can't come back into Cochtonville. I'm sorry."

"Of course, I'll comply."

The guard peered at the tattoo.

"Say," he said. "Saaay."

Ulysses swallowed a lump in his throat. My mouth was dry.

The guard slapped Ulysses on the arm. "Gus Adams! You must be a history buff. Most people don't know about Gus. He's so much greater than his brother Grizzly, don't you think?"

"Of course," Ulysses said. Crickets chirped in the beauty of the summer evening.

The guard went on, ogling the tat. "The two traveled together with Gus making watercolors of the bears. One inspired the California state flag. Little known fact—those guys were my relatives."

"Oh, so interesting!" I said, my foot hovering over the accelerator.

"Of course, and the noble grizzly went into decline from all the ranchers and miners taking its habitat," Ulysses said. I cringed. This sounded too critical of civilization. He'd come off as a radical, and of course his enthusiasm was accompanied by a slight wrinkling of his facial skin. Probably the guard hadn't taken much note of the age on the ID.

"You're right. It only stands proud on the flag now," the man said

"And Gus stands proud as the triumph of art over violence," Ulysses said.

"Spoken like a true Renaissance man. Not everyone understands the intersection of art and science. I could either shoot you at this point or let you pass...though I couldn't shoot you even if I wanted to. We've got these trial guns and they're no damn good. I get to be a consultant, though, and we get the improved version, based on our recommendations, at a reduced rate. That new Chief of Vice with the hot wife set it all up. So get out of here! Ma'am, on your return, stop and I'll show you my watercolors of our corn. It's got a kinetic beauty all its own. Not everyone sees it at first."

Scuffles, squeals, and a sound like noses being blown drifted across the cornfield as hogs trotted into view.

"I'll be damned," the guard said. "Get a load of that. They're loose. The hogs have been busting out lately." A siren went off.

"Air raid." The man shrugged. "Can't keep you any longer. I've got to duck and cover. It's been a pleasure to meet the fantastic Mr. Butz. You sure helped a lot of us get by. Take care, you two. Safe travels."

Ulysses shook the man's hand, jumped in the car, and we were on our way. After a few miles, the world came clear. Sweat poured off me. "Whew. He recognized you."

Ulysses put one hand over the other to stop the trembling. "We didn't dupe him at all. Keep going at a steady pace in case he changes his mind." When he'd stopped shaking, he wiggled the ID from his tight pocket.

"Weapons violation. That's too ironic." He rolled down the window and tossed the rectangle of plastic out. "Are you sure you don't want to leave me after you get your grass? I don't think you can even marry a man without a country."

"You can seek asylum. Wilma prepped Valentine and me on how to do it. Valentine's leaving too."

"Never thought I'd be thankful for how easy people in Cochtonville are to fool, Doc Bliss." He touched my hair.

"We've made it," I said. "We made it together. They didn't beat us down this time. I had a lot of help, and that's the key—working together when life is unjust. Hey, speaking of fooling people, I've got a surprise for you. Open the glove compartment."

He put his hand in carefully and pulled out a packet of *Muscuna cochtonus*.

"Beautiful. You have a permit for these, right?"

"Of course. How many chances can one woman take? Keep going."

He fished out the pair of blue booties I'd stashed there to hint at my surprise. I'd hoped to break the news under more relaxed circumstances.

He held them in his cupped hands. He lifted one up and turned on the interior light, for night was upon us. "What's this mean?"

"You're a smart man. Figure it out. I had an illegal ultrasound."

He laughed, and that laughter washed away the anxiety of the past month. "Blue? Really? The kid's already going against our parental expectations."

"He's got an identity all his own," I said. "There's a theory that says we chose our own sex in the womb. He is what he is."

"Just like brewing a beer. You think you've created one thing and it comes out completely different—but still good."

His breath paused. For a second, I worried. I needed to hear his breath.

He whistled. "It's just that a man can get himself into a lot of trouble."

I patted his leg. "Trouble is an equal-opportunity employer."

"I don't know what that is. We'll have to come up with a new name for the baby," he said.

I poked at his tattoo. "How about Gus? It's been lucky so far. What did you say? Art over violence?"

"I like it. Maybe next time for Nellie Noel."

"Next time," I said. "I put away money from my patent. I got your cash from behind General Grant. We're going to be okay if we land someplace merciful."

A car passed us in the other direction. Its undimmed headlights flooded the car. Ulysses and I met eyes as I looked away from the glare. Color was back in his face. His eyes were clear beneath the thick lashes.

"Let's grow beans and add them to beer," he said as the light receded. "We could have a goal of exporting it to Cochtonville."

"If you want to stir up a rebellion."

He smiled halfway. "I was thinking about it."

"Back to brewing, in other words?"

"Let's give it a shot. If the beans turn out like Mother, we won't even need a guard dog. Just a strong set of walls to keep people away from danger. How about you? What's your heart's desire?"

"Besides you, I've got this attraction to beach grass."

The corn was smaller now, and as we drove, it thinned and became soybeans. The glow of cars on a highway flickered ahead. Fast-moving lights came up behind us. Ulysses slumped in his seat and covered his face with his hand as the car passed us and disappeared in the darkness.

He sat up. "Reminds me of the night we met."

"When the bus broke down?"

"Christmas Eve. When we became one and I decided to marry you."

"It was simply chemical attraction at that point."

"Who can argue with that? I knew it would be more."

We came to a crossroads. I carried a list of sympathetic innkeepers in my head—all friends of Jan and Hans—and both directions held such a place. Each was over a hundred miles away.

I pulled over to the side of the country road. "I'm too tired to go much farther. I don't know where to go."

"I'll take the wheel. After sleeping like the dead, I can drive all night. It's as if anything's possible."

"It is. Look at all the stars." I took a deep breath. My heart was opening like a blossom.

The night was moonless, and without the light pollution of the city, the sky was freckled with incandescence. We got out to change drivers and took the time to lean on Old Gold and hold each other as we stared up in awe.

"Everything you'd need to make a world is up there," I said. "Every element you'd ever need."

"Here too," Ulysses said.

A streak of star and then another cut through the night sky.

"Is that a dream?" I asked.

"If it is, we're in the same dream."

We left in the direction that held the falling stars and headed for what we'd call home.

THE END

Thank you for reading! Did you enjoy?

Please Add Your Review! And turn the page for a sneak peek of LOST IN WASTE, book 2 in the Unstable States series!

SNEAK PEEK OF LOST IN WASTE

I was high for a Midwesterner, six feet up on a poured concrete stage with fifteen feet of gold-and-green curtains behind me, held up by three giant concrete hands. Mom was in the mostly female crowd, standing in the town square among the Pesto women with their long ratty prairie skirts and the Cochton Enterprises employees in their polos and khakis. She mouthed, "Good luck, Cali."

Today's contest was a big one. I swear, the nation of Cochtonia had more competitions for its female citizens than an ear of corn has kernels, but we had to have some way to determine who was allowed to bear and birth a baby boy. After the great spill in Cochtonia thirty years ago, we still had more pigs than weeds. We still had more corn than our air had particulates. We even had insects, although it was an insecticide pipe that broke and shot its load into the Cedar River. Nine months later and beyond, people had baby girls now and then—I had been born three years after the incident—but a boy? Nope. Nobody had a male child without undergoing an expensive technique allowed for the best of female citizens, those awarded InVitro status.

A contest for InVitro status is why I stood six feet above the crowd on this cool spring day next to my boss in his supervisory role, and the Icon who had the fate of being my partner in this challenge. The Icon, Eve Whitehead, was low-level glitterati in the fledgling nation of Cochtonia. Her features were small and even. She might have been plain without makeup. She was muscular. I had to swallow my jealousy every time she moved her arms to fluff her perky mahogany bob or adjust the lacy beret she wore.

Eve was well known around Cochtonia. Her claim to fame was appearing in cautionary one-minute videos, where she disobeyed petty laws and did things like reading a paper book or planting a garden. For her crimes she was arrested by the Vice Patrol, the ubiquitous law enforcement group we citizens casually called Washers because they washed society of its human dirt. It was mandated that citizens log on to these videos each week. I'd already seen a lot of Eve. She was even better looking in person.

I worked as a chemist for Cochton Enterprises. Yet today I was with Eve on Team Beautiful and Damned. Looking at the downtown of the capital city of Cochtonville, with its red brick buildings and the gleaming Pavilion of Agriculture, bars, pawn shops, laundromats, and my mom's medic shop, I knew if we didn't win this contest, I'd be the damned. Living in Cochtonia and having a flunky lab job as I did was like living in a trench. InVitro status was the only way a female could dig her way out. I'd be Lady Van Winkle. I'd clear the family name, forever associated with lazy drunkenness. I'd have a genetically modified baby without the bother or expense of a husband who was certain to be older and on his second or third wife. Even better, it came with money and a chance at a house in a classy suburb. Mom could live with me in the luxury she deserved. *I* was going to be the best of citizens. Yes, I'd prove myself a success.

Carefully, I shrugged my supervisor's hand from my shoulder as he leaned into me and whispered, "Cali, forgive me if this becomes uncomfortable." My boss, once known as Richard Bux, had been a regular boss who wore polos and khakis. Last month he'd been promoted to the title of sir, and the new Sir Bux wore a uniform. He was more flighty than usual since he'd gotten his status as a member of the Order of the Pig, following which I'd been selected to participate in this competition. His shiny new Order of the Pig medal shook on his yellow sash across his new green suit. The pin was kind of like the British Order of the Garter star, but a hog instead of cross sat inside the gaudy burst of what I was sure was a thin layer of gold over plastic since we were resource poor. It was accompanied by three copper soybeans, one for each decade of devotion to Cochton Enterprises. According to his decorations, this man had served our nation well. Until recently, he'd been a father figure to me, more stable than my own father, and by that, I mean sober. But since he'd told me we were to be featured in the latest state-sponsored competition, he'd been weirdly touchy-feely and talked about how he cared for *me* rather than about my data. And he'd grown a scraggly goatee.

Previous contests were simple tasks such as a national anthem contest and bake-offs featuring cornmeal. The crowd was mildly interested in this event. Entertainment wasn't a thing in Cochtonia. We worked and were serious and consumed corn-based products. The people were mostly here for the food. In the sea of people, I caught Mom's furrowed brow as she stood next to the corn liquor stand set up by the Pestos at their all-corn food and beverage booth. She was there to watch my introduction but also to run interference in case my dad showed up and drank too much.

The Pestos, thus named because they were associated with pesticide application in Cochtonia (and sold a tasty corn-based sauce), were rural folk who came to town when there was a festival or announcement where they could sell their products in the town square—the only spot in the whole nation freely open to the public. Pesto women, their corn silk hair tied back in buns, were the only females in Cochtonia who seemed able to have children without any intervention these days, although all of their babies were girls. None of the kids were here, nor were their husbands, the pesticide appliers of the nation. The babies they blatantly nursed had bandanas wrapped across their eyes.

The Cochtonia manager, Norman Allen, a figurehead because he was the last male conceived naturally, held up a microphone and spoke to all of us in his slow Iowa drawl. Cochtonia was once known as the state of Iowa and in the United States, but it had declared independence and broken away, and no one fought for our return. We were like a detaching skin tag. It first founded itself as a city-state called Cochtonville but expanded by foreclosing on farms, doing this quickly—before other countries could buy them, as was happening at the time—until it declared itself a new nation: Cochtonia.

A mosquito landed on Norm's head as he spoke. "We are having this competition because our nation isn't growing economically or population wise. We must work harder and smarter. Each team of two women will find a resource associated with their assigned project, along with a practical use for the site. I will now introduce the teams, although I'm sure you're all familiar with the Icons associated with each group." He slapped the mosquito.

As he introduced us, each team of two women stepped forward and greeted the audience.

"You all know Private Eye. She reminds you the Vice Patrol is always looking for criminal behavior. She and her science support will repurpose an abandoned library." A black-haired woman and someone who worked in the lab down the hall bowed to the crowd.

"The Icon known as Report 'Em Raw discourages unauthorized sexual conduct. She and her partner will find a use for an abandoned chicken farm." A thin-nosed woman and a blonde gave the crowd a thumbs-up.

"Icon Keep It Tidy and her colleague will find a way to use loose garbage and abandoned lots in our city. We know, although we highly applaud single use items, a creative use for them will encourage all to pick them up." Two women with neat buns and wrinkle-free rompers ran forward and did the splits as the crowd clapped.

"Our Beautiful and Damned Icon shows us the folly of disobeying Cochtonville's laws. She and her teammate will find a use for the WasteBin." I stepped forward and waved with a closed hand and forced smile as Eve did. My stomach was in knots. The WasteBin was a remote site filled with effluent from sewage lagoons. Everyone knew what was there—hog waste, garbage, and worthless rocky soil that couldn't grow corn. Getting there required a journey on rural roads. Some of them needed manual driving. Mom's face screwed up as if she was smelling it. We had the worst assignment of the bunch.

The manager took a dramatic pause before saying, "The prize will be InVitro status awarded in conjunction with the Corn Days Festival."

Upon hearing the words, the tangible consequence, I wanted to win as much as I wanted to breathe. Success was closer than it had ever been.

Eve grabbed me too tightly and cried, "I have always desired this. We can get our own men. Man rental is a perk of InVitro status!"

"Yuck," I said, looking at Sir Bux and Norm. "A perk I can do without."

"Silly, the rentals are probably robots. Where else would young men come from?"

Lady LouOtta Maliegene, a bobble-headed woman with InVitro status and a close-cut tailored dress, came from behind the curtains and took the microphone from the city manager. "Will all patriots join me in singing 'Bombs and Tassels'?" She'd won her status by writing this—the Cochtonia anthem. Her voice was bubbly, almost childish, as she nodded too much and flashed her huge teeth.

Norman Allen held up an image of a green square with yellow silhouettes of an ear of corn and a fat hog. This was our national flag. Immediately, as required, we all pressed our foreheads with our index fingers to show we were thinking of Cochtonia.

"Ohhh." LouOtta held the first note, a high C, to help the people of Cochtonia get started. This was the only song we were allowed to sing these days and we'd lost our sense of pitch. All joined in, finger to forehead. The smell of manure and insecticides drifted on a lazy breeze.

"Bombs and tassels, tassels and bombs,
Come father, come brothers,
Hear the sound.
As bombs and corn tassels burst around,
Defend our enterprise.
We will stand against enemies
And favor our friends
As we please.
We are the Cochtonians, right.
Defend. Defend and fight."

I was never sure who I was to fight nor had I ever seen a bomb or even a brother. Yet I sang because to not sing was to risk arrest.

We were dismissed to the backstage area. Sir Bux came up to us. "I'm giving you the best of resources for this competition. Cali, I've got permission to send you to the field with a UTI."

I clapped my hands together. "A Universal Testing Instrument? I've always wanted one of those!" A UTI was a handheld spectroscopic and chromatographic device. It detected a wide variety of atoms and molecules. Despite my shitty assignment, this gadget would give me an edge at figuring out what was in the sewage. From there, I'd find a use for it.

My mom rushed backstage and flew up to Sir Bux, giving him the stink eye.

"How can you send my daughter there? It's dangerous."

He opened and closed his mouth like a carp before blurting out, "Forgive me. The assignment was out of my hands. I care about Cali as much as you do."

A man in a white coat and white Stetson, a Vice Patrol agent, grabbed Sir Bux by his scraggly goatee. "You're sending my daughter to the WasteBin. If anything happens to her, you'll rot in prison."

My boss flailed his arms like a spotted cucumber beetle. "Commissioner Whitehead, I can explain. It wasn't my choice. These orders came from the Cochtons."

"I, for one, am going to the WasteBin," I said. "I'm used to shit."

Eve linked arms with me. "I, too, wish to go. The WasteBin is my future."

"Medic? Is there a medic?" The city manager had the microphone and called from the front of the stage. "We have somebody down."

"It's just a Pesto," Lady LouOtta added. "No rush."

Mom backed away from my boss, and the Vice Patrol agent let go of his beard.

"I'm a medic. I'll handle it," Mom said. I followed her to the crowd, where a circle had formed around a Pesto woman collapsed on the grass next to a bawling blindfolded baby. Mom knelt beside her, took her pulse, and examined her eyes as the other Pesto women pressed close.

"She's damn weak," one said.

"I don't want her ugly baby," said another, holding her own colicky baby.

"She's a martyr," said a third.

Eve strode over. "The problem?" she said in a feminine voice.

"I suspect she fainted," Mom answered. "I need to get her to my clinic, XX Success, across the way."

Eve hoisted the limp woman to her shoulder as a Pesto woman shoved the fallen woman's baby into my arms.

"Let's go," said Eve.

The clinic bent around a corner on Maize Street. The building had once been a grocery store and had windows with six panes of glass, now covered with wooden blinds. Shelves packed with health and beauty products lined the walls. A bar sat adjacent to XX Success on one side, a laundromat on the other. Mom was a medic who treated minor injuries. She was an alternative to doctors for those who had few resources. Her patients rarely had the money to pay, but Mom made ends meet selling beauty products to the InVitros, who had money. She spent much of each day behind the counter with the glass display case that held wands filled with eyelash extenders and wrinkle smoothers and a Mercury purse—worth more than she made in a year.

"Thanks for your help. Put her here in the exam room." Mom indicated a screened-off area, not a room at all.

Eve and I waited on the other side of the wall. The baby bawled like a cat in heat.

"Don't be put off by the baby. We'll have nannies to help," Eve assured me. "It comes with InVitro status. Of course, you have to pay them, but not much, and we'll make publicity appearances for which we'll be paid."

The baby screamed so hard its bandana was wet from tears, and slobber flew from its tight lips.

"I'm not sure I like babies," I said, peeling the wet bandana from the baby's face.

We both gasped. The little girl had tiny eyes, the size of the quarter-inch gumballs in the machine by the door. I'd never seen such eyes before, but Mom had mentioned there'd been a rash of babies born with small eyes following the introduction of a new pesticide.

"It's true," Eve whispered. "The kids are mutated."

"Old man's a Duster. I'm late. Are you hip?" The Pesto had awakened and was talking in a harsh word salad. "The baby has pin eyes. She's up all night like a vampire bastard. She's not blind. The eyes are overly sensitive to light. I can't get a lick of sleep. I'm about to lose my mind."

"I'll take a look at her." Mom came from behind the screen. She grabbed a lollipop from the counter and unwrapped it. "Hold this in her mouth," she said, handing it to me. I did as instructed while she examined the baby's eyes with a penscope. She went back to talk to the woman.

"The reflection in her eyes is white instead of red. I could give you some drops to help her see without pain during the day. She might sleep at night after the treatment."

"Be cool, girl. *I'm* the sick one. I need a period restorer. Help me. I'm begging you as a martyr."

A Vice Patrol van pulled up in front of the store.

"It's Dad. Alright, I'm out of here," Eve said. "I'll see you tomorrow. Sorry to leave you with the baby." Her last sentence was insincere. She gave me a perfunctory hug as I clung to the baby, now nursing a lollipop.

As soon as Eve had gone, Mom called out. "Cali, lock the door. We're closed." She grabbed a device from her rack of gadgets before returning to the woman.

"A gun?" the woman said from behind the screen. "I thought I'd get a pill."

"I prefer physical methods to chemical ones. They're quicker and neater. Less painful. Faster too. Lean back and relax. It's just energy." A high-pitched pinging squealed out. The baby pinched her eyes together.

"You'll find relief in no time," Mom said.

The woman appeared from behind the screen, her blouse mussed, her hands on her belly. "I don't feel a thing."

Mom handed the woman a package of menstrual pads, Collection Pad brand. "That's the beauty of it."

"I got no money," said the woman. "I can't even pay for *this* with money." She pulled a ring off her hand and gave it to Mom. "It's cleared with the husband. He says if I have any more girls with tiny eyes he's gonna kill me."

"I'm not doing this for him. I'm working for you."

"Bitch, *I* wanted this. I can't go through having another tiny-eyed girl again. My own life is hard enough."

"I understand," said Mom.

"I knew I could trust you," the Pesto said.

Mom put the ring on the counter and pulled out another device from her rack of gadgets. She pointed a card-sized XRF gun at it, which pounded the ring with a stream of X-rays. Mom read the display. "It's copper," she told the woman. "I'll take it in trade. Sometimes women come in and I have to break the news to them that their rings are mostly lead."

"I'm cool," the woman said.

"How about I treat the baby? Let's put some drops in her eyes while she least suspects it."

Mom opened a locked drawer and got out a massive book. Paper books—references included—were illegal. Officials needed to track everything we read, every page, every word for the good of Cochtonia. Books, all nonfiction, were online and updated frequently. Paper books were not only illegal, they were unreliable. Using a paper book meant one thing—Mom didn't want any trace left behind of these people getting a cure.

Mom put her finger on a page. "Yes."

"Is that a paper book? They're illegal," the woman said.

"No. It's an offline nonfiction reference," Mom replied. "I have to make the drug. It's nanoparticles. The opposite of making crystals."

"Spare the details, brainiac. I never went to school. Are you going to help her or not?"

"Yes. The waiting time on nanos is mercifully short." Mom hunched over the counter. She got out two jars and poured them together, then funneled them into a dropper bottle and shook it.

Mom pulled open one of the tiny eyes and added a dropperful of liquid. The baby startled awake and Mom put medicine in the other eye before the baby cried forcefully and filled her diaper.

"Damn, it made her poop," the Pesto said.

"I've got what it takes," Mom said with strained cheerfulness. "Let's change her before you leave."

The Pesto watched as Mom changed the baby and sprayed the dirty cloth diaper with ConTain, a scent remover we'd concocted together. The smell vanished. She put the diaper in a plastic bag and handed it and the blinking baby to the woman. Mom unlocked the door and ushered them out. On the sidewalk in front, a Vice Patrol in a long white coat and a Stetson decorated with pins of pigs and corn was getting an earful from a citizen of Cochtonville, a woman Mom's age. The Pesto went out to face them.

"What have you done?" the citizen said to her. "I know why you people come here."

"Got some eye drops for the brat and period pads for me. Is it any of your business?"

"Period pads. Officer. Take note." The woman snatched the Collection Pads from the plastic bag as the broad-shouldered Vice Patrol officer shifted her belt laden with devices uncomfortably.

"I won't take notes on such a delicate subject," she said.

The intruder pointed to Mom. "This woman is spreading regrets."

"Regrets I can deal with." The Vice Patrol agent took a No Regrets scanner from her belt. She passed it over the Pesto's cheek. A green light appeared.

"She's clean. No infections, not pregnant," the patrolman said, holding up the screen. "What kind of regrets are you talking about? What else does a woman have to regret? We've got plenty of deviants without you creating trouble with the savages." She grabbed the complainer by the neck and threw her to the cement. "You live in the greatest nation on earth. Act like it. Stop stirring up trouble."

"I have no regrets," said the Pesto as she and her baby swooshed past the fallen woman.

The woman, her chin bloody, called as she struggled to sit up, "You selfish Pest."

"Do *you* want this baby?" The Pesto turned and shoved the child at the woman, who shrank away at the sight of the tiny eyes. The baby smacked her lips diabolically as her mother held her out. "Take her and my husband and my life. Or shut the crap up, ya dig?"

"If you don't want your kids, keep your legs together."

"How about *you* dirty dance with my husband then? He's rough. Can you put your crotch where your mouth is?"

"This talk has to be illegal," the woman complained, wiping her chin.

"It is. Word Crime. I'm arresting both of you." The Washer pressed a gadget on her belt. A Washer van pulled up and Eve's dad got out. "What's happening here, Ursula?"

"Word Crime and being a nuisance, commissioner," said the Vice Patrol. She took the baby as Eve's dad escorted the swearing mother and the crying complainer to the van.

"What're you doing with the baby?" I asked in alarm.

"Don't bother about it. This kind of thing happens all the time," said Ursula. Eve's dad shut the door to the van.

"Get some rest," he said to me. "My daughter will win the contest and you're not dragging her down."

Mom and I walked to her old car, parked a ways from her shop.

"They resisted at first," Mom said as we swiped our sidewalk passes at the corner meter.

"The Pestos? Resisted what?"

"The takeover of their land by Cochton Enterprises. They slaughtered all of their animals. They poured ButtOut on their fields."

"The herbicide?" We crossed the street and spotted the car.

"Yes, but the scientists at Cochton Enterprises developed ButtOut resistant corn." We got in the car and closed the doors.

"I never learned this in school. I was told they were backward people who only partially appreciated the civilization we brought to them," I said.

"My dad told me. He was one of the scientists who worked on the resistant corn. He would've done anything for Cochton Enterprises. At the end of his life, he came to regret it. It's why I'm worried about your assignment. I don't trust Cochton Enterprises."

"Mom, I'll be fine. I'm twenty-five years old. If I'm going to be an InVitro, it may as well be now. I want to be a success. Don't you want to be a grandma?"

"I'm sure there's a catch. Be careful."

Don't stop now. Keep reading with your copy of LOST IN WASTE available now.

Find book two of the Unstable States series, LOST IN WASTE, and discover more from author Catherine Haustein at www.catherinehaustein.com

———————

Chemist Cali Van Winkle and media icon Eve Whitehead, residents of the agricultural nation of Cochtonia, are forced from the capital city of Cochtonville to a remote area where garbage and hog waste overruns everything.

Their dreadful assignment is to devise a plan to make the disgusting place turn a profit. The prize is In Vitro status—the opportunity to have a genetically modified baby. With few men and fewer young women, it's the only way to have a child in their country—a land tainted by a chemical spill.

The WasteBin is a dangerous dump, but the women are focused on success. But they find more than trash at the remote site. It's home to abandoned people: a lonely castaway, a pack of motherless girls, and best of all, two exiled males genetically modified to please women.

Cali and Eve grow to adore the wasteland. But the explorers have to go back to society, and when they do, life won't be the same for any of them.

———————

ACKNOWLEDGMENTS

I'd like to thank the following for their assistance:

Steve Bray owner of Green Gable Inn (Cedar Rapids, Iowa) and Diane Chaplin owner of Chaplin's (Arnolds Park, Iowa) for their insights on the life of a bar owner.

Sarah E. Gold for initial proof-reading and copyediting, Suzanna Sturgis for suggestions on plot and character, Kay Van Wyk for giving the manuscript a first reading, and Amy Sue Nathan for advice on the first chapters. Amanda Roberts for her expert editing.

Mary Ann Emerick for my author photo!

ABOUT THE AUTHOR

Born under a half-illuminated quarter moon, Catherine Haustein is never sure if she favors light or shadow. Her *Unstable States* series contains ample portions of both. The author and chemist lives and teaches in a tidy town in Iowa on the shores of a lake which sometimes is cited for elevated fecal coliform levels. A graduate of the Iowa Writers' Workshop, Catherine weaves the passions and optimism of science with the absurdities of  the present and dark possibilities of the future throughout her books.

www.catherinehaustein.com

 twitter.com/hausteinci

 pinterest.com/catherinehauste

ABOUT THE PUBLISHER

City Owl Press is a cutting edge indie publishing company, bringing the world of romance and speculative fiction to discerning readers.

www.cityowlpress.com

Made in the USA
Monee, IL
25 February 2020